THE DISAPPEARANCE AT PÈRE-LACHAISE

THE
DISAPPEARANCE AT
PÈRE-LACHAISE

A Victor Legris Mystery

CLAUDE IZNER

Translated by Lorenza Garcia and Isabel Reid

Minotaur Books ✖ New York

THE DISAPPEARANCE AT PÈRE-LACHAISE. Copyright © 2003 by Éditions 10/18, Département d'Univers Poche. English translation copyright © 2007 by Gallic Books. All rights reserved. Printed in the United States of America. For information, address St. Martin's Press, 175 Fifth Avenue, New York, N.Y. 10010.

www.minotaurbooks.com

The Library of Congress has cataloged the hardcover edition as follows:

Izner, Claude.
    [La disparue du Père-Lachaise. English]
    The disappearance at Père-Lachaise : a Victor Legris mystery / Claude Izner ; translated by Lorenza Garcia and Isabel Reid. — 1st U.S. ed.
        p. cm.
    "First published in France as La disparue du Père-Lachaise by Éditions 10/18"—T.p. verso.
    ISBN 978-0-312-38375-6
    1. Booksellers and bookselling—France—Paris—Fiction. 2. Paris (France)—History—1870–1940—Fiction. I. Garcia, Lorenza. II. Reid, Isabel. III. Title.
    PQ2709.Z64D513 2009
    843'.92—dc22

                                                        2009016579

ISBN 978-0-312-64956-2 (trade paperback)

First published in France as *La disparue du Père-Lachaise* by Éditions 10/18

First Minotaur Books Paperback Edition: September 2010

10   9   8   7   6   5   4   3   2   1

To all the usual people!
And to our dear Invisible Ones

'Are you still there? You are undoubtedly dead, but from where I am, you can speak to the dead.'

Victor Hugo

'We are all ghosts . . .'

Élisabeth d'Autriche

CONTENTS

THE PÈRE-LACHAISE CEMETERY

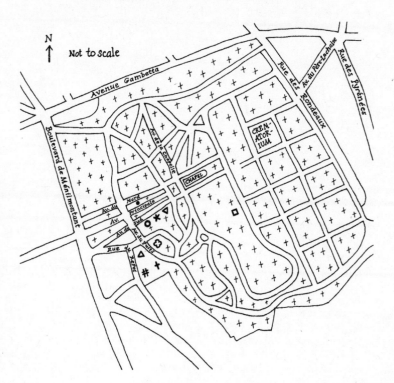

✝	Hélöise and Abélard
•	Musset
▲	Rachel
◻	Molière
✱	Armand de Valois
○	Delambre
♯	Baron James de Rothschild
▽	Tenon
✛	Chenier

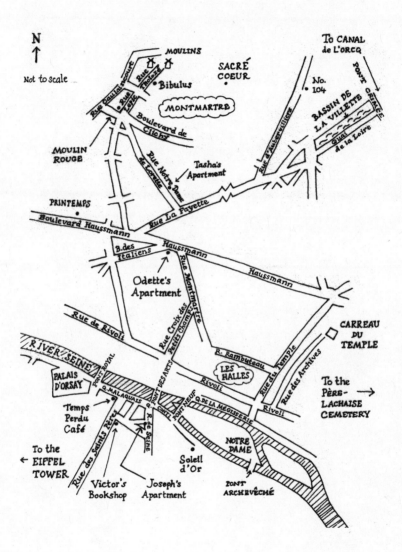

PROLOGUE

Cauca province, Columbia.
November 1889

They had finally reached Las Juntas after a difficult descent through forests dripping with humidity. A bearded man led the way. Behind him were two Indian bearers, carrying a fourth man in a hammock slung between two poles that rested on their shoulders. They were about half a mile outside the village on a stony path bordered with flowering lavender. The twenty or so shacks surrounded by meagre plantations of maize and tobacco stood out against the charred foothills of the Andes Cordillera. Down below, the restless waters of the river Dagua rolled towards the Pacific Ocean.

The path they had been following ended in front of the grandly named Hacienda del Dagua, an abandoned house dating back to the time when Las Juntas had been a lively centre of commerce between Cali and Buenaventura. All that remained of it now was rubble overgrown with weeds. Only one bedroom, its roof caved in, was still standing.

The bearers placed the improvised stretcher on some straw-filled crates and left hurriedly, muttering the words, *'Duendes, duendes.'* The bearded man pulled a face. Under normal circumstances a haunted house would have aroused his curiosity, but for three days now nothing had gone as planned, and he felt a growing indifference to the world around him. He watched the Indians leave, removed his haversack and looked around the room.

A mass of cobwebs hung like a thick veil over a jumble of broken carriage wheels, metal cogs, the remains of a telegraph machine and dozens of empty bottles. The man picked up a yellow, worm-eaten volume – the pages almost turned to dust: *Stances à la Malibran* by Alfred de Musset. He laughed to himself. Musset, here of all places! How absurd! He dropped the book and bent over the body lying across the straw-filled crates. The dying man was about the same height as him, but of heavier build. His unbuttoned shirt revealed his chest bathed in sweat, each intake of breath rattling as though it were his last. Red froth bubbled from his mouth. The bullet had hit him in the back, piercing his lung. He's not long for this world, thought the bearded man, surprised at how detached he felt.

He opened the haversack and spread its contents on the compacted earth: a wallet, a couple of cartridges, some under-clothes, a knife, some ordnance survey maps. An envelope was sticking out of the wallet, addressed to 'M. Armand de Valois, Geologist with the Inter-Oceanic Company, c/o Señora Caicedo, Hotel Rosalie, Cali, Colombia'. He opened the letter and read it out in a low voice:

29th July 1889

My dearest Armand,

How are you, my duck? Your letter was waiting for me yesterday on my return from Paris. I thoroughly enjoyed my stay at Houlgate. My friend Adalberte de Brix (President Brix's widow, you remember) was renting a villa close to mine. We went on a few pleasant walks together and played lawn tennis,

2

badminton and croquet and met some charming people — in particular the well-known English spiritualist M. Numa Winner. Just imagine, he predicted both M. de Lesseps's bankruptcy and the cessation of work on the canal as far back as two years ago! I visited him at his house several times in the company of Adalberte. Since her son Alberic was taken in his prime, she has developed a boundless passion for séances and has consulted several mediums, with no real success, until she encountered M. Numa Winner. And now, my darling, can you imagine, she has spoken to young Alberic through him. I should never have believed it had I not seen it with my own eyes. It was astonishing! Young Alberic implored his mother to stop mourning his departure and said that he was happy where he was, and cried out 'Free! Free at last!' What a comfort, don't you agree? I asked M. Numa some questions of my own, and he assured me that your troubles will soon be over and that you will enjoy a well-earned rest. You see, my duck, your little wife is thinking of you. Did I tell you that your bookseller M. Legris, from Rue des Saints-Pères, was involved in a series of sordid murders at the Universal Exposition? Raphaëlle de Gouveline told me that he was seen about with a Russian émigrée, a loose woman who poses nude as an artist's model. Nothing would surprise me about that man; he doesn't wear a top hat and has a Chinese servant. I shall end here as I have a fitting with Mme Maud, on Rue du Louvre. It's a wonderful dress; the cut is quite . . . But hush, now, it's going to be a surprise. Your little wife wishes to look pretty for your return. Write to me soon. I send you a thousand heliotrope-scented kisses.

Your Odette

The sky was clouding over. The man put the letter back in the envelope and replaced it in the wallet, which he slipped into the dying man's pocket. As he did so, something darted through the air above him, then disappeared. He lit a candle and moved it about slowly. He could see nothing. But he had recognised the flight of a vampire bat – an animal that sucked the blood from people's toes as they slept. In a fit of disgust, he seized a bottle and hurled it. It shattered against the wall. The wounded man coughed; he was suffocating. His breathing quickened and he fixed his eyes on the tall figure standing over him. He tried to sit up, but his strength was draining away with the blood oozing from his mouth and he fell back. It was over. The bearded man crossed himself mechanically, murmured, 'May his soul rest in peace, Amen.' He closed the dead man's eyes.

Now he had to carry out his plan without fail. He would wait until dawn before washing the body – and, most importantly, concealing the wound. Then he would notify the local official, who would come and certify the death and arrange with the magistrate for the speediest burial possible. Las Juntas had been chosen because it had no priest or carpenter; the body would be buried in the ground wrapped in a simple shroud, and in a few months only the bones would remain.

The man threw himself down without taking off his boots. But despite his exhaustion, he could not sleep. He was thinking about what he needed to do. When it was all over, a good mule would get him to the port of Buenaventura in five or six days' time, and there he'd board a Panama-bound steamer from the English Steamship Company. He'd arrive in Barranquilla in time to catch the train. Twenty-four hours later, the ship *La-Fayette* would leave Colombian waters and in mid-December she'd drop anchor at St Nazaire.

He searched in the dead man's pocket and pulled out a half-crushed cigar, which he lit. The vampire bat, hanging from a joist, watched anxiously as the tiny red eye glowed in front of the man's mouth.

CHAPTER ONE

Four months later . . .

'Lord, he was so good and kind. We loved him so dearly! Lord, he was . . .'

The words, tirelessly repeated, filtered through the veil masking the face of a woman who sat huddled against a carriage window. From time to time, another woman, seated opposite, emphasised them with a hurriedly executed sign of the cross. This litany, barely audible above the screech of axles and the clatter of wheels over paving stones, had long since ceased to have meaning, like a monotonous nursery rhyme.

The cabman pulled on the reins and the carriage came to a halt beside the entrance to the Père-Lachaise cemetery on Rue de Rondeaux. He came down from his perch to settle up with the gatekeeper and, having slipped the man a coin, clumsily heaved himself back on to his seat and gave a crack of his whip.

The carriage entered the cemetery gates moments ahead of a funeral cortège and proceeded down one of the looped avenues. The rain formed a halo of light above the vast graveyard. On either side of the avenue was a succession of chapels, cenotaphs and mausoleums adorned with plump cherubs and weeping nymphs. Among the tombs was a maze of footpaths and avenues invaded by undergrowth, still relatively sparse in these early days of March. Sycamores, beeches, cedars and lime trees darkened an already overcast sky. On turning a bend, the carriage narrowly avoided colliding with a tall, white-haired man who was engaged in contemplating the ample posterior of a bronze nymph. The horse reared up, the cabman let out a stream of oaths and the old man shook his fist and cried out: 'Damn you, Grouchy![1] I'll cut you down!' before stumbling off. The cabman muttered a few threats, reassured his passengers and, with a click of his tongue, calmed his horse, which set off towards an avenue running southwards, where it stopped beside the tomb of the surgeon Jacques René Tenon.

A very young woman in simple black clothes consisting of a woollen dress, a waisted jacket covered with a shawl, and a cotton bonnet from which a few strands of blonde hair had escaped, opened the carriage door and jumped to the ground to help another woman, also blonde, but more buxom, of heavier build, and in full mourning. It was she who had invoked the Lord from behind her veil. In her chinchilla hat and astrakhan coat she looked more suitably dressed for a polar expedition than a visit to a cemetery. The women stood side by side for a moment, staring at the carriage as it gradually darkened into a silhouette against the fading afternoon light. The fur hat leaned towards the cotton bonnet.

'Tell him to wait for us in Rue de Repos.'

The younger woman passed the order on to the cabman and paid him. He doffed his oilcloth topper and with a loud 'Gee up!' hastened away.

'I ain't waiting about for queer birds who don't know 'ow to tip a bloke. They can go 'ome on foot!' he muttered.

'Denise!' cried the woman in the fur hat.

'Yes, Madame,' the young girl replied, hurrying to her side.

'Come along now, give it to me. What are you gaping at?'

'Nothing, Madame. I'm just a bit . . . scared.' She pulled a flat rectangular package out of her basket and handed it to her mistress.

'Scared? Of what? Of whom? If there's one place where the Almighty is sure to be watching over us, it is here in this cemetery. Our dear departed are close by, they are all around us, they can see us and speak to us!' cried the woman.

Denise grew more flustered. 'That's what scares me, Madame.'

'You poor, foolish child! What am I to do with you? I shall see you shortly.'

Alarmed, the young girl grasped her mistress's arm. 'Am I not going with you?'

'You will remain here. He wishes to see me alone. I shall return in an hour and a half.'

'Oh, Madame, please. It'll be dark soon.'

'Nonsense, it's not yet four o'clock. The gates close at six. If you don't want to die ignorant, you've plenty of time to visit the tombs. I recommend Musset's, over there in the hollow where they've planted a willow. It isn't very grand but the epitaph is most beautiful. I don't suppose you know who he is. Perhaps you'd better go up to the chapel. It'll do you no harm to say a prayer.'

'Please, Madame!' implored the young girl. But Odette de Valois was already walking away briskly. Denise shivered and took shelter under a chestnut tree. The rain had turned to drizzle and a few birds had resumed their singing. A ginger cat moved stealthily amongst the tombstones, and the lamplighter, carrying his long cane in one hand, crossed the avenue and winked at the young girl. Telling herself she couldn't stand there for ever, she tied her shawl over her bonnet and wandered about beneath the gas lamps, around which raindrops formed haloes.

She tried to put her mind at ease by recalling the walks she'd taken in the Forêt de Nevet with her cousin Ronan, with whom she'd been in love when she was thirteen. How handsome he had been and what a shame that he had chosen another! Lost in thought, she gradually forgot her fears as she relived the few happy moments of her childhood: the two years spent in Douarnenez with her uncle the fisherman, her aunt's kindness, her cousin's attentiveness. And then the return to Quimper, her mother's illness and death, her father's increasing violence after he took to drink, and the departure of her brothers and sisters, leaving her all alone at home, dreaming that a prince would come and whisk her away to Paris . . .

She was suddenly reminded where she was when she came upon a dilapidated, pseudo-Gothic mausoleum adorned with interlocking names. She walked over to it and read that the remains of Hélöise and Abélard had lain there since the beginning of the century. Was it not strange that her memories of Ronan had brought her to the tomb of these legendary lovers? And what if Madame was right? What if the dead . . .

'Soldiers, your general is relying on your bravery! It'll be a bloody battle, but we'll take this enemy stronghold and plant our flags here! Zounds! Let them have it!' roared a drunkard, popping out from behind the monument.

Denise recognised the old man who'd nearly been knocked

over by the carriage. Arms flailing, he rushed towards her. She turned and ran.

Odette de Valois stood motionless in front of a funerary chapel that was more substantial than its neighbours, its baroque pediment decorated with acanthus and laurel leaves in bas-relief. After looking around to make sure she was alone, she placed the key in the lock of the fine wrought-iron gate. The hinges creaked as it opened. She entered and descended the two steps that led to an altar at the back of the chapel. She placed her package between two candelabra and proceeded to light the candles. She looked up at a stained-glass window depicting the Virgin Mary, and crossed herself before kneeling on a prayer stool. The candles illuminated the stucco plaques with their gilded names and dates:

Antoine Auguste de Valois
Division General
High-ranking officer
of the Legion of Honour
1786–1882

Anne Angélique
Courtin de Valois
1796–1812

Eugénie Suzanne Louise
His Wife
1801–1881

Pierre Casimir Alphonse
de Valois
Notary
1812–1871

Armand Honoré Casimir
de Valois
Geologist
1854–1889

Straightening up, Odette read out in a low voice the words inscribed on a marble tablet:

Lord, he was so good and kind!
We loved him so tenderly!
You have given him eternal rest
In the bosom of a strange land.
We are stricken by your justice.
Let us pray for him and live in a way
That will reunite us with him in heaven.

She placed her hands together and, raising her voice, began to recite the Lord's Prayer. Then she stood up and, unwrapping the package, cried out excitedly:

'Armand, it is I, Odette, your Odette! I am here, I have brought what you asked for in the hope you might forgive the past. Give me a sign, my duck. Come to me, come, I beg you!'

The only reply was the sound of rain splashing on stone. She sighed and knelt down again. The shadow of a tree, resembling a Hindu goddess with many arms, danced between the candelabra. Her eyes glued to it, the woman moved her lips silently. She stared in wonder, hypnotised by the dancing shape that grew and grew, until it reached the stained-glass window. She wanted to cry out but could only find the strength to whisper, 'At last!'

Denise was wandering, lost, in the Jewish part of the cemetery. She walked past the tombs of the tragedienne Rachel, and Baron

James de Rothschild, without noticing them. She was afraid of bumping into the old drunkard again, and had only one desire: to find Tenon's tomb.

Finally she got her bearings. There in front of her stood the memorial cenotaph to André Chenier, built by his brother Marie-Joseph. She read one of the epitaphs, finding it beautiful: *'Death cannot destroy that which is immortal.'*

Musing over the words in an attempt to forget how dark it was becoming, she turned right. She had no watch, but her inner clock told her it was time to go to the meeting place. When she arrived, there was no one there. She stood for a while, shivering with fright and cold. Her shawl was soaked through by the fine rain. Finally, she could wait no longer. She ran back up the avenue. She remembered from a previous brief visit with her mistress that the chapel dedicated to the de Valois family was a little further up, a few yards from the tomb of the astronomer Jean-Baptiste Delambre. She cried out as she ran:

'Come back, Madame, I beg you! Saint Corentin, Saint Gildas, Holy Mother of God, protect me!'

At last she could see the funerary chapel where a faint light was glowing. Looking anxiously around, she began to walk cautiously towards it. All of a sudden, a shadow darted out of a bush, chased by another. She recoiled in terror. Two cats.

'Madame . . . Madame. Are you there?'

It was raining more heavily now and she couldn't see. She slipped, grabbing hold of the open gate to stop herself from falling. The chapel was empty. One of the two candles, burnt half down, dimly lit the altar where a lifeless object, resembling a sleeping animal, lay. In spite of her terror, she leaned closer and recognised the puce-coloured silk scarf her mistress had used to wrap the package she had brought with her. She was about to pick it up when something struck her wrist. A stone bounced on to the altar.

She turned round. There was no one there. She rushed out into the avenue. It was empty. Scared out of her wits, she ran as fast as her legs would take her towards the Rue de Repos exit with only one thought in her head: to alert the gatekeeper.

She had scarcely left when a man's figure emerged from a corner of the chapel by the gates through which she had just hurried. A gloved hand gathered up the puce scarf, seized the flat, rectangular object lying between the candelabra, and slipped them swiftly into a shoulder bag slung over a dark frock coat.

The man walked round the funerary monument to a grove of flowering elder trees. He took off his gloves, placed them on a tombstone and crouched down. He seized the ankles of a woman dressed in full mourning who lay senseless on the ground and dragged her over to a handcart that leant against a crypt. Catching his breath, he straightened up and began to remove a tarpaulin from the cart, which contained a strange assortment of objects: chisels, a parasol, a cabman's frock coat, two dead cats, a woman's ankle boot, a battered top hat, a fragment of tombstone, some scattered white lilies, the hood of a perambulator and sundry other items. The man tipped out the bric-à-brac and raised the handles of the cart to make it easier to slide the body in from the front. He had to struggle to lay the woman's inert body out on the cart, then he concealed it under the frock coat and the perambulator hood, piled the parasol, top hat, flowers and cats on top, higgledy-piggledy, and covered everything with the tarpaulin.

Only then did he look around him. And satisfied that there was nothing but bushes and statues, he picked up his cane and slipped away.

Sitting at a table cluttered with papers, Denise was dabbing at her eyes, unable to regain her composure. The gatekeeper, a small, lean man with a large moustache in cap and uniform, was doing his best to calm her by patting her on the shoulder. If he'd been more daring, he'd have put his arm round her.

'You must have missed each other, or maybe she took the other exit, on Boulevard de Ménilmontant. A lot of people do that around closing time. They're afraid they'll get locked in and rush out in a panic, forgetting there's this exit. That must be the explanation. Don't you think I'd have seen her going past otherwise?'

'But what if . . . something's happened to her?' Denise sniffled.

'Now, my dear, whatever could have happened to her? Surely you don't think the good Lord took her straight up to heaven? Or a ghost spirited her away? You're young all right, but not young enough to swallow that nonsense!'

Denise smiled weakly.

'That's more like it!' said the gatekeeper, in an approving voice, squeezing her shoulder lustily. 'It's a shame to spoil that pretty face of yours with tears.'

Denise blew her nose.

'The best thing for you to do is go straight home. I'll wager your mistress is there already making you a drink of hot milk.'

Denise felt her pocket to check she had the spare key to the apartment. Like the man said, Madame probably was at home. Even so, she persisted.

'I told the cabman to wait for us on Rue de Repos.'

The gatekeeper frowned.

'I went out to smoke my pipe on the pavement and I didn't notice a carriage. He must have cleared off. Those fellows have no patience at all. Don't you worry, there's a cab stand not two minutes from here, on Rue de Pyrénées. I suppose you have some money?'

'Yes, I've got the week's grocery money that Madame gave me.'

'Well, off you trot, young lady!'

Denise blushed and grew a little flustered as she waited for him to let go of her shoulder. But, rather than letting go, the gatekeeper tightened his grip. She was about to make her escape when a rasping voice made the moustachioed man jump.

'If you go to Place Vendôme, don't forget the noble conqueror of kings!' declaimed the white-haired old man lurching through the doorway.

Denise used this opportunity to escape. The old man addressed her, hiccupping, 'Whoa, camp follower! All quiet here in the bivouac, soldier Barnabé?'

'Busy actually, Père Moscou, we're about to lock up,' the gatekeeper replied, in a haughty voice.

'Hold your horses, Barnabé, hold your horses. Didn't you promise me a tot of rum a moment ago if I could catch you a dozen? Well, here they are!' cried the old man triumphantly, brandishing a battered basket full of snails. 'Nothing like a rainy day to bring these fellows out. We'll run 'em through, cut their little throats!'

The gatekeeper grumbled into his moustache and filled a small glass, which the old man knocked back in one go.

'This is hardly generous of you, Barnabé. The Emperor will be most displeased!'

'Go on and fetch your things; I've got to ring the bell. We're closing in fifteen minutes!'

'May glory and prosperity be yours!' cried the old man, giving a military salute.

Doing his best to walk in a straight line, Père Moscou weaved between the tombs, leaning on them to the left and the right, and carrying on an indignant conversation with himself: 'Five *petit-gris* and seven *Bourgognes*! Lovely, especially with a bit of garlic and parsley butter, and some shallots! Worth more than one for the road! Never mind, we'll make up for it! Ah, I hear the signal!'

There was a clanging noise as the gatekeeper began to ring his bell in Avenue du Puits.

'It's time to launch the attack, Major . . .'

He leant over and read the name on a tombstone.

'Major Brémont, assemble two companies of hussars and reconnoitre the area as far as those woods on the hill. As for you General . . . General . . .'

Another tombstone provided a second name.

'General Sabourdin, take your regiment to the bridgehead. We must hold it at all costs! Get rid of this lot and bring on the artillery. Cannons, we need cannons! Oh! A pair of gloves . . . A challenge? Who dares challenge Père Moscou? Is it you, Grouchy? You'll have to wait! Bang, bang, boom. We'll run 'em through! Prepare to die!'

He thrust his arms forward, imitating a bayonet charge, and took off at a gallop through the pouring rain until he reached the grove of elder trees where he had left his cart.

'Victory!' he roared. 'We've saved the city. We can return to camp, heads held high!'

After stuffing a glove into each pocket, he positioned himself between the handles of the cart, strapped the leather harnesses over his shoulders and, heaving himself upright, lifted his cargo, which moved off with a jolt and bounced along behind him.

'Damnation! Why's this thing so heavy? It's Grouchy's doing. He's loaded me down with bricks. I couldn't care less, Emmanuel. You didn't deserve to be a peer of France! Softly does it, cut their throats then how we'll laugh!'

At this last roar a startled ginger cat scurried off.

Père Moscou reached Boulevard Ménilmontant as the bumps and hollows of the graveyard began to vanish in the twilight. With a little luck and a lot of effort he hoped to make it back to his bivouac by nine o'clock.

Denise could hear the clock in the sitting room chime seven times. She had rung and knocked on the door, but there had been no reply. The concierge, Monsieur Hyacinthe, was adamant that Madame hadn't returned but she had refused to believe it.

She was seized again by panic, and her hand shook so much that she could barely put the key in the lock. What had become of her mistress? Perhaps she'd had a dizzy spell after leaving the funerary chapel and was still in Père-Lachaise cemetery? If so, she was sure to die of fright in that terrible place. She said she wasn't scared of ghosts but she'd be singing a different tune tonight . . . Denise hesitated, her hand gripping the key. Should she go back there and knock at the gatekeeper's lodge? Would anyone be there? What if it were the skinny man with the moustache and he pounced on her? Or the old drunk with the wild eyes? She thought better of it. There were other possible reasons for Madame's absence. She might have gone to see that woman, for instance, that . . . Denise could feel her pulse racing.

The corridor yawned before her, pitch black. She recoiled and propped open the door with a chair so that the light from the gas lamp on the landing shone into the hallway. She reached for a small box that lay on a pedestal table next to a petrol lamp, struck a match and lit the wick. The smell made her feel queasy. She pushed the chair away, closed and bolted the door and hurried into the sitting room where she lit all the candles in the candelabra. Too bad if Madame accused her of being wasteful and scolded her — she was never satisfied anyway. She had regained her composure enough to pick up the lamp and have a look around the apartment. It occurred to her that Madame de Valois might have had time to come back and leave again without being seen by the concierge. If so, she might have left a note — unless she felt unwell and was lying down. These possibilities jostled for position in the frightened girl's head as she made her way tentatively towards the bedroom.

'Madame, Madame. Are you asleep?' she whispered.

All was quiet. She decided to go in, not really knowing what she was frightened of finding. The room was in disarray. Since her husband's death, Madame only allowed it to be cleaned fortnightly. Otherwise it was strictly out of bounds, though Denise flouted this rule as soon as her mistress's back was turned.

She was familiar with every inch of the room's décor: the black veil hanging from the canopy of the four-poster bed; the ebony crucifix recently purchased at auction; the palm tree festooned with black crêpe like a funereal Christmas tree; the mirror in the bathroom draped in black gauze . . . Even the bed was in mourning, as Madame had chosen black for her sheets and silk quilt, which she slept under every night and tucked in every morning. The thick, velvet curtains drawn across the windows were also black. Only the mauve wall hangings with their motif of violets had escaped the macabre choice of colour, but Madame was already planning to replace them with charcoal grey. Near the ottoman where Madame sat for hours reading her missal, stood a small, mahogany table she had converted into an altar, upon which she had placed a photograph of her husband flanked by candleholders and incense sticks.

But most terrible was what Madame kept locked up in the enormous rosewood wardrobe with the full-length mirror, acquired shortly before her husband's death. Besides her mourning clothes, it contained a skull, various lithographs illustrating tortures inflicted on heretics and books. The books!

How they'd horrified Denise when she'd been foolish enough to glance through them one day! Even more than the skull with its hollow eye sockets.

She shivered. Although it was draught-proof, the apartment was cold and damp. Anxious to economise, her mistress had turned off the heaters the week before, declaring that spring was round the corner and it would soon warm up.

Denise explored the room, forcing herself to open the wardrobe and peek into the bathroom.

She took a quick look in the dining room, Monsieur's bedroom, the linen room, the galley kitchen, the tiny boudoir, the storeroom and even the water closet. The apartment was empty. She stood for a moment on the sitting-room balcony trying to calm herself. She leant on the guard rail and observed how the glare of electric street lamps had transformed Boulevard Haussmann into a glittering palace. She felt calmer, but as soon as she set foot on the parquet floor her fears came rushing back.

She snuffed out the candles, picked up the lamp and walked down the corridor – looking away as she passed Madame's bedroom – and hurried to her room at the far end next to the kitchen, where she threw herself on to a small iron bed, hoping to sink into sleep. The light from the lamp cast ghostly shapes on the ceiling. She put it out.

'Hell and damnation! It's darker than a tomb! Who blew out the candle?' Père Moscou roared, shaking his fist at a roving cloud that had eclipsed the crescent moon.

He was worn out from his slog across the eleventh and

twelfth arrondissements and along the Seine. He was also hungry and cold. It had stopped raining some time ago, but the wind was blowing from the north now, which meant frost.

He crossed Pont Royal and standing before him, on Quai d'Orsay, were the ruins of a vast building occupying a quadrangle that stretched from Rue de Poitiers to Rue de Bellechasse: the palace that housed the Conseil d'État and the Cour des Comptes,[2] and which was burnt down by the communards in 1871 and left to fall into decay.

The ruin, whose windows no longer contained a single pane of glass and whose roof had caved in, was reminiscent of a modern Pompeii reclaimed by nature. Badly lit by the widely spaced street lamps, a jungle had grown up around the charred stones, creating a patch of virgin forest in the heart of the capital.

Père Moscou walked along the side of the building and turned off into Rue de Lille to come round to the front. Behind him, a shadow with no shoulders and a tiny ball for a head stretched out in the light of a street lamp before contracting into a grotesque silhouette and vanishing into the night. Père Moscou did not notice it. Leaving his handcart unattended, he climbed up a flight of steps to the ground floor of the main building, which was slightly set back from the street, and pulled on a cord. There was the sound of shuffling feet and a plump and greying woman, bulging out of a fluffy, purple housecoat, opened the door cautiously.

'Oh it's you! About time. I was just off to bed.'

Père Moscou went back down the steps to fetch his cart.

'I hope your wheels are clean after all that rain. My word

you're puffing like a pair of old bellows. Hold on, I'll help you. What've you got in here? Lead?'

'Don't know. The usual. I'll just put it at the back of the yard and I'll be right with you.'

A few moments later he opened the door to the small cosy kitchen that smelled pleasantly of cooked vegetables. Madame Valladier, the concierge who reigned over the crumbling building, stood in front of her stove, moodily stirring some soup.

'That bread soup smells good,' Père Moscou said, leaning over the pot.

'Not so fast, you dirty old man. Go and wash your paws at the pump before you sit down to eat. God knows what you've been fiddling with in that graveyard of yours!'

When she turned round with a steaming bowl in her hands, the old man was already seated, a greedy look on his face and a bunch of lilies lying beside him on the table.

'Where'd that come from? You been to a wedding?'

'Comrade Barnabé told me I could take them. Some toffs buried a newborn. There were flowers everywhere, enough for a regiment.'

'That's terrible! You ought to be ashamed!'

'Bah! You've got to look at it this way. The lad's dead. He has no need of flowers, so why not offer them to a beautiful woman, eh, Maguelonne?'

'I've told you a thousand times that my name's Louise!'

'I know, but Maguelonne is more noble,' the old man replied, cutting himself a large chunk of bread. 'I found that name on a lovely pink marble tombstone.'

'Oh, you and your graveyard!' cried the concierge. 'Get a

move on, will you. I'm worn out. I've spent the whole day running from courtyard to courtyard chasing away those rascals who want to kiss the girls. Ah, young people today!'

Père Moscou lapped up his soup noisily.

'Don't be such a prude, Maguelonne. Let the boys make their final assault. If they're victorious it'll produce little conscripts for the army of the Republic. Empire and kings may be dead but the army is still alive and kicking!'

'Why don't you go and get some sleep instead of talking drivel!'

As soon as the old man had left, Madame Valladier's expression softened. She gathered the lilies and arranged them in an earthenware jug before burying her face in them.

Lighting his way with a lantern tied round his neck, Père Moscou hitched himself to his cart at the foot of a colossal stairway with a rusty, twisted banister. He groaned as he crossed the main courtyard that had once been covered in sand and was now a field of wild grass with a street lamp protruding from it. Amidst the wild oats and sweet clover the old man had planted a little vegetable garden whose harvest he shared with the concierge.

He continued along an arcaded gallery overrun by climbing plants that had broken through the floors and thick walls, until he reached a hallway strewn with rubble that crunched beneath the wheels of his cart. He stopped at the doorway of a square-shaped room, formerly the secretariant for the Conseil d'État, and lifted a moth-eaten curtain that covered the entrance.

He entered what he called his bivouac. The dividing walls of the room were riddled with cracks stuffed with bits of old newspaper. The ceiling was missing and the loose floorboards above let in dust and draughts. The ground was covered with coarse matting and in one corner an acacia tree served as a coat stand. The bivouac also contained a wood-burning stove that he used in mid-winter, a mattress piled high with quilts, a pair of rickety old chairs and a stack of wine crates filled not with bottles but with Père Moscou's carefully arranged treasures. There was a crate for odd pairs of shoes, another for hats, a third for walking sticks and umbrellas, all destined for re-sale at Carreau du Temple. It was what the old man called his retirement capital. Once a week he went looking for treasure in Père-Lachaise cemetery, where for many years he had been employed as a gravedigger and occasional stone mason, and now and then, during good weather, he would take visitors on a guided tour.

'I'll sort this lot out tomorrow,' he told himself, parking the cart, 'but these tomcats can go in the cooler.'

He lifted the tarpaulin and seized the two carcasses lying on the frock coat, two black cats he'd found behind Parmentier's tomb, already dead. Père Moscou was too fond of animals ever to kill them. He stuffed them in a box, which he covered with a piece of sacking.

'I'll offer Marcelin the skins on Sunday and then sell the rest to Cabirol as hare's meat. But first I'll have to get hold of some rabbit heads at Les Halles. I've got a lot on my plate!'

Père Moscou lay down. He was exhausted, but pleased with what he'd achieved. He snuggled under the quilts and smiled at a plaster bust sitting on a chair.

'Goodnight, my Emperor,' he mumbled, 'and death to Grouchy!'

He put out the lamp and was soon snoring.

Although her brother Erwan had been dead for three years, Denise found herself walking with him beside the sea, and was surprised to see him looking so well. A sudden crash woke her from her dream and she curled up in bed, terrified.

What had roused her was only a creaking sound magnified by the silence. She heard it again, and then again. It was too evenly spaced to be the furniture shifting, she decided. It was coming from the corridor, muffled and menacing.

Mastering her emotions, she got out of bed and dragged her washstand against the door after first removing the jug and basin. She listened. Silence. Trembling with fear and cold – her room faced north and was not heated – she curled up on the narrow iron bed. A pale light shone through the window. Denise fixed her eyes on the door handle and saw it move slowly downwards. Someone was trying to get in. A chink appeared as the door opened slightly and was blocked by the washstand, which stood firm. The intruder gave a slight push, to no avail. The door closed and the handle went back to its original position. The unseen visitor moved stealthily away.

Denise relaxed her jaw and lowered her hand, which had been pressed against her mouth. She made herself count up to two hundred. Vaguely reassured, she got up and hurriedly straightened her clothes and hair. The large purple cotton shawl that had carried her meagre belongings from Quimper three years earlier was spread out on the bed. Behind a worn curtain, two patched dresses and the velvet skirt that Madame de Valois had given her hung on a clothes rail. She placed them on the shawl with some stockings, a petticoat and two carefully folded white blouses and, before tying the four corners of the shawl together, she added a tarnished silver crucifix, a mirror and an embroidered tucker — objects that had once belonged to her mother and which constituted her entire inheritance.

On her guard, Denise listened carefully and, hearing nothing, decided to slip on her coat and put back the washstand. She was just about to leave the room when she realised she had forgotten something. She lifted the mattress and pulled out a chromo-lithograph fixed to a thin piece of wood, which depicted the Virgin Mary, dressed in a blue robe, standing in front of some yellow rocks. She wrapped it quickly in a pillowcase, wedged it under her arm and, picking up her bundle, opened the door.

The grey dawn hadn't dispelled the menacing gloom of the apartment. Denise held her breath as she had before plunging into the River Odet as a child, and raced down the corridor. She had to get out of that haunted place as fast as possible. When she reached the landing she hesitated. The keys! What had she done with the keys? Had she put them above the fireplace in the sitting room before lighting the candles or mislaid them in her room? It was too late! She slammed the door impulsively, tore down a flight of stairs, then stopped dead in her tracks. Where would she go? The only money she had was the change from the grocery money. She ought to have left it on the hall table, or she might be accused of stealing. But then again Madame de Valois owed her some wages. The money could be considered an advance payment. In any case she did not have the courage to go back up there.

She carried on down the stairs. Where would she go? She didn't know a soul in Paris. Was there a place that took in homeless young women? Then she remembered Madame's former lover, Monsieur Victor Legris, the attractive gentleman with dark eyes who always had a kind word for her and occasionally slipped her a coin. She remembered having accompanied Madame de Valois to his bookshop on the Rive Gauche, near the Seine. What was the name of that street? It began with Saint . . . and there was a hospital nearby.

As she crossed the entrance hall Monsieur Hyacinthe called out to her.

'You're abroad early this morning, Mademoiselle Le Louarn. Is anything the matter?'

She shook her head and walked out into the deserted boulevard, unaware that the door to the building had opened behind her and a young boy wearing a gilt-buttoned tunic and a peaked cap had slipped out.

The sun's early rays shone through a grove of plane trees on to a ruined ivy-covered baluster and lit up a copper brazier that suddenly glinted, startling a small, slender animal with a pointed nose.

'Come back here, Madame Stone Marten, you coward. Come back, my pretty one, and I'll give you a big chunk of this crispy pork rind! An offering from Mother Valladier, that paragon among women who still has a fine bosom despite her age . . . You refuse? You're a fool. Victory is ours, boom, bang, boom!'

Père Moscou combed his fingers through his hair as he waited for his coffee to boil. He had slept soundly and was fully sober. He wished he had a drop of something with which to toast the beautiful dawn, but it was his principle never to drink anywhere but leaning against the bar of a tavern or, if pressed, at a friend's house.

'Being drunk on one's own patch is unworthy of Antoine Jean Anicet Ménager, otherwise known as Moscou the Brave, grandson of the Emperor of the *grognards*[3] and of the *grognard* of the Emperor. Remember, I am accountable to the nation for the lives of my men. If the enemy attacks, we'll run him through, we'll slit his throat!'

This speech was directed at a few pigeons and a crow attracted by the breakfast scraps. Père Moscou rubbed his neck.

'Speaking of throats, mine's a little rough this morning. I must have had a bit of a tipple last night. Moscou, you're an old lush and for your trouble not a drop of plonk before midday! Come along, it's time you got to work.'

He poured the remains of his coffee on to the brazier, which billowed with smoke, and made his way through the under-growth and wild lilies, disturbing a flock of sparrows as he went. He tripped over a pile of plaster debris, bounced off a fig tree and landed in a tangle of clematis.

'Prepare to die!' he cried, rushing at the invisible enemy.

He charged across his bivouac, sabre to the fore, then stopped in his tracks and walked nonchalantly over to his cart, which was standing by the wall. He lifted the tarpaulin, and glanced at the contents for a moment.

'What a load of old rubbish!'

Seizing the parasol, the ankle boot and the top hat, he went to deposit them in their appropriate boxes.

'It wouldn't surprise me if people left their underwear behind in that cemetery.'

He returned to the cart.

'Not to mention their children. First they dump the pram,' he said, dropping the hood of the perambulator on the floor, 'and then they toss the brat in the nettles!'

He was anxious to try on the coachman's frock coat and grabbed it, twirling it around as he threw it over his shoulders.

'I should dye it green or red or the second coachman will jeer at me. It's not bad, it'll make a nice coa—'

He stood rooted to the spot with his mouth wide open. A woman dressed in black was lying on the cart, her head resting on a piece of tombstone and a closed umbrella on her chest. Her eyes were shut and her cheeks deathly pale.

'Well, I'll be damned! A stowaway!' He brushed the anonymous woman's forehead with his hand and cried out as though he'd been stung. There was no doubt about it, she was quite dead. He noticed a brownish stain on her coat collar and pulled it back to reveal a patch of dried blood on the nape of her neck. He lifted her fur cap and pushed her head to one side. The back of her skull had been smashed in. A murder. He let go of the woman's head in alarm.

'That's a serious corpse. I've seen enough to know and never balked at burying them. But . . . a murdered woman on my cart!

That's going too far! I know I didn't do it, that's for sure. I'll fight anything that moves, like a lion I am when I've had a few and I'm fired up for battle. But never a woman. Never! Who's trying to lay the blame for this wickedness on Père Moscou?'

With trembling hands he replaced the tarpaulin and harnessed himself to the cart, which he dragged to the far side of the courtyard and left in a tangle of elder and viburnum bushes while he ran to fetch a spade from his bivouac.

'Lucky it rained last night so the ground's soft . . .'

Removing the tarpaulin again he examined the corpse carefully. He decided he would take the hat but not the coat — too much blood. There was a chain round the woman's neck with a silver locket on it. I'll sell that to the jeweller on Rue de Pernelle together with this diamond ring, he thought, as he slipped it off the third finger of her left hand. The wedding ring proved more stubborn and he gave up, considering it improper to deprive a dead person of such a sacred ornament.

Having pocketed the jewellery, he spat on his hands, rubbed them together, picked up the spade and began digging, whistling a marching tune to give him courage. He tried to convince himself the dead woman was a soldier killed in battle and that he, the man's general, was burying him on the battle-field. It took him a good hour to dig a deep enough hole, and when he stood up straight he was dripping with sweat despite the chill in the air. He pulled the dead woman by the feet. As she slid off the cart her coat and dress became hitched up, exposing her silk-stockinged legs. Père Moscou turned away in embarrassment. The body fell to the ground with a thud. He rolled it into the pit with his umbrella, hurriedly shovelling back the loose earth. When he'd finished, he flattened the grave and scattered it with stones, bits of rubble and grass. He cast a critical eye over his work and found it wanting. The most important thing was missing. He went off, inventing another story to reassure himself.

'I'm certain it was he, Emperor. Emmanuel Grouchy's behind this. Remember Waterloo? If he'd stopped Blücher from joining forces with Wellington, victory would have been yours. I reported it to you. He found out, and has hated me ever since. This is his revenge.'

Père Moscou returned carrying two uprooted lilac bushes, which he very carefully replanted. After he'd finished, he thrust his fists in his pockets and stepped back to consider his work.

'No one, not even Grouchy, would say a woman's buried there, God rest her soul. I'm not done yet; I need a pick-me-up after that, a drop of hussar's elixir.

The overgrown garden was so serene he might almost have imagined the strange ceremony. But the jewellery he was rolling between his fingers was real enough.

CHAPTER TWO

It was almost nine o'clock when Denise reached Pont des Arts. The crisp, clear morning set off to perfection one of the most beautiful views in Paris. She stopped halfway across the bridge, mesmerised by the sights around her. To her left lay the towers of the Palais de Justice, the spire of Saint-Chapelle and the imposing bulk of Notre-Dame with the point of the Île de la Cité and the Vert-Galant garden glinting behind them in the sunshine. To her right, far in the distance, the Eiffel Tower soared into the sky. The Seine seemed to arch its back as it curved under Pont Neuf, its current breaking against the hulls of the laundry boats before settling into a smooth yellowish flow, dotted with ducks.

She walked past the L'Institut and the École des Beaux-Arts, watching the second-hand booksellers and the medal traders setting up their stalls on the other side of Quai Malaquais. She had to pluck up courage to ask a portly man the way, but he smiled at her from behind an enormous moustache and pointed out Rue des Saints-Pères.

The houses here were less ostentatiously grand than those on Boulevard Haussman, but Denise found them much more beautiful, perhaps because their weather-beaten façades had stood the test of time. There was a calm, provincial air to the street that she found reassuring. There were several bookshops, but she couldn't see Monsieur Legris's. It was only when she spotted the sign saying 'Elzévir' above the number 18 that she was certain that she had come to the right place. Behind the shop windows, which were set in wood panelling of a greeny-bronze colour, large red-bound gilt-edged volumes were lined up next to more recent works. Amongst the latter, the latest book by Émile Zola, *The Beast in Man*, the extremely controversial *Noncoms* by Lucien Descaves and a Shakespeare play, left open at a lurid illustration of witches, took pride of place. One corner of the window display was dedicated to some novels whose titles Denise read out haltingly in a low voice: *The Lerouge Affair* by Émile Gaboriau, *The Exploits of Rocambole* by Ponson du Terrail, *The Mystery of Edwin Drood* by Charles Dickens, *Fifi Vollard's Gang* by Constant Guéroult and *The Moonstone* by Wilkie Collins. A small notice in red ink read:

If you like murder mysteries and thrillers, do not hesitate to ask for advice. It will be our pleasure to assist you.

A little alarmed by these words, Denise pressed her face against the window and saw a blond young man inside the shop, engrossed in a newspaper. She was startled by the sound of whistling. A schoolboy, his cap pulled down over his eyes, was standing beside her, so close that he nudged her arm. She moved away slightly and then took refuge under the awning of a packaging shop on the other side of the street, hoping that Madame's ex-lover would soon appear. The schoolboy positioned himself a little further off, in front of Debauve & Gallais, makers of fine chocolates.

The door of the building beside the bookshop opened and out came a woman as round as a ball, enveloped in an apron and armed with a broom. As she scanned the street, looking from right to left, she caught sight of Denise and stared at her suspiciously. Then she disappeared into the hall, reappearing a moment later with a bucket, which she emptied on to the pavement just as a costermonger's cart appeared beside her. The water narrowly missed the woman pulling the cart.

'Watch out, Madame Ballu. You almost drowned me!'

'I'm sorry, Madame Pignot, my mind was elsewhere. I was thinking about my cousin Alphonse, the one who went to Senegal. He's caught it!'

'Caught what?'

'Influenza. They've given him syrup of snails, but he's still coughing and coughing.'

'Not to worry, Madame Ballu, I'm sure he'll get better. Good day!'

'And good day to you, Madame Pignot.'

Madame Pignot waved in the direction of the bookshop and set off again pulling her cart. The young blond man rushed out of the shop. 'Maman, wait!' he cried.

He caught up with the costermonger, grabbed a couple of large apples from the top of her fruit and vegetable basket, planted a kiss on her cheek and went back into the bookshop.

Denise did not budge from her spot. She saw the blond boy reappear on the pavement and call to a man leaning out of a first-floor window, 'Give me ten minutes, boss!'

The man nodded his assent, then closed the window. Denise had time to notice his slanting eyes. She remembered her mistress mentioning Monsieur Legris's Chinese valet disapprovingly.

The Oriental man was dressed in the English style in a fully buttoned tweed jacket with narrow lapels and flap pockets, a white shirt, grey trousers with an impeccable crease and brown leather shoes. He went over to a table with a row of inkwells on it, and picked up some rail tickets, which he slipped into his wallet. He gazed for a moment at the two new prints recently hung on the wall to brighten the room. One, *Boat ride under the Azuma Bridge*, was by Kiyonga[1] and the other, entitled *Lake Biwa*, was by Hiroshige.[2] He pushed open the door of the bathroom, which was equipped with a copper bath. Leaning towards the mirror over the basin, he straightened the knot of his green silk tie, put on a checked worsted bowler hat and, apparently satisfied, smiled at the photograph on a marble shelf in front of him. Gazing out of the image was a young woman with brown hair who was tenderly holding a boy of about twelve. At the bottom was the inscription, *Daphne and Victor, London 1872*.

The man went back into the spacious sitting room, which was furnished in the style of Louis XIII, slid back a slatted paper partition, and entered a Japanese-style bedroom. A recess housed a thick cotton blanket and a wooden pillow, a Japanese trunk with ornamental hinges, Noh theatre masks, sheathed swords and a lacquer writing desk. He closed a suitcase, covered in multicoloured labels, and attached a rectangular tag to the handle bearing the following identification: *Monsieur Kenji Mori, 18 Rue des Saints-Pères, Paris, France*.

As he prepared for his departure, Kenji was reflecting on

how, finally, Iris was going to be living near him. In her last letter she had expressed her joy at the thought of living in France, no longer having to wait weeks for him to find time to leave his business associate and cross the Channel to be with her. Saint-Mandé was very close to Paris and he would be able to visit her every Sunday. She would enjoy living comfortably in the heart of the countryside. Mademoiselle Bontemps's boarding house, an agreeable dwelling on Chausée de l'Étang, was opposite the Bois de Vincennes. He would, however, have to use all his wiles to keep her away from the bookshop. It was out of the question that she should meet Victor! He would find a way. His thoughts were interrupted by the noise of wheels in the street. He went over to the window: a carriage was drawing up in front of the bookshop. The blond young man got out and shouted triumphantly, 'Your cab awaits, M'sieu Mori!'

'Coming!'

Denise watched the blond boy come out of the bookshop weighed down by a suitcase dotted with labels. He was followed by two men: the Oriental, and a good-looking man of medium height aged about thirty. He had brown hair and a moustache. She stiffened – it was Madame de Valois's old lover! She heard him cry, 'Have a good journey, Kenji, be good!' as the Oriental took his seat in the cab, which set off.

As soon as Victor Legris and the blond boy had gone back into the shop, Denise crossed the road in what she hoped was a confident manner and went in after them. The blond boy was busy dusting the books on the shelves with a feather duster. At the tinkling of the door bell, he turned his large round head, crowned with dead-straight hair, and smiled at Denise, who gazed at him, blushing, not knowing what to say.

'Good morning. May I help you?' When she didn't reply, he went up to her, smiling more broadly. 'Are you looking for a book? Any author in particular?'

She noticed that he was hunchbacked. Her brother Erwan had told her once that meeting a hunchback brought luck. She was reassured, without knowing why, although now the boy was scrutinising her in a slightly condescending way. 'I would like to speak to Monsieur Legris,' she whispered. 'It's . . . important.'

Intrigued, the boy took in the young girl's attire. She was badly turned out, her shoes were in a pitiful state and her crinoline was rather skimpy. He noticed the rectangular package that she was clutching to her bosom and from this he concluded that she must be one of those provincial girls convinced they were the next George Sand, come to sell her writings to the booksellers of Saint-Germain. He sighed, and going behind the counter, disappeared up the spiral staircase that led to the first floor. Left alone, Denise stared at the bust of a man wearing a wig and a faintly mocking expression, which was positioned on a black marble mantelpiece. She tried to read the name of the figure.

'So, you like my Molière?'

The deep voice made her jump. Victor Legris was regarding her with a questioning air. The young man had taken up his duster again and was humming as he dusted.

'I'm in the service of Madame de Valois, and I . . . I've . . .'

'Madame de Valois?' Victor frowned. The image of his former mistress came to him, her blonde hair loose, her round pink breasts revealed beneath the sheet she had thrown back. It all seemed such a long time ago . . . how long ago had he left her? Nine, ten months? 'Yes, I recognise you. Remind me what your name is.'

'Denise Le Louarn.'

'Denise, of course. Did Madame send you?' He suddenly felt guilty.

'No, no, Monsieur, I came of my own accord. I don't know anyone in Paris except you, and . . .'

She cast an embarrassed look at the assistant who was listening to the conversation. At a sign from Victor, he made himself scarce.

'I have to speak to you, please, Monsieur . . . It's about Madame de Valois, I'm so worried.'

Feeling uncomfortable, Victor noticed that the young girl looked pale and uncertain and seemed on the point of collapse. He gestured vaguely, then let his hand fall. 'Have you had any breakfast?' Without waiting for a reply, he took her arm and went on, 'No, neither have I. Come on. Joseph, if anyone asks for me, I'll be at the Temps Perdu. Leave your things here, behind the counter, Mademoiselle.'

The door bell sounded. Joseph shook his feather duster in exasperation over a rectangular table covered with a green cloth in the middle of the bookshop. '*Temps perdu*, time wasted. How apt – he certainly knows how to waste time. And, what's more, he leaves me to run the business on my own, poor Jojo!'

He put down his feather duster and, settling himself on a stool, took an apple and a newspaper out of his pocket. He glanced at the front page.

Stop press: In Germany, Paul Lafargue, the son-in-law of Karl Marx, rejoiced at the 4,500 votes received by the socialist Bebel in Strasbourg.

He shrugged his shoulders; he wasn't very interested in politics. He leafed through the daily until he came to the heading *Miscellaneous News* and read out loud:

A strange robbery. Last night, unknown individuals broke into the stables of the Omnibus Company depot on Rue Ordener and cut off the manes and tails of twenty-five horses. An investigation is underway . . .

'That's not normal! What on earth are they going to do with horse hair? Make wigs?'

As quick as a flash, he jumped down from his perch, snatched up a pair of scissors and a pot of glue, and pulled a thick black notebook out of his other pocket. He cut out the article and stuck it into the notebook with all the other unusual snippets. Then he bit into his apple and went on with his reading.

The Temps Perdu was on the corner of Rue des Saints-Pères and Quai Malaquais. At that early hour, the café was almost empty. They sat down at a table in one of the little booths opposite the bar. Victor ordered tea. Denise didn't want anything to drink but she ate some bread and butter and a croissant. She was ravenous.

'The French are incapable of making tea correctly, even though it's so simple! This brew is like dish water.'

'Madame always tells me that I make her hot chocolate badly.' The young girl wiped a crumb from the corner of her mouth.

Mildly irritated, Victor pushed his cup away. 'If I understand correctly, you want to leave Madame de Valois. Is she really so unbearable?'

Denise hesitated, lowering her eyes. 'She was different before . . .'

'Before what?'

'Before the death of Monsieur. Yes, she was demanding and strict, like all bosses, but she also had her good points. This summer, in Houlgate, she was actually very kind; she let me go for walks by the sea while she went to her meetings with Madame de Brix.'

She stopped suddenly, her fingers moulding some crumbs of bread, and cried: 'She's the one who put all these foolish thoughts in her head!'

'Thoughts?'

'You'll laugh, Monsieur . . . Well, that the dead aren't dead, that there's an afterlife, not in paradise, but here on earth with us, that they come back to visit us without us being able to see them . . . things like that. In Houlgate, Madame de Brix took Madame to see a medium. He lived in a beautiful house where very strange things went on. Monsieur Numa, the medium, would lend his voice to the dead so that they could converse with the living. Madame de Brix talked to her son who's been dead and buried for ages. I didn't see it myself, it was Sidonie Taillade, her maid, who told me. It made her laugh. She said that her boss was a bit loopy.'

Denise emphasised this statement by tapping her forehead with her index finger. She went on: 'Madame de Valois changed overnight when the telegram announcing Monsieur's death arrived from America. It was the end of November and . . .'

Victor was no longer listening. He was remembering how the Comtesse de Salignac had told him the news with relish: 'I believe you know Armand de Valois? You can cross him off your customer list – he's no longer of this world, poor thing, carried off by yellow fever.' Taken up with his love for Tasha, a painter he had met at the Universal Exposition, Victor had not found the courage to present his condolences in person to Odette and had made do with sending her a rather impersonal note. Tasha . . . He could picture her as clearly as if she were before him, with her green eyes and red hair tied back at the nape of her neck. He could even hear the slight lilt of her Russian accent. How he missed her! She had been giving him the cold shoulder for two long weeks. And over something so stupid! He had merely dared to disapprove of her proposal to exhibit her canvases at the Soleil d'Or. 'That insalubrious dive on the Place Saint-Michel? Why not choose somewhere with a better clientele?' he had suggested. Of course she had taken offence; she was so touchy! 'Admit it – you're just jealous! You can't stand me living an independent life; you would like to shut me up like a concubine!' she had retorted, flaring up with anger. Jealous . . . Yes, she was right, but wasn't that natural when he saw the familiar way the other artists treated her, especially that Maurice Laumier, whom he loathed and who loathed him back?

'. . . know that perhaps I shouldn't say this to you, Monsieur, but . . . Monsieur, are you listening?'

Victor came back to earth. 'Yes?'

'You understand, Monsieur, I think she was worried that the Good Lord had punished her because . . . well . . .' She lowered her head.

'Punished? What do you mean?'

'For her affair with you – I don't mean to be rude.'

Victor forced himself to smile. 'Come on, my dear, I wasn't the only one and, besides, Monsieur de Valois was scarcely a paragon of virtue himself. You worked for them; you must have been aware of that. By the time he died, your mistress and I had long since separated.'

'I know. But that doesn't stop her praying several times a day, on her knees, in front of a portrait of Monsieur, framed in black crêpe. I've heard her begging him to forgive her. "Armand, I feel your presence, I know you're here. You see everything. You hear everything. Give your little sugar plum a sign, my duck, I implore you!" Fancy calling a dead man "my duck"! And there's another thing. She had me close the shutters and pull the curtains on the pretext that Monsieur feared the light, so we live constantly by candlelight. The apartment is like a tomb! And you wouldn't believe Madame's bedroom . . . if you could see how she's decorated it and what she keeps in her wardrobe . . . She would have liked a grand funeral with no expense spared on flowers, wreaths and the whole works, but since he was buried amongst the savages, she had a marble plaque engraved, which cost an arm and a leg because of the gold lettering, and she had it placed in the Vallois family chapel in the Pères-Lachaise cemetery. All that frightened me. I've tried to convince myself that being widowed has driven her a little mad. She started disappearing every Monday and Thursday afternoon, and when she returned she was . . . trans . . . trans . . .'

'Transfigured?'

'Yes, that must be it. You know, like the saints you see on stained-glass windows in churches. The day before yesterday she asked me to go with her. We took a carriage and went to a handsome building in a part of Paris I didn't know. A lady let us in. I didn't see her face, she was wearing a veil, but I gathered from the tone of her voice that she was displeased. She took Madame to one side and lectured her because she had not come alone. They shut themselves in a bedroom at the end of a long corridor. I had to wait more than two hours for them to come out. Madame had been crying; she was dabbing her eyes. The lady in the veil said to her: 'Tomorrow, your mourning will be over on condition that you obey your husband and bring him what he asked for. Then he will be freed from his bonds and you will be able to start a new life.'

'What did she have to take?'

Denise bit her lip. 'A picture that Monsieur was very fond of, at least that's what Madame told me. I went to get it; it was very dark in Monsieur's bedroom and Madame was in a hurry. We went to Père-Lachaise and that's where Madame disappeared, I've . . .'

Victor lit a cigarette and blew out the smoke, watching a large brunette woman on the other side of the road. If he had had his camera with him, he would have been able to take a good shot of the light figure against the dark wall. Meanwhile the girl was still prattling on . . .

'You have to believe me. I'm not making it up, Monsieur Legris, I swear that it's true! When I reached the chapel, Madame had disappeared. There was only the scarf that had been wrapped . . . just the scarf, there on the ground. I went to pick it up, but something struck me, a stone perhaps. But I saw no one. I was terrified and ran as fast as I could to the gatekeeper's lodge and he advised me to go home. When I got back to Boulevard Haussmann, I looked everywhere, but she wasn't there. I shut myself in my room and early in the morning someone tried to break in! I sensed an evil presence just as I had in the chapel. If you call up spirits, they appear!'

While the young girl continued her lamentations, Victor, amused, was wondering why Odette had had to think up such a far-fetched strategem just to stay out all night. He found it hard to believe in Odette's new incarnation as a sorrowing widow desperate to communicate with the spirit of her husband, whom she had betrayed over and over again. Perhaps this time she had two lovers on the go and was trying to fool one of them in order to spend time with the other.

'Please, Monsieur Legris, I implore you to help me. I don't want to go back there. I'd rather sleep under the bridges than stay another night in that cursed house!'

'Don't worry, my dear, Madame de Valois has no doubt had to go away unexpectedly.' To be with a loved one, just like Kenji, who is off courting his dear Iris, he thought.

'But, Monsieur, there really was . . . a presence outside my door; I didn't dream it. And Madame hasn't taken any of her clothes. I would have noticed when I searched . . .'

While maintaining an air of interest, Victor studied the girl's lips, but really he was thinking of Tasha. He suddenly had an inspiration. Thanks to this voluble little maid, and to Kenji, he had the opportunity to effect a reconciliation. He stubbed out his cigarette and threw a few coins on to the saucer.

'It's all right, my dear. I'll sort something out.'

Two customers were leafing through some books, one sitting at the big table and the other at the counter where Joseph was standing. Victor beckoned him discreetly.

'I'm leaving you to look after this young lady. Her name's Denise – keep an eye on her. I'll be right back.'

'But, boss . . .'

Victor had already gone.

'Would you believe it! As soon as Monsieur Mori turns his back, Monsieur Legris disappears too! I can't be everywhere at once,' grumbled Joseph, giving Denise a black look.

'Don't worry about me, Monsieur. I'll just sit on this stool and wait. If you need any help, please just ask me,' stammered the girl.

Slightly mollified by this offer and by the girl's use of 'Monsieur', Joseph deigned to smile before turning to help a customer.

In high good humour, Victor set off up Rue Lepic, whistling the opening bars of a waltz by Fauré. He turned into Rue Tholozé and pushed open the doors of Bibulus, a smoky bar with a sign representing a suckling dog. After the dazzlingly bright sunshine, the darkness took him by surprise. He slowly crossed the low-ceilinged room that was furnished with barrels for tables. Two customers, sprawled in front of their glasses of beer, were shuffling greasy cards.

At the counter a large ruddy-faced fellow was drawing pints.

'*Ave*, Firmin!' Victor greeted him.

'Amen,' grunted the barman.

Victor went along a narrow corridor and entered a room on the same floor with a glass roof that was kitted out as a painter's studio. A charcoal stove gave out a powerful heat and the air was heavy with the smell of tobacco. Half a dozen young people were bent over their easels working on studies of the model, a half-naked lady leaning against a pedestal on which a vase of carnations had been placed. To one side, a petite redhead, whose chignon was coming loose, was concentrating on her canvas, covering it with nervous brush strokes. She was wearing an oversized stained smock that came down to her ankle boots. A large man with long hair and a beard was leaning towards her, proffering advice. With flushed cheeks, Victor observed them for a while before making up his mind. 'Hello Tasha,' he said, ignoring the bearded fellow.

Surprised, the petite redhead jumped.

'Can I talk to you in private?' he added.

'What happy event brings our friend the bookseller-cum-photographer here?' asked the bearded man in an aggressive tone.

Victor greeted him stiffly.

'Maurice, make yourself scarce for a moment, would you?' said Tasha, giving him a friendly pat.

'Right away, my beauty, for you, anything . . . anything at all. In fact, I could frame your pictures for you.'

'Why are you always so rude to him?' asked Tasha, putting down her brush. Victor immediately adopted a penitent air.

'I think I should apologise,' he said.

'I don't expect you to do that; nothing will change his personality. I did warn you though that I will not be treated like an object.'

At that moment enthusiastic cries greeted Firmin who was carrying a tray of glasses. Maurice gave Victor a mocking glance and joined the others crowding round the large fellow, calling him the Bacchus of modern times and the saviour of oppressed artists.

Adjusting her chignon, Tasha took off her smock to reveal a white bodice and mauve skirt, then put on a coat that tied at the waist. 'Did you want something?'

'Just a little favour. Would you be able to lend your room to a girl who has nowhere else to go?'

She looked at him in amazement, one glove still in her hand, the other half on.

'And where will I sleep?'

'Rue des Saints-Pères. Number 18. The Elzévir bookshop.'

She slowly finished putting on her gloves.

'You could have thought of a better excuse.'

'It's the truth. The girl's name is Denise and I don't know what else to do with her. But, even if that weren't the case, I would have come anyway with some sort of proposition. Two weeks without you; it's an eternity.'

She hid a smile, pleased to have scored some kind of victory.

Several times during the past two weeks she had been on the point of rushing round to see him, risking bumping into his Japanese business associate, who behaved coldly towards her, for some unknown reason. But she had held back, not wanting to be the first to make the move, out of pride, but also out of caution. Victor was too possessive. If she allowed herself, even once, to seek his forgiveness, he would think he had the right to decide upon whom she saw and what she did, and to smother her with love. And that would be the end of the affair . . .

'You seem to have forgotten Monsieur Mori.'

'Kenji is in London until the end of the week.'

'You've thought of everything! How organised you are! Am I supposed to fall into your arms sighing, "When do we leave for your house?"?'

'You're supposed to do what you like, knowing that nothing would make me happier than a yes.'

'I would be able to come and go as I liked?'

'How could I stop you? I haven't the strength,' he said, laughing.

'Well, in that case . . . a truce may be possible. Does this poor little homeless girl want to move into my palace this evening?'

He almost kissed her, but already she was moving away to put her hat on in front of the mirror at the end of the studio. Maurice Laumier approached him.

'What do you think of this canvas? Our friend is getting better all the time, don't you agree? Exhibiting her work at the Soleil d'Or will be a real opportunity for her. Gauguin has decorated the basement, and two Saturdays a month he gets all the artists who contribute to the magazine *La Plume* to gather there. You're always going on about literature; you should come along to listen to the poets – they're the real thing.'

Victor had no desire to get into an argument with Maurice Laumier. He studied Tasha's composition, in the centre of which the carnations flared like a flame, throwing the languid silhouette of the woman into shadow.

'I'm surprised that you encourage the study of such conventional subjects,' he murmured.

'My dear chap, you pretend to know about photography, so surely I don't have to explain to you that the subject is unimportant, it's the style that distinguishes the artist.'

'You're absolutely right. And I like Tasha's style enormously. I hope you don't object to that?'

'Don't start that again! See you tomorrow, Maurice, we've got to go.'

They went out, leaving Maurice fuming. Enraged, he knocked over Tasha's stool as he sat back down on his own.

'To hear them, you'd think I was a rum baba, and they were silly schoolboys fighting over me in a pâtisserie,' she murmured, walking quickly up Rue Durantin.

'What did you say?' asked Victor, who was struggling to keep up with her.

'Nothing, I was talking to myself!'

Worried, he hurried to catch up with her. What if she changed her mind? She had calmed down by the time they reached Rue Berthe and he was able to walk next to her.

'I'm sorry about earlier. I didn't mean to be unpleasant to Laumier.'

'When will you stop being jealous?' she cried, turning to face him.

'Me? Jealous?'

'Listen to me, Victor Legris, we have to sort this out now, once and for all! I had a life before I met you and I will not put up with you interfering in my friendships. You're suspicious, vindictive and you have no self-control!'

'I'm sorry, I swear that—'

'No vows!' she exclaimed, laughing, in spite of herself. 'You won't be able to keep them.'

They reached Rue des Martyrs. Above them towered the scaffolding of the Sacré-Coeur construction site whilst, lower down, the sails of the Moulin de la Galette hung over the tiered houses that sat cheek by jowl.

'What about your exhibition? Are you ready for it?' he asked sheepishly.

'I'm only exhibiting two or three canvases. Framing is so expensive . . .'

She slowed down. Now he would think she was asking him for money. Of course, he reacted immediately.

'Tasha, I can pay for it.'

'No.'

'Don't be stubborn! I can afford it and it would give me pleasure . . .'

'Liar. You told me you disapproved of the venue, too vulgar for your taste.'

'I was being stupid, yet again. I take it all back. I believe in you, in your talent. It would be ridiculous to give up now! Let me do this for you. It's not as if it's jewels I want to buy for you, just some bits of wood, for heaven's sake!'

She walked along in silence nibbling her thumbnail through her glove. He edged closer to her and pulled her to him. She let herself be drawn into his embrace, indifferent to the clatter of the hansom cabs passing each other on the road.

'That ringing noise is deafening! Oh no, young man, you'll never convince me!'

An elegant lady with greying hair was staring at Joseph over a lorgnette. Nearby, a thin young girl whose nose was slightly too long gazed at him adoringly. Hunched over on her stool, Denise was doing her best to escape the notice of the ladies.

Joseph was showing off an apparatus resting on the desk.

'It's child's play, Madame la Comtesse. I'll show you how it works. And you too, Mademoiselle Valentine. Imagine that you want to talk to your aunt. First you press the bell hard, two or three times, then you lift the receiver and bring it to your ear. You say "allô" – that's an English word, you don't say *bonjour*. The telephonist replies "allô" and you give her the name and address of the person you want to speak to. I'll demonstrate.'

He put the receiver to his ear, pausing to observe the effect on his audience.

'Allô . . . Yes, Mademoiselle, I would like to speak to Madame la Comtesse de Salignac, 22 Rue du Bac, Paris.'

He smiled at Valentine.

'Here you are, Mademoiselle. You keep the receiver next to your ear until you hear your aunt. Never fiddle with the bell while you're in the middle of a conversation, because you'll cut the connection. Speak clearly, without raising your voice, holding the mouthpiece an inch or two from your mouth.'

He turned to the Comtesse.

'When the conversation is finished, you hang up and press the bell to let the telephonist know that the line is free.'

The Comtesses de Salignac sniffed disdainfully.

'I don't see the advantage of owning such an instrument. If you want conversation, there's nothing better than a tearoom! I'm sure that no sensible person will want to be encumbered with such a device. Tell me, young man, have you received my Georges Ohnet?'

'Which one?'

'*Spirit of Stone* and this time I have the name of the publisher: it's Ollendorff.'

'No, Madame, not yet, it's only just come out, although we do expect to receive it soon. In the meantime I can recommend the latest Zola.'

'You can't mean *Beast in Man*! You must have taken leave of your senses, young man! I counted the deaths: six, you hear me, six! President Grandmorin, assassinated, that makes one. Madame Misard, slowly poisoned, that makes two. Flore, committed suicide, three. Séverine: assassinated. And finally, Jacques and Pecqueux, run over by a locomotive. That Monsieur Zola soaks his pen in blood. He's not a writer, he's a butcher!'

Joseph caught Valentine's eye. She was trying to stifle a laugh. The Comtesse tapped her on the shoulder with her lorgnette.

'Valentine, we'll come back when Monsieur Legris does us the honour of being here.'

As they were leaving, a schoolboy stood aside to let them pass. From outside the shop window, Valentine risked an amorous glance at Joseph, who was then in seventh heaven.

Meanwhile, the schoolboy, a slender lad whose voice was breaking, was asking for the poetry section. Joseph distractedly pointed out a shelf at right angles to the counter, behind which Denise was still patiently waiting.

Victor looked in cautiously.

'Has the battleaxe gone?'

Three heads turned in unison and Joseph exclaimed, 'You might warn me when you're about to appear like that from the apartment, I almost jumped out of my skin! You can come in, the coast is clear.'

Tasha appeared behind Victor.

'Mademoiselle Tasha! How lovely to see you!'

'I'm happy to see you too, Jojo. I've been missing your moujik features.'

She went up to Denise, who got to her feet, blushing.

'Hello, Mademoiselle, you must be Denise? Monsieur Legris told me about your troubles. I can help out for a few days if that would suit you. I have a little room in Rue Notre-Dame-de-Lorette. It's not luxurious, but you no one will disturb you there and you will have a superb view of the rooftops of Paris.'

'Thank you, Madame, it's too good of you!'

'Call me Tasha. And it's a pleasure – I know what it's like to be homeless. Here's the key. Joseph will take you; he knows where it is. I hope you don't mind, Joseph?'

'You can take a cab,' put in Victor.

'A cab? No, I don't mind at all! Shall we go straight away?'

'If you like,' replied Tasha. 'I've left some provisions; don't hesitate to help yourself. And . . . please excuse the mess. Oh, one other thing. The roof leaks, and the owner keeps putting off calling the tiler, so don't move the buckets.'

Not knowing how to show her gratitude, Denise nervously crumpled her dress between her fingers. She looked anxiously from Victor to Tasha. 'Monsieur Legris, would it be too much to ask you to get me a reference if you see Madame de Valois, because it will be very difficult for me to find a position if I don't have a reference and . . .'

'Don't worry, I'll write you one since your mistress is not here.'

The schoolboy made his way towards the door, murmuring, 'I'll think about it.'

No one paid much attention to him. Uneasy, Victor tried to appear nonchalant by tapping the bust of Molière. Tasha gave him a stern look and murmured in his ear: 'Well, what a coincidence – the girl just happens to be employed by Madame de Valois? Suppose we discuss your dear friend Madame Froufrou?'

'Women, they're all devils, they would lead a saint astray! That Josephine, for example . . . Hey, are you listening to me?'

Père Moscou's neighbour nodded, slowly pouring some water on to a slotted spoon with sugar in it. The liquid dripped into a glass half full of clear alcohol that bubbled and thickened like a magic potion and turned a yellowish colour, verging on emerald green.

'Ferdinand, you shouldn't touch the green fairy; it eats you from the inside and you'll become addicted to it – it'll drive you crazy. Do as I do: stick to the juice of the grape, or beer, even though all they serve in this dive is cat's piss!'

While the other man mumbled and groaned, Old Moscou looked around in disgust at the tavern, where he had wasted the last hour. It was next to the undertaker's at 104 Rue d'Aubervilliers and the room, with its black wall hangings, was full of undertakers' men, who had come to relax after a trip to one of the many Parisian cemeteries. Whether they had been to officiate at Charonne, Montparnasse or Vaugirard or whether they had gone as far as Ivry or Bagneux, the coffin bearers only wanted one thing: to cheer themselves up with a glass of rough red wine whilst exchanging bawdy anecdotes. That is, if they didn't prefer to abuse themselves with absinthe.

'I buried her, that treacherous Josephine Bonaparte. She sold the secrets Napoleon told her in bed to Fouché[3] and I swear, Ferdinand, that no one will ever discover her body!'

There were guffaws and a man with three chins shouted: 'Hey, Moscou! You're pickled, you're seeing bodies everywhere! If I were you, Féfé, I'd change tables – he might mistake you for a stiff and dig you a hole!'

Père Moscou swung round furiously in his chair. 'You'd better belt up! That's just like you, Grouchy!'

'Grouchy? Who on earth's that?' asked the fat man, guffawing.

'Someone who didn't dare face the cannons!' thundered Père Moscou.

'You and your cannons! You've been knocking them back, haven't you, old man?'

The undertakers laughed even louder. The old man rose in a dignified manner and, hand on heart, launched into a tirade.

'I've also had my time with the dead. The rich ones we called salmon, the poor ones herrings. I dug graves at Père-Lachaise for thirty-seven years, while you were all still wet behind the ears! Then one day they said to me, "Your time is up; make way for the young uns!" If my mate Barnabé hadn't looked out for me, if he hadn't let me collect things and show people around on the quiet, I might as well have curled up and died. That's what you can look forward to! When your paws are covered with callouses from burying folk, it's you who will be balancing on the edge of the abyss. So, a bit of respect, please!'

Shifting his weight from his right leg to his left, he tore off his hat and angrily scratched his head.

'You mark my words, you'll see!'

In the silence that followed, he sat down again. Hunched over his wine, he mumbled to himself, but the names 'Grouchy' and 'Josephine' could be heard. When he was certain that no one was paying attention to him any more, he felt around in the recesses of his trousers and pulled out some gloves rolled in a ball, some nails, three five-sou pieces, a handkerchief, and then let out an oath. Still cursing through his teeth, he began to rummage feverishly in his other clothes.

Confound it, hell and damnation, where have they got to? I've lost them! . . . No, here they are!

He pulled out the jewels that he had removed that morning from the dead woman and rolled them in the palm of his hand,

56

considering them, confusedly persuading himself that they belonged to 'Chausette Fine Deux Boyards Ney'.[4] He opened the cover of the locket. Bewildered, he looked at a portrait of a smiling young man with a moustache. Narrowing his eyes, he leant over to examine the face more closely and he thought he saw it move.

'Who are you? Fouché? Grouchy? You're certainly not the little corporal, that you're not! You want to make a fool of me, eh? You're wrong, Hector! I might be a bit fuddled, but if ever I crossed you in the street, I would remember you as if I'd always known you. Your mug is engraved on my memory.'

He drained his glass, stowed away all his odds and ends and, holding the jewels tight in his hand, went out into the street, where rows of hearses were parked.

Just as Joseph was helping Denise out of the cab that had taken them to Rue Notre-Dame-de-Lorette, a cyclist came screeching to a halt. She was wearing culottes, revealing plump calves, made more so by her tightly laced ankle boots. Her plaited grey hair was tied up on the top of her head, making her look like a little girl dressed up as a middle-aged woman. She was tangled in the pedals and was about to fall off when Joseph rushed over to catch her. The bicycle fell to the ground with a metallic thud.

'Mademoiselle Becker, you'll have to learn to control that animal!'

'Monsieur Joseph! *Danke schön*, so kind, so kind. Without you I would have fallen flat on my face.'

As she straightened her clothes, a second carriage slowed down on the other side of the street. The curtain was pulled back slightly. Mademoiselle Becker, Denise, Joseph and the bicycle disappeared into the carriage entrance of number 60. The curtain fell back in place and the second carriage moved slowly on.

Out of breath, Joseph put the bicycle down on the mat outside an apartment on the first floor. 'There, the beast is tethered! Don't let it escape.'

'*Danke*, Monsieur Joseph. Are you going to see Mademoiselle Tasha? I think she's gone out.'

'She's entrusted her key to me; she's putting up a cousin who's come to visit Paris.'

'Have you just arrived from the Ukraine?' Mademoiselle Becker asked Denise.

Joseph added, 'One of my cousins. I'm going to act as her guide. See you soon, Mademoiselle Becker.'

They hurried up the stairs, not pausing until they reached the fourth floor.

'That was the owner,' explained Joseph. 'They call her Madame Vulture, because she's constantly on the watch for tenants trying to scarper without paying their rent. So it's better if we make her think that you're my cousin. I hope you're not too tired – there are still two more floors to go.'

'I'm used to stairs.'

'I'm not. I haven't even been up the Eiffel Tower; heights give me vertigo. Have you been up it?'

'I would love to,' murmured Denise, 'apparently it's worth it for the view.'

'It's also worth coming here for the view!' exclaimed Joseph who had just opened Tasha's door.

The garret was full of frames and paintings – views of rooftops and a few male nudes – perched on easels or lying on the floor. Several pairs of gloves were strewn over the hastily made bed. The chairs were covered with clothes and the table was barely visible under a heap of sketches, dirty plates, palettes and paintbrushes.

'It doesn't matter. I'll tidy up – I'm also used to doing that.'

'Don't tidy too much, otherwise Mademoiselle Tasha won't be able to find anything,' Joseph advised her, as he went into the tiny room that served both as kitchen and bathroom. He fetched a jug of water and two glasses that he wiped with his handkerchief. He went back to the bedroom to find that Denise had put her packages on the bed.

'What are you hiding in there? Notebooks?'

She opened the package and revealed the chromolithograph of a Madonna praying, her head wreathed in a halo.

'It's *The Madonna in Blue*, she watches over me. There's a similar one on one of the windows in the Saint-Corentin Cathedral in Quimper. Every Sunday I prayed to her to make my wishes come true.'

'And you lug it around everywhere with you? It's a bit of an encumbrance. My mother gives me a rabbit's foot as a lucky charm each time she cooks a . . .'

Denise burst into tears.

'Don't cry, the rabbit is already dead, of course.'

'Madame's going to be furious, because that picture doesn't belong to me. It's the one she wanted to take to Monsieur's funerary chapel, but I switched it for the Archangel Saint Michel. When I ran away, yesterday evening, I took it with me because I like it so much, but it's not stealing, just borrowing. I'm going to give it back, I swear.'

Not understanding what she was talking about, Joseph awkwardly offered her his handkerchief.

'The Virgin Mary, Archangel Saint Michel, what's the difference? Come on, dry your eyes or you'll have a nose as large as a potato. You'll like it in this room, you'll see, everything will work out.'

While he was comforting her, he discreetly turned the nudes to face the wall.

'I imagine it's not much fun being all alone in Paris without any family. Especially living with Madame Odette. That woman came several times to the shop acting like the Empress of India. She was not the right kind of woman for Monsieur Legris. Look, tomorrow's Sunday, why don't I show you around the neighbourhood? We could stroll as far as the Grands Boulevards where there's a carnival on and a roller coaster. Afterwards we'll go to my mother's house for dinner – she's the queen of *frites*! You do like *frites*, don't you?'

She nodded yes. 'You're very kind.'

'I'll read you the first chapter of my book.'

'You write books? Do you know *The Oracle for Ladies and Girls*?'

'I specialise in crime stories.'

'Like the ones that I saw in your shop window? What's the title?'

Joseph hesitated, it was the first time he had revealed his

secret. No one, not even Valentine de Salignac, the love of his life, knew about his literary activity.

'It's called *Blood and Love*.'

'Love . . . I prefer love to blood.'

'Don't worry, there's much more love than blood, but, you know, you have to make some concessions to please the reading public.'

He bowed somewhat grandly, and kissed her hand, happy to be able to try out his best manners on this naïve young girl, before addressing himself to the niece of the Comtesse. Blushing, Denise stayed rooted to the spot long after the young man had departed.

He rushed down the stairs imagining himself in an embrace with Valentine. As he left, he gave a friendly greeting to a young man hanging about on the pavement clutching a bouquet of flowers.

CHAPTER THREE

D ENISE was roused from her slumber by a regular tapping noise. She got out of bed in her undershirt and petticoat. Tiny drops were trickling from the flaking ceiling and splattering into the three pails placed under the main beam. Balancing on a rickety stool, she opened the skylight. On the edge of the gutter two magpies were busily pecking at the zinc, but she took little notice of them. What caught her attention was the sea of slate roofs that stretched out as far as the eye could see, punctuated by the red or grey stalks of the chimneys. The cold forced her to retreat.

Once she had dressed and made her bed, she breakfasted on a glass of water and the apple Joseph had given her the night before. The juicy acidity of the fruit reminded her of that September afternoon when Ronan and she had gorged themselves on mulberries in the Forêt de Nevet, while dreaming of their future. She had promised herself that if she ever became rich, she would never again go near a kitchen stove.

She took the time to brush her hair thoroughly in front of the mirror above the sink and with a moistened finger fixed a lock of hair in place on her forehead. Would the hunchbacked boy who had promised to come later in the morning approve? He wasn't very handsome, but he was so kind! Would he think she was pretty? When she was a little girl, her mother had loved to stroke her hair, calling her 'my pet'. But Madame had treated her like a slattern, and old Hyacinthe had said she was skinny as a rake. As for pretty, was she? No man had ever told her so.

She returned to the bedroom to tidy the things on the table. A little bookcase built into a recess in a wall aroused her curiosity. She read out the gilded lettering adorning the spines of some of the beautiful bound books that were on the shelves along with some tattered paperbacks: *Bel-Ami*, *Treasure Island*, *An Island Fisherman*. Leaning against the books were two sepia-tinted photographs, one of Tasha, the young redhead whose room it was, the other of Victor Legris. She opened her bundle of belongings, took out her silver crucifix, and placed it next to the chromolithograph of *The Madonna in Blue* on an easel bearing a large painting of a male nude. Standing back to judge the effect, she felt pleased at having managed to add a personal touch to the room. But, almost immediately, her fear came rushing back. She hurriedly thrust the crucifix under her bodice and then hid *The Madonna in Blue* between the frame and the canvas of the nude.

Sitting on the bed, she tried to concentrate on the numerous pairs of lace gloves scattered around the garret. But she couldn't help it: her gaze was continually drawn back to the repository of her secret, the nude, a three-quarter study of a slightly round-shouldered man, his arm raised to reach for an open book on a chest. Although the picture shocked her, she couldn't take her eyes off the buttocks, round as pearls. She closed her eyes and let herself fall backwards, giggling. Was it a picture of the bookseller? Who would ever think of looking for *The Madonna in Blue* behind his naked figure?

The chiming of bells in the distance told her that it was ten o'clock. For the first time in years, her time was her own. Surely this was happiness? A room of one's own, the prospect of a stroll with a young man and no mistress to give her orders. To accentuate the enjoyment she felt at lounging on the bed, she took pleasure in running through the things she would have had to do that morning, had she still been in Madame's service. At this moment she would have been hurrying through the streets, burdened with a shopping basket, scouring the stalls for vegetables and cakes that would please her mistress. With half-closed eyes, she drowsily repeated to herself: 'If Madame returns, what will she eat? Sticks and stones . . .'

'Two rabbit heads, surely you can spare them? Come on, Goglu, do a good deed and God will reward you a hundredfold!'

'What would I want with a hundred rabbit heads, Père Moscou?' asked the butcher mockingly, fixing a side of beef on to a hook. 'I know your type, you old fraudster, you'd pass catmeat off as rabbit!'

'And so what! When it's well cooked, meat is meat!'

'Catch!' cried the butcher, throwing him the two bloody heads. 'And don't come back, Moscou. I've got more important things to worry about than dishing out ingredients for your soup – they don't come cheap!'

'My heart bleeds for you, Goglu. You make me want to blub!' cried Old Moscou furiously.

He narrowly missed one of the market porters of Les Halles bearing down on him, a carcass on his shoulders, yelling: 'Watch out, watch out in front of you!'

He crossed the Pavillon de Baltard, where all the meat was displayed. The tortured flesh, destined to satisfy insatiable appetites, was spread out in a symphony of red. Meat cleavers were crushing skulls, carving knives slicing haunches. Men in vermilion-stained aprons barked out orders while wagons piled with carcasses just missed crashing into each other. The sweetish odour pervading this slaughterhouse was making Père Moscou feel ill and he swayed, incapable of moving, a rabbit head clutched in each hand. He was haunted by the image of the woman's body in his cart; it was suffocating him. What had he done with the body? He could picture himself digging a hole under the trees of his courtyard, but had that really happened or was it a nightmare?

'Josephine, you filthy traitress, you're making me see things! Or maybe it's you, Emmanuel!'

'Oi, tosspot, go and sleep it off somewhere else! The rest of us is doin' an honest day's work 'ere,' a butcher's boy shouted at him.

Père Moscou jerked back to life like a mechanical toy and started walking, muttering: 'And I'm not? I may work for the King of Prussia and collect bugger all, but it's better than nothing.'

He glanced at the rabbit heads before shoving them into his pockets. He could now go to Marcelin's or to Cabirol's but first he would have to take the cats back to the Cour des Comptes. While he was there he would check if he really had buried a Josephine on his turf.

He walked past a stall of eels. There were about a dozen of them, soft and slimy, intertwined on a wicker trug. He spotted his friend Barnabé.

'Well, well! What you are you doing here?'

'As you can see, I'm stocking up, the missus likes *matelote*.'

'Ugh! It's rotten, that filthy mess.'

'Yes,' laughed Barnabé, 'but it's cheap. With a good sauce on top, it slips down nicely. A drop of wine?'

'No time!' barked Père Moscou, feeling sick.

A dull, persistent fear, such as he had never before experienced, gripped him as he emerged into the freezing day. Every couple of minutes he turned round to check that he had not been followed. Two girls of easy virtue, finding this amusing, taunted him on Rue Rambuteau and some urchins followed him to an area full of vendors' wagons. The vendors had piled their wares on the pavement and were starting to sell them, their street cries ringing out.

Stopping near a soup seller, Père Moscou extracted a ten centime piece from his old frock coat and greedily seized a steaming bowl. One of the urchins threw a stone at him, nearly overturning the bowl.

'The guillotine for you!' bellowed the old man, shaking his fist.

'Cowardy cowardy custard, your nose is made of mustard!' cried the urchins, running away.

Fortified by the piping hot liquid, he carried on through the streets, which were gradually filling with a weary mob. Carriages and omnibuses passed each other noisily on the bridges, the swearing and whip-cracking of the coach drivers competing with the groaning of the wheels. Flocks of sparrows swooped down on the piles of horse dung strewn across the wooden cobbles.

Père Moscou, exhausted, dragged himself along Quai Conti.

For a while he thought he had conquered the fear that had overcome him in Les Halles. But, as soon as he had set foot in Place de l'Institut, it came flooding back. Shakily, as if hounded by an invisible menace, he walked along Quai Malaquais without even pausing when he crossed Rue des Saints-Pères.

Tasha was stretched out in the bath, gently stewing in the hot water. Victor looked in. 'You're just like Kenji — he loves boiling-hot baths. Be careful, you're all red; you might burn.'

He plunged his hand in the water and withdrew it as if he'd been burnt, caressing the breasts of the young woman as he did so.

'Get out!' she cried, splashing him.

Returning to her reverie, she reflected on the night they had just spent together. Victor had been both tender and passionate, and she had only resisted him so she could abandon herself more completely. When their passion was finally spent, she had curled up against his chest. Their relationship fulfilled her emotionally as well as physically, and yet she still felt on the defensive, disinclined to put up with Victor's bouts of jealousy.

Her thoughts wandered to that other passion of hers, which enraged and pained Victor, but filled her life to the exclusion of all else: her painting. Victor had offered to pay for the framing of her canvases, so there was nothing to stop her exhibiting them at the Soleil d'Or alongside the paintings of Laumier and his friends. So why was she worrying? She had been preparing for the exhibition since the summer; she had put heart and soul into her rooftops of Paris series and into her male nudes. But now that she was finally going to reveal them to the public, even to a public of vulgar barflies, as Victor had dubbed them, she was scared. She knew that her canvases would never receive the acclaim of the renowned art salons. Her work displayed too much rebellion against the style of the Academy painters and reflected too many diverse influences such as Impressionism and Symbolism. She also knew that, sooner or later, Laumier's group, who worshipped Gauguin and Syntheticism, would reject her. In fact, what she feared most was having to confront these contradictions.

Wrapped in a towel, she crossed Kenji's apartment, hurried into Victor's and got dressed. Above the chest, facing her, she caught sight of another Tasha, a naked head and shoulders, painted last year by Laumier. Despite Kenji's antipathy towards his mistress, Victor obstinately displayed the little picture, which she felt was better proof of his love than any declaration.

'Where are you hiding?'

'I'm shaving.'

She joined him in the little bathroom. 'I have to return a caricature of Zola to *Gil Blas*,[1] then I'm going to Bibulus to put the finishing touches to the painting I'm working on,' she gabbled, not daring to look at him.

Without replying, Victor wiped his face and turned towards her, smiling.

'I know it's Sunday, but I won't be back late,' she promised him.

'You can come back whenever you like.'

'Of course, if you wanted to, you could come with me . . .' she began, her tone hesitant.

'That's kind, but I have an errand to run. I . . .' He interrupted himself. It would serve no purpose to tell her that he proposed to go over to Odette's to try to get to the bottom of Denise's story.

He embraced her, planting a kiss on her lips. Freed from the tension she had felt since she woke, she relaxed. 'You know, I'm wondering if I should continue to limit my painting to one subject.'

He moved away from her, astonished. She almost never confided her artistic doubts to him.

'What do you mean?'

'Sometimes I would like to forget everything I've learnt at art school, about fashions, about technique, and just let myself go, using my paintings to express my . . . my inner world. What do you think?'

He stayed silent for a moment, and then almost reluctantly replied: 'The more solid the base of knowledge we have, the more we can build on it. I think it's the same with photography. I have to learn. When I feel ready, I'll forget all the learning and start inventing.'

'So you think it's too soon for me?'

He frowned, visibly struggling with himself.

'Yes. Only when you have acquired a technique that is perfect in all respects will you be able to eliminate the aspect of that technique which you don't judge to be important,' he said snatching up his hat.

'Is it really you giving me this advice?'

She looked at him in amazement. Suddenly she went over to him, removed his hat and kissed him passionately. They stayed standing for a moment, then collapsed on to the bed, where their ardour tousled their hair and crumpled their clothes.

'What's come over you?'

'I love you,' she breathed, putting her fingers inside his collar and starting to unbutton it.

Madame Valladier hastily shrugged on a jacket. Someone was banging on the door with such force that the furniture in the sitting room was shaking. She was exasperated to see Père Moscou planted on the doorstep, looking terrified, the bottom of his frock coat stained.

'Drunker than a lord! You've spilled wine all down yourself!'

'My dear Maguelonne, it's only rabbit blood. I swear on the life of the Emperor that I have not touched a drop. But I'm not myself; I've got the collywobbles!'

'What have you done now?'

'Me? I'm as innocent as a newborn babe, I am. Hmm! Something smells good . . .'

'I'm simmering some artichokes with marrow. I'll bring you a plateful in a little while.'

'That woman, she's top notch,' Père Moscou declared, heading for the Cour D'Honneur.

He changed his mind. To recover his peace of mind he had to perform a ritual. He set off down a wide staircase, its cracked steps sprouting tendrils of weeds, which had once led to the salon of the Conseil d'État. The walls, originally decorated with frescoes by the painter Théodore Chassériau, had been blackened by the fire of 1871, but, as at Pompeii, some of the paintings remained partly intact. Père Moscou marched straight over to a peeling war painting depicting horses and three figures representing 'silence', 'meditation' and 'study'. He paid no attention to *Force and Order* higher up, or to a group of blacksmiths. Women suckling children alongside men harvesting also left him cold. It was only when he reached the panel of *Commerce rapprochant les peuples* that he stopped to contemplate an Oceanid at the bottom of the fresco.

The half-naked lady, painted in pale grey, seemed to be looking at him in a strange and provocative manner. He kissed the tip of his finger and touched her breast.

'Hello there, beautiful child, look after Père Moscou – never let him fall into the slough of despondency – and in exchange he will promise that while he lives you will never have to sleep in the open.'

Reassured by this speech, he went back down the corridor leading to his bivouac. The curtain covering the entrance had been half torn down. He stopped on the threshold, dumbstruck by the devastation that had occurred in the room. The crates in which he kept his treasures were spread out over the floor in a trail of canes, hats and shoes. Someone had gone through them furiously, tearing them apart and trampling on them. The two chairs, one of them broken, lay on their backs next to a wall. The stove had been pulled from its iron pipe, and someone had crammed the carpet, rolled up in a cylinder, into the hole. As for the bed, it resembled a battlefield on which the disembowelled quilts were losing their entrails. But what disturbed Père Moscou the most was the realisation that three branches of his acacia had been broken. He raced to the end of the corridor, to what had once been the secretariat of the Conseil d'État, to make sure that his cart was still beneath the pile of firewood where he had hidden it the previous evening. Still there. But his relief was shortlived. Unable to face the devastation of his bivouac alone, he hastened to find Madame Valladier.

When she saw the chaos, the concierge raised her hands to her face. 'Heavens above! It looks as if it's been hit by a whirlwind!'

Still shocked, Père Moscou could only repeat: 'Damnation, Grouchy, you've really done it this time! Damnation . . .'

'Hold your tongue, you old gas bag, and help me tidy up. I'll wager it was them scoundrels I chased away the other day who came back to get even. I don't like coppers, but I swear to God if this carries on any longer I am going to report it!

She leaned down to try and restuff one of the quilts. 'A fine mess, but I should be able to mend it for you. Come on, lend a hand!

Red in the face, his mouth hanging open, Père Moscou pointed to a wall where a message had been scrawled:

WHERE HAVE YOU HIDDEN THEM?
A.D.V.

Madame Valladier brushed the letters with her fingertips. 'That's recent. What could it possibly mean? A.D.V. . . . Adieu something? Do you understand it?'

Père Moscou could only swallow as he fingered the dead

woman's jewellery in his right pocket, beneath the sticky rabbit's head.

'He was the grandfather of the detective novel. Died in 1873 at the age of thirty-eight. I hope I live much longer than he did, and that I too shall be a famous writer,' concluded Joseph, as he and Denise left number 39 Rue Notre-Dame-de-Lorette, the last home of Émile Gaboriau.

The streets were busy and they were walking quite far apart, a little embarrassed. Denise was intimidated by the erudite young man, whom she would have liked to impress.

Joseph didn't know if he should offer the young girl his arm, and felt vaguely guilty that he was being unfaithful to his sweetheart, Valentine de Salignac.

They arrived in silence at Notre-Dame-de-Lorette Church. Denise crossed herself. Without even glancing at the façade, which he found ugly, Joseph turned into Rue Laffite which led straight to Boulevard des Italiens. He racked his brains for a way to break the ice.

'Lorette sounds pretty, doesn't it? It's even become a Christian name. Fifty years ago, many courtesans who lived in this quarter were named for the church, and it became common.'

Embarrassed by his reference to women of easy virtue, she didn't reply, so he set about continuing his discourse on semantics until finally she took up the conversational bait that he had offered.

'In Brittany it's the other way round. We choose everyday

names to make surnames. Take mine for example, Le Louarn means The Fox.'

'How long have you lived in Paris?'

'I moved here three years ago. I remember it as if it were yesterday. Coming out of Gare Montparnasse, I was bowled over; I had never seen so many people. I almost had to fight to get on to a tram. I had the address of an employment agency on Rue Coquillière behind the Bourse de Commerce, but I nearly got lost several times before finding it. Then I had to wait for two hours in a room full of sad-looking girls sitting on benches. One of them made fun of me – she told me they would never take me on because they only wanted the freshest meat.'

'Meat?'

'That's what they call the girls looking for positions. I was lucky. When my turn came, the mistress liked me because I was the only one wearing a hat – all the others were bare-headed – and because my dress was clean. I had only ever worked for one person, and then only part-time, an old woman named Quemener who lived in Penhars, on the outskirts of Quimper, who had just died. Her daughter was kind enough to write a letter of recommendation, praising me. So, on that same night, I was employed by Monsieur and Madame de Valois, where I have been ever since.'

From time to time, Denise interrupted her story to read the names on the corners of the boulevards. She was filled with delight at the sight of theatres, cafés and luxury shops that seemed to possess all the wonders of the universe. What pleasure to taste such freedom! Her animated face, lit by her grey eyes and set off by her ash-blonde hair, was rather attractive. She smiled at Joseph, who had been watching her unobtrusively.

'And what about you, Monsieur Joseph, are you a Parisian?'

He nodded and, grabbing her hand, dragged her across to the other side of the road.

'We're not far from Carrefour des Écrasés . . . Honestly, wouldn't you have preferred to stay in the country?' he asked, making a face at the volume of traffic that was dominating Boulevard des Italiens.

'Definitely not! My father used to beat me, and working in the fields is slave labour. Although being a servant isn't much better. I had to toil from seven in the morning until ten at night, preparing food, brushing clothes, cleaning shoes, polishing brass, ironing . . . I didn't have a minute to draw breath. When Monsieur was there it was hard. Every week there was a dinner with many guests and I had to stay until they'd all left, which was sometimes not until two or three in the morning. I would make up for it when I went out to do the shopping; I would take quarter of an hour here, quarter of an hour there, and look in the shop windows. When Monsieur left for Panama in September '88, my life became easier. And every time Monsieur Legris came to visit Madame, he was kind to me; he would always slip me a coin. That's why I went to find him.'

'You did the right thing. He's a splendid boss. I've been lucky. I've never regretted being his assistant. It's thanks to Maman that I got the job. And the other boss, Monsieur Kenji Mori, Monsieur Legris's adoptive father, he's also splendid. He was born in Japan and he's very learned. He's knocked around the Orient and has brought back loads of strange and interesting objects. We've arrived! You see, there's the roller coaster at 26, we can go there one evening, but with empty stomachs!'

On Boulevard des Capucines there were booths from which the enticing odour of aniseed and melted sugar wafted. A crowd of people flowed slowly past the showmen who were promoting extravaganzas, wrestling matches and wild animal fights.

'Wild animals, my eye – a moth-eaten panther or a mangy lion more like. Come on, I'm sure we can find something better,' said Joseph to Denise, who was open-mouthed at the sight of the beautiful dresses the passers-by were wearing.

A barrel-organ started playing 'Les Pioupious d'Auvergne'. This lively air seemed to bring the wooden horses of the merry-go-round they were sitting on to life, and they burst out laughing.

Her head spinning, Denise found herself in the middle of a deafening brass band. She wanted to listen to it but Joseph had already moved on.

'What would you say to a visit to Madame Topaz?'

Dressed in a brilliant costume, the colour of the sun, and wearing a turban adorned with feathers, a large bony woman was inviting people to venture inside her caravan to have their fortune told.

'Shall we go in?' suggested Joseph.

Her face suddenly dark, Denise obstinately refused.

'Why not? She can't be very frightening – look at her!'

'I'm not sure if Monsieur Legris told you . . . but Madame disappeared while we were at the Père-Lachaise cemetery. That's why I ran away: I thought that the spirits were angry with me. Before, I didn't believe in that sort of thing. But when

I went into Monsieur's funerary chapel, I felt a presence. And later, in the apartment . . . an evil force. It all comes from that woman Madame went to, that clairvoyant. She cast the evil eye on us, I'm sure of it,' she finished, moving away from Madame Topaz.

'A clairvoyant? Does she really predict the future? Give me her address; I'm interested! I'd like to know if I'm going to become a bookseller or a writer, and whether, with my help, Maman will find financial security.'

'I don't remember the address, it was a beautiful building near a panorama. There were . . . naked women on each side of the door, statues. We went up to the second floor . . . I'll never set foot in that house again – it's worse than visiting the devil!' she cried.

'All right, don't worry about Madame Topaz. I'm going to try to hit the jackpot; I'm a crackshot with an air rifle.'

He made his way over to a shooting gallery where you could win plaster figurines or fake jewellery if you hit the target six times in a row. Spurred on by his desire to please Denise, he succeeded every time. Gloomily, the stallholder handed over a brown boar on a yellow plinth, but Joseph went over to the tray where the necklaces and earrings were displayed.

'Could I have one of these instead?' He pointed to a bracelet decorated with a charm.

'You need twenty-four points for that,' said the stallholder.

'And if I give you this?'

Joseph held out a twenty-sou piece that he kept in his trouser pocket for emergencies. His mother would not be happy, but he would think of something to tell her.

Denise's smile when he put the bracelet round her wrist was ample reward. She studied the charm, a little golden dog with a pointed nose and eyes of red stone.

'It looks like a fox . . .'

'That's why I chose it.'

'Roll up, roll up, ladies and gentlemen! Come and see the re-enactment of the most frightening murders of all time! The shocking crime committed by Pranzini, who killed Claudine-Marie Regnault alias Régine de Montille, her chambermaid and her little daughter in Rue Montaigne. The unsolved assassination of Dante Caicedonni, stabbed to death in his hotel room on Boulevard Saint-Michel, his murderer is still at large! The town of Millery's famous bloody trunk, in which the decomposing body of Gouffé,[2] the porter was found. Don't delay, come in! Five sous, two if you're a soldier. But sensitive souls beware!'

Stopping in front of a man in a striped shirt who was hollering into a megaphone while brandishing a knife dipped in red, Joseph murmured, 'Good God!' and turned to Denise. She stared at him, as white as a sheet.

'Would you mind very much if I went to see? It's just that I have to take notes for my writing.'

'Of course, I understand,' she said in a small voice. 'I'll wait for you over there.'

She went towards the wooden horses whilst Joseph disappeared under the awning.

In the semi-darkness of candle-light, podiums were arranged in a circle. The scenes were mimed by street entertainers and narrated by showmen, and watched by an audience hungry for sensation. Joseph chose the Gouffé case.

'. . . month of August '89 at Millery, near Lyon, the inhabitants were disturbed by a nauseating odour that was emanating from thick bramble bushes. Finally the local constable discovered a hessian sack in the shrubbery. Show us the sack!'

A person dressed in black held the sack up for the audience.

'When he split it open with his knife, he found the half-decomposed head of a man. Show the audience the head!'

The same person took a bloody head from the sack, arousing shrieks of horror.

'Scarcely had the autopsy been completed, when a farmer collecting snails on the banks of the Rhône came upon a strange trunk broken into several pieces. Here it is!'

He pointed to a trunk, which the man in black started to open. The mime that followed was about the Caicedonni affair, a case which interested Joseph. In front of him, a young woman in a pink dress was sitting next to a curly-haired man who had his arm slung round her waist.

'Marie Turnerad was only sixteen when she became Dante Caicedonni's mistress, in 1878!' declaimed another showman.

He began to sing, accompanied by a fiddle:

> *Oh listen to this tale of woe*
> *Of a poor lass wrongly accused,*
> *Of the murder of her treacherous beau*
> *For her trust he had sadly abused.*
>
> *This Romeo who trod the boards*
> *Played only villains never lords.*

He beguiled the little barber's maid,
Swearing their love would never fade.

The chorus:

Marie Turnerad who coiffed the toffs
At Lenthéric's Paris barber shop
Fell for an artiste, blond and cunning
Who stole her heart and spent her money.

Second verse!

But Joseph didn't wait to hear the rest of the edifying little ditty and went back into the fresh air, humming. He joined Denise who, with her hands over her ears, was watching a saxhorn player. Wanting to make up for having abandoned her, he bought her a marshmallow. When they left the fair, the boulevard seemed rather quiet.

'*Marie Turnerad, who coiffed the toffs . . .*' hummed Joseph, then interrupted himself with a groan.

'Now I'll have that dreadful tune stuck in my head for two months. Whenever I hear a song or read a text, they imprint themselves here,' he said indicating his forehead. 'The memory fairy was leaning over my cradle, which makes me very useful in the bookshop. Perhaps I get it from my father who was a secondhand bookseller. He died of a chill three years after I was born. My mother inherited his stock, so I was brought up surrounded by old papers.'

Denise thought he'd been lucky. She wished her father had

disappeared when she was little. That idea led to another.

'Apparently yellow fever transforms you into a living skeleton . . .'

'What made you say that?' exclaimed Joseph.

'Because I was thinking of Monsieur,' she replied, without adding that she feared the ghost of someone who had fallen victim to that terrible illness. 'The day Madame received the telegram she almost fainted. Yet he cheated on her, he even made a pass at me. And it's not as if he had any money – she held the purse strings.'

'People say that love is blind!' replied Joseph, who didn't like Odette enough to feel any sympathy for her predicament. 'It's very sad, but there have been thousands of deaths in Columbia because of that canal. Frankly they might as well not have dug it for all the good it's done: so many people have been ruined by it, when there were already quite enough who were hard-up.'

'Hard-up?'

'Poor. Maman, she was also poor when she sold *frites*. As a costermonger, she earns a bit more, but she would never have bought shares in a canal, or, if she had, she would have chosen a French canal; I don't know, maybe the Canal de l'Ourcq. Are you hungry?'

She nodded.

'We're going to take the bus. Maman has made us calves' foot with *frites*.'

The carriage had to wait for an omnibus to go past before stopping opposite a handsome building at number 24 Boulevard

Haussmann. Victor got out and, while the concierge was deep in conversation with a chambermaid a little way up the street, he slipped stealthily through the open carriage gate. He went up to the fifth floor. When there was no answer to the door bell, he knocked, then automatically turned the door handle. Surprised to find it unlocked, he called out, 'Odette, are you there? It's me, Victor.'

He took a few steps along the corridor. The apartment was dark and smelt stuffy. He drew back the sitting-room curtains. He glanced around and saw that the room was in disarray, but he couldn't tell if that was because someone had recently broken in. A net curtain topped with delicate lace obscured the windows, making it hard to see. Victor remembered that Odette often used to say, 'The light ruins my complexion.' On the mantelpiece a huge clock was ticking ponderously, surrounded by a forest of golden candelabra, bronze sculptures and plants. A coat and a veiled hat lay on a wing chair. A baby grand piano draped in a velvet cover nestled in a corner, bearing a host of knick-knacks and vases filled with dying flowers. Musical scores were strewn across the floor. Had Odette, who played the piano rather badly, been overcome by a sudden musical tantrum? Victor also noticed that the cushions of the two sofas in the room were rumpled and that, in the dining room leading off the sitting room, one of the many chairs round the Henri II table was lying crookedly against the wall.

Going into the bedroom, he was taken aback by the macabre décor. The bed was made up to look funereal. That very bed, on which Odette had so many times offered herself to him and which back then had been a sea of liberty-print flowers, now resembled a coffin. Everything seemed in order except for one detail. A framed photograph lay face down beneath a mahogany table laden with candles and incense sticks. He picked it up. Under the broken glass, Armand de Valois stood erect, with a vaguely bored expression, in dress coat and top hat.

Just to ease his conscience, he resolved to look through the rest of the apartment. Apart from a general air of disorder, suggesting a hasty departure, he could see nothing out of the ordinary. He would willingly have searched each room more thoroughly, but had no valid reason to justify such an indiscretion. After all, Odette was free to do as she pleased. If she had bolted, that was her business, unless Denise had invented her disappearance in order to commit a robbery and get away with it. He had some idea where Odette's valuables were kept, so perhaps he should check them over? But then he told himself that had the little Bretonne been guilty of theft, she would hardly have come looking for his help. 'And yet . . . suppose she's a compulsive liar and there's a hidden meaning to this scenario . . . No, she doesn't have the wit to fabricate . . . Come on, Victor! Can't you just admit that Odette has slipped away with someone? Surely you can't be jealous of her as well?'

He was about to close the sitting-room curtains when he noticed something glinting in the sunlight. It was Odette's key-ring. He knew that Odette was scatterbrained but not to the point of leaving without her keys. He pocketed them so that he could lock up, telling himself that he would return them to Denise. He could feel a strange excitement mounting, similar to that he had experienced last summer when he had embarked on his first investigation. But this time, he reassured himself, it would all be much easier to resolve than the mystery of the Universal Exposition.

He went downstairs again and knocked on the concierge's door.

'I'm coming, I'm coming! What do you want? Oh, it's you . . .'

The concierge regarded him coldly. He seemed to have forgotten the tips that Victor had showered him with when he visited his mistress.

'Did Madame de Valois notify you that she was going to be away? We had a rendezvous this evening; I'm a little concerned . . .'

'No need to make a fuss just because a lady stood you up.'

'It was a business meeting,' retorted Victor drily.

'All I can tell you is that the night before last she came back at an ungodly hour. These people, they do as they please and think nothing of asking to be let in even if it's the middle of the night, and afterwards there's no hope of my getting back to sleep . . .'

'Are you certain it was Madame de Valois? It could have been another resident.'

'Absolutely certain. She gave her name and also used mine, Hyacinthe. I'm not mistaken.'

'But her maid insists that she has not been home since Friday afternoon . . .'

'Her maid? Denise? She's a whining good-for-nothing and as thick as two short planks. She's always complaining. Don't get me started about Bretons! It wouldn't be the first time that she's come up with some cock-and-bull story just to get herself noticed.'

Victor made his escape under the mocking eye of the concierge. 'That'll teach him to come poking his nose into other people's business,' muttered old Hyacinthe.

As soon as he reached the boulevard, Victor felt as if a weight had been lifted from him. Kenji was right to rail against the clutter of western homes. Too many wall hangings and knick-knacks and too much furniture – and also too many concierges. What was the meaning of that palm decorated with black crêpe, the veiled mirror and the incense? Was Odette really overcome with grief, or had Armand's death been the pretext for her to launch a new fashion: the grieving widow?

'A strange fad, that one,' he said to himself, leaving Rue de la Chausée-d'Antin and crossing Boulevard des Capucines to avoid a street fair. He decided to walk. It would give him a chance to clear his mind of the painful memories awakened by his visit to the apartment.

'I don't know any more; I can't remember where I put that Josephine!' moaned Père Moscou, charging around the court-yard.

He crashed through the branches of fig trees and honey-suckle tendrils, cats and rabbits scampering out of his way, then bumped into a lamp-post entwined with vegetation struggling upwards to find the light. Cursing, he let himself fall against a section of crumbling wall then, his head in his hands, waited for the pain to abate. 'My brain has turned to mush! I can't think straight now that my bivouac has been turned upside down. I know I buried a good lady somewhere in this scrub, but I'm darned if I can find the spot. 'Where have you hidden them?' Someone knows about the jewels. Grouchy? I'm going to have to ditch them pronto. But first the moggies.'

He went back to his bedroom, where Madame de Valladier was sitting on the bed, furiously sewing up a quilt that lay on her lap. Paying her as little heed as if she had been part of the furniture, he made for the drawers, still overturned, and gathered up the two cats, which were giving off a fetid odour. Shoving them into a sack, he took his leave.

'Old camel,' murmured the concierge. 'One day he offers me flowers, the next he makes off without even saying goodbye!'

Jean Marcelin ran his business behind Marché des Carmes.[3] He was busy brushing a white rabbit skin, which he planned to make into an ermine muff, when he saw Père Moscou approaching, preceded by the smell of gamey meat. The old man threw the two dead cats on to the counter. 'Skin these for me quickly will you? I'm in a hurry.'

Disgusted, the skinner touched one of the two creatures lightly. 'These mogs are putrid.'

'Skip the humbug; you can pickle their skins in vinegar. How much?'

Marcelin turned up his pointed nose, indicating that he was considering the price. 'Eighty centimes the pair.'

'Pull the other one – a franc or no deal.'

Marcelin hestitated, about to refuse, but then remembered that he had a sable coat to finish. The black fur could be dyed brown and then it would do nicely. 'Don't move, I'll be back in two minutes.'

'Cut their heads off, while you're at it.'

Marcelin took the cats and came back a few moments later holding a parcel wrapped in newspaper and a coin. Père Moscou seized them and bolted without saying goodbye.

He only had to cross Place Maubert and go up Rue des Trois-Portes to reach Ernest Cabirol's workshop. As soon as he entered the shop he was overcome by a coughing fit. Three cauldrons simmered on an enormous stove, giving off a cloud of noxious steam. A bent old man bounded from one to another like a little imp, stirring their contents with a large wooden spoon. The diverse scraps of meat provided by all the restaurants in the area were in these infernal cauldrons, to which he would add salt and pepper and make the resulting stew into pasties called 'harlequins'. These he sold for a sou a piece as feed for domestic animals or as nourishment for down-and-outs who couldn't afford anything better.

'I've brought you a couple of hares,' said Père Moscou, taking the parcel out of his sack. 'Oh, mustn't forget the heads,' he added, pulling them out of his pocket. 'What on earth's this?'

He held up two blood-stained gloves. 'Well, you could always add these to your soup!'

'I don't put filth like that in my soup!' objected Cabirol indignantly. 'I want nothing to do with those rags. Besides, there's a finger missing.'

Père Moscou looked more carefully at his find. The thumb of the left hand had been cut off at the first joint. 'You're right,

Ernest, I hadn't noticed. Bah! It doesn't matter; I'll wash them and make them into mittens.'

Cabirol considered the skinned cats nonchalantly through half-closed eyes. 'They're off,' he concluded. 'Two sous.'

'Come on, be generous: three. They'll add flavour. What are you cooking up today?'

'Beef with cabbage, offal, calf's head and sparrow. It's a dish to revive you – see how it foams! It'll be on sale tomorrow at Mère Froment's, on Rue Galande. All right then, three sous.'

Feeling sick, Père Moscou left the master chef's shop and found himself face-to-face with a schoolboy in uniform. The schoolboy raised his cap in an affable manner and received a grunt in reply.

Gripped by fear and doubt, Père Moscou went to prop up a bar on Rue de la Bûcherie. He made sure that no one was watching before taking another look inside the locket, which was sticky with blood. 'Someone is after me . . . ADV, is it you?'

A draught of cold air made him shiver. The door to the street was ajar, but he hadn't noticed anyone opening it. Looking as if he had just seen a ghost, Père Moscou rose and, without pausing to finish his drink, hurried towards the Seine.

CHAPTER FOUR

VICTOR turned over in bed with a groan and pulled the pillow over his ears. Why did that stupid clot always feel the need to burst into song when he was opening the shop?

> *Marie Turnerad who coiffed the toffs*
> *At Lenthéric's Paris barber shop . . .*

Joseph broke into a whistle – a sign that he'd forgotten the rest of the words. The heavy wooden shutters came down with a clatter and the shop assistant, puffed out, fell silent. Victor was just drifting into a delicious slumber when another, more rhythmic refrain began straining towards the high notes.

He leapt out of bed, exasperated, and charged through the apartment, slamming the hallway door that opened on to the spiral staircase. Joseph must have taken the hint because he went quiet.

Wide awake, Victor stood gazing at Tasha, who was in the middle of a dream – one arm stretched out above her head, the other hanging over the side of the bed. He lay down next to her, allowing his hand to stray beneath the sheet. Almost immediately the young woman's fingers found his and she drew him to her before pushing him away.

'What would your friend Monsieur Mori say if he could see us?' she said, lazily running her fingers through her hair.

'Nothing, for the simple reason that he's busy doing the same thing in London in the company of a certain Iris.'

'We have five days left if I'm right. I really must have my apartment back by then, my dearest man. So, you'll have to deal with this problem between Madame Froufrou and her maid, or else find another position for Denise.'

'I promise I'll sort it out later,' Victor said, his hands and mouth busying themselves again.

Tasha granted him a kiss, then extricated herself, giggling.

'Not later: now! I'm going to see my editor to show him the illustrations for *Pantagruel*[1] then I'll be at Bibulus until eight o'clock this evening. Will you come and pick me up? We can have dinner together somewhere.'

Without waiting for him to agree she disappeared into the bathroom, locking the door.

Victor dressed and went downstairs, yawning. He greeted Joseph's, 'Morning, boss, did you sleep well?' with a black look, and walked groggily over to where a couple of old catalogues that Kenji had compiled were lying on a desk. He flicked through them absentmindedly, his thoughts elsewhere. He didn't know why, but he kept coming back to the morbid décor of Odette's bedroom and the sitting-room clock ticking the minutes away in the empty apartment. He closed the catalogues.

'Joseph, I am going to La Madeleine to value a collection. I shall be back by lunchtime.'

He was in a hurry to leave, eager to question Denise about how her mistress had been occupying her time of late.

*

Victor was breathless when he reached the top of the six flights, which seemed all the steeper because he'd climbed them without stopping. He walked along the dark passageway towards Tasha's garret, recalling for a split second her former neighbour the Serbian singer Danilo Ducovitch, knocked, and waited.

'It's Monsieur Legris!' he said in a clear voice, his ear pressed to the door.

The girl must have gone out. He tried his own keys in the hope that one would fit. He was about to give up, his irritation mounting, when he realised they were Odette's keys.

This is too much! And now I'll have to go and leave them with her wretched concierge.

He rattled the door handle in frustration and the door opened.

Not locked – after all that!

He stood there, flabbergasted. The entire contents of the room had been dislodged as though in preparation for a removal. Picture frames were piled on chairs. The mattress and pillows were lying on the floor. The sheets and covers had been torn off and were hanging from an easel propping up a canvas of a nude male, which he recognised immediately as himself – thank God it was a three-quarter profile, so no one else would! The bookcase in the recess stared back at him vacantly, and its contents, strewn over the bed base, reminded him of an impatient heir whose ageing aunt had died, and who had brought her books to the shop bundled up in green sacking. The table looked out of place pushed under the skylight, and its usual clutter lay in a pile on the floor. The dresser doors hung open and the chipped crockery sat on the ground gathering dust. Two trunkfuls of clothes had disgorged their contents on to the ceramic stove.

Victor stepped over a puddle and entered the tiny room which served as both kitchen and bathroom. A cluster of pots that usually resided on a shelf formed a circle around three stacked buckets.

Although nothing appeared to have been damaged, the fact remained that the room had been systematically ransacked and the rain had flooded the floor. He felt his anger rising. This was what happened when you trusted strangers! His first intuition on entering Odette's apartment had been right: Denise was a thief. He looked around in vain for her bundle. So she'd run off. It remained to be seen what she'd taken with her. A canvas perhaps? Tasha's paintings weren't worth anything yet and a dealer wouldn't give five francs for them. She possessed nothing of value, no jewellery, no ornaments. What about her clothes? The lace gloves she had brought from Russia . . . Perhaps the Breton girl had been content just to add a few pieces of clothing to her trousseau. He felt disheartened, incapable of making a decision. Should he tell Tasha? No, she'd be furious and blame him. Reluctantly, he began to put the furniture back in its place. After half an hour of tidying – an activity he was unaccustomed to – he peered, exhausted, into the cracked mirror hanging on a piece of wire next to the recess, and had difficulty believing that the feverish face he saw in it was his. He smoothed his hair and glanced once more around the over-tidy garret. You'd be able to find a needle in here now, but Tasha wouldn't be able to find anything. She'd be livid. All of a sudden he had misgivings. Granted, Denise had abandoned the nest, but what if someone else had ransacked the room after she'd left?

He rushed down the stairs and, crossing the courtyard, knocked at the concierges' lodge. Monsieur Ladoucette, dragging his leg, opened the door. He lifted his grey cloth cap from his frizzy white head and waved a crumpled newspaper as if he were trying to shake the crumbs from it.

'A very good day to you, Monsieur Legris. 'Scuse my excitement, sir, but it isn't every day you get to see your own name printed in the newspaper. It's me in here! You see, yesterday evening I was out walking my dog, Choupette, on Rue des Martyrs, when a waitress from Bouillon Duval . . .'

'I wanted to know whether anyone went up to Mademoiselle Kherson's yesterday or this morn—'

'Yes! Don't move, I'm coming!' a voice screeched from the back of the lodge.

Monsieur Ladoucette continued his monologue, oblivious to the interruption.

'. . . emptied a bucket of slimy water right under her feet. Just then, a big fellow with a beard, who was coming the other way . . .'

A small weasel-faced woman appeared next to Monsieur Ladoucette and greeted Victor with a nod.

'Ah! The old rheumatics. Ever so bad. Always flare up when the weather turns cold. Yes, someone came yesterday evening while I was peeling the potatoes. With a telegraph. Wanted to know where Mademoiselle Tasha lived, so I told him the sixth.'

'. . . slipped up on the pavement right under my nose. Mad

with rage he was. Rushed at the waitress with a knife. And Choupette . . .'

'Pipe down will you! You're getting on Monsieur Legris's nerves!' his wife bellowed in his ear. 'You mustn't mind him. Battle of Sedan. Cannons going off. Deaf as a post,' she said to Victor.

'He wants to know about Mademoiselle Kherson!' she bawled in her husband's ear again.

'That reminds me. Mademoiselle Becker told us Mademoiselle Kherson's putting up your shop assistant's cousin. Will she be staying long? I have to know because of the letters and so forth,' the concierge asked Victor.

'There's no need to be bothering Monsieur Legris about that, Aristide. The girl's gone. Found a position,' his wife told him.

'What time did she leave the building?' Victor asked, feeling a headache coming on.

'This morning. About seven o'clock, when I was emptying the rubbish bins. Why? Didn't she leave Mademoiselle Tasha's key under the mat like she said she would?'

'Yes, indeed, under the mat,' Victor replied hastily.

'I'm glad to hear it. We're the ones responsible for everyone who comes through here, you know.'

'Did she tell you where she was going?'

'Of course she did; we had a nice little chat. She's a bit lost all alone here in Paris, poor creature. When you're in service, there's not a lot of time for promenading. She wanted to know how to get to Pont de Crimée. Said she had an appointment at an employment agency there. As far as I could gather, her last mistress was no picnic. I said she should take the omnibus, since

Pont de Crimée isn't exactly next door. "Oh, I think I'll walk," she says, "I'll see a bit of the city. I've got time, they're not expecting me until midday." If you ask me, she was in no hurry to start her new job.'

Victor turned to leave, but Monsieur Ladoucette held him back.

'So Choupette jumped up and bit him hard on the backside and he let go of his knife. "Stinking mad dog!" he cries. "Pavement biter!" I snap back at him. And just then . . .'

'Aristide!' Madame Ladoucette cried reprovingly. 'Go and shell the peas! By the way, Monsieur Legris, would it be too much to ask if you could bring me the beginning of the Xavier de Montépin?[2] The fifth volume ends so beautifully: "I have suffered, but now I am in paradise. God is good!" But I still want to know what happens to the little bread delivery girl in the first four!'

'Yes, I promise. I must go upstairs again; I've left something behind.'

Like Monsieur Ladoucette's dog, Victor felt angry enough to bite someone and it took him six flights of stairs to calm down. He checked under the door mat as soon as he reached the top. No key. He was puzzled. Why would Denise have spun such a tale, worthy of Xavier de Montépin himself? He couldn't help admiring the way she had inveigled him with her story at the Temps Perdu last Saturday. 'She's a good little actress. She ought to try joining the Comédie-Française instead of wasting her time playing the part of the faithful servant!' How was he to go about unravelling this mess? He must begin at the beginning. He would go to Père-Lachaise. What better way of making the gatekeeper talk than setting his camera up amidst the tomb-stones? The light was good. He would spend a peaceful after-noon surrounded by greenery and then go and leave Odette's key with Hyacinthe. But first of all he must collect his equipment from Rue des Saints-Pères. Once again his appetite for solving puzzles was awakened, and life suddenly had a spice to it that excited him.

Joseph was spending his lunch break perched on his library steps scanning the morning papers for news items.

'Have there been any sales?' Victor enquired, depositing his hat on Molière's head.

'A Crébillon fils[3] illustrated by Moreau le Jeune. A gentleman of independent means bought it, pretending he was only interested in the morocco binding. And three copies of *The Beast in Man*,' Joseph mumbled. 'There was a telephone call for Monsieur Mori and I took the liberty of telling the caller he was absent but that you might go and have a look.'

'At what?'

'An inheritance, on Avenue Ternes, the complete works of Bossuet in ten volumes, and an incomplete Saint-Simon. I wrote down the address just in case; it's on the desk. Oh! Listen to this, boss . . .'

With his nose pressed to the newspaper, he read out:

Early on Thursday morning at St Nazaire, a macabre discovery was made under somewhat strange circumstances. Foreman Aimable Boudier, upon descending into the hold of a ship whose cargo of grain had just been unloaded, was shocked and horrified to come across a man's body in an advanced state of putrefaction. A few hairs were still sticking to the skull, but the face was unrecognisable. Monsieur Pinot of the Harbour Police contacted the head of the Paris Police who arrived promptly at the scene.

'Monsieur Goron is going to have his work cut out for him, considering he hasn't even bothered to arrest the main suspect in the Gouffé affair. What do you think, boss?'

Joseph glanced up to find that Victor had gone.

'I don't know why I bother. He has no interest in anything these days. Love! Women! Granted, women are decorative in the home and indispensable to its function, but they distract a man from his true passions!'

He promised himself he would never renounce writing for the love of Valentine. Victor returned with a bag slung over his shoulder.

'I'm going out, Joseph. I'm leaving you in charge of the shop.'

'Again? Where are you off to now?'

'To have a look at that inheritance, of course.'

'I thought you hated Bossuet! And what about lunch? Madame Germaine will think I forgot to tell you she's prepared *tripes à la mode de Caen*.[4] You only need to heat it up.'

'I donate the frugal meal to you.'

The carriage dropped him at Place des Pyrénées and he made his way to the cemetery via a narrow pathway running alongside a patch of wasteland where a few scrawny goats were nibbling at the scrubby grass.

He went to the chapel first, hoping to photograph the magnificent view of Paris from there. Beyond a piece of raised terrain lined with cypress trees, the grey and white city stretched out, its towers and domes outlined against the sky like an uneven row of teeth: the Pantheon, Notre-Dame, Les Invalides, the Eiffel Tower. Removing a detachable tripod from his bag, he fixed it to his camera, a Photo-Secret 9/12 with a bellows chamber, and peered into the viewfinder. A few inquisitive passers-by gathered round him and he hurriedly gathered up his equipment and moved on. A few yards above the chapel in a fenced-off enclosure, he could see the front of the crematorium with its painted trellis, and on top the two chimney flues. He had little sympathy for the idea of burning people's bodies and he hoped it would be many years before this custom, imported from England, took root in France. Since its inauguration the previous year, the crematorium had been used on a hundred or so occasions and had already sparked off a passionate debate within the Catholic community: the arch-bishop of Paris had spoken out strongly against cremation. But these wrangles did not concern him; he liked cemeteries because they were little islands of green in the middle of cities where one could listen to the birds singing. And as a photographer he found the tombs highly interesting. This one, for instance, he said to himself as he set up his tripod: a headstone, two bronze hands in a tender embrace and the epitaph below:

My wife, I await you
5 February 1843
My husband, I am here
5 December 1877

Although tempted to smile at such a display of devotion, he was moved by it too. Just then, a funeral cortège passed along the avenue and he lifted his hat.

He asked one of the keepers for directions to the Valois family chapel and after losing his way a couple of times found the funerary chapel, unlocked. He entered and read the inscriptions on the walls. Odette had stood there only a few days before. He examined the altar and then the floor for clues, but found nothing.

He went back out into the avenue to photograph the chapel. As he was fixing the shot, the upside down image of a dishevelled-looking old man with white hair appeared in his viewfinder. He straightened up. Surprised, the old man stared hard at him and all of a sudden began to shout:

'Dammit! It's you! I know you! It's you, in the flesh! I said I'd recognise you. Just like in your photograph. So you've come to get me, eh? Well, you won't have me! Oh no! Not you! No one can get Père Moscou, not even Grouchy! To the slaughter!'

He turned and ran off, waving his arms in the air. Victor hurriedly packed his equipment away with the intention of following the old man, but he had vanished into thin air.

He wandered aimlessly, haunted by the name the old man had shouted at him. Grouchy. Had he been referring to Marquis Emmanuel de Grouchy, Marshal of France? What possible part could he play in all this? Unable to find his bearings, he wandered about until he arrived at the Rue de Repos exit, where he walked resolutely into the gatekeeper's lodge. He found a skinny little man with large whiskers smoking his pipe and playing solitaire. On seeing Victor, the man hurriedly covered the cards with his cap and began to get up.

'Please stay seated. Perhaps you may be able to help me – it concerns our maid. She returned home on Friday evening in a state of utter panic. My wife and I are terribly worried about the girl. We're beginning to wonder whether she isn't slightly unhinged.'

'Friday, you say? She wouldn't happen to be a blonde slip of a girl?'

'My wife arranged to meet her in Rue de Repos, and waited there until closing time. When the girl didn't appear, she decided to return home, assuming she would find her already there. When Denise – that's the girl's name – finally turned up, she was in a terrible state, stammering and gibbering about ghosts and apparitions and goodness knows what else. I couldn't make head or tail of it, which is why I wondered whether you might have heard something about this unfortunate incident? Naturally we don't wish to keep an hysteric in our employ.'

'I thought as much. She didn't seem normal to me, and I trust my instincts. Yes, she told me some unlikely story about her mistress vanishing into thin air. But don't be too hard on her. Cemeteries can have a strange effect on people.'

'Did you also see her mistress – I mean my wife?'

Barnabé rubbed his chin and glanced suspiciously at Victor.

'How could I have seen her if she was standing outside in Rue de Repos?'

Victor winked at the man.

'You never know with women. I'm not normally distrustful, but, well . . . it's only natural. Having concluded that Denise must be slightly touched, it occurred to me that perhaps my wife . . .'

Barnabé fiddled with his cap and screwed up his face, which relaxed suddenly as he began to laugh.

'Oh, I get it. You think your missus might have slipped off to an appointment with her . . . doctor! All I can tell you is I never clapped eyes on her, and your maid was in such a state she practically threw herself on me. Lucky for her it was me. I soon calmed her down and sent her packing. I'm a married man, I told her.'

'She mentioned something to us about a tall, white-haired fellow who chased her.'

'That'll be Père Moscou. He's a trifle eccentric, but harmless enough – a good sort. Hankers after the Empire – wouldn't hurt a fly, not even when he's the worse for drink. He's worked here a long time. I've known him for fifteen years. He looks after the tombs, does odd jobs here and there, so I turn a blind eye.'

'Where might I find this Père . . . What did you call him?'

'Moscou. His ancestors were in the retreat from Moscow, hence the nickname. He lives in the Cour des Comptes on Quai d'Orsay – the one they burnt down in '71. But you'll be lucky if you catch him there, he's always on the move. Do us a favour, Monsieur, don't pick a quarrel with him or it'll come back on me. I've got my job to think about and six children to feed. In any case, your maid was wrong to complain about him. If he did talk bawdy to her, it's only on account of his being somewhat forward. But he's no worse than your average cabman.'

'Have no fear, I simply wish to ask him a few questions. Here, take my card. If you see him, tell him to pay me a call. I'll make it worth his while.'

During the carriage ride to Boulevard Haussmann, Victor's mind was engaged in an intoxicating ferment of speculation. Denise claimed she had last seen Odette at Père-Lachaise, and yet could he trust the servant girl after what he had found at Tasha's apartment? The gatekeeper's description of her as an impassioned female who had made advances towards him was hardly favourable. And as for Monsieur Hyacinthe, he insisted that Madame de Valois had returned home on Friday night.

I must find out the truth. And the old man in the cemetery, this Père Moscou. What was that gibberish he shouted? 'I know you . . . just like in your photograph.' What photograph? Bah! The man was probably drunk. It has no bearing on this affair.

The carriage had been halted by an enormous traffic jam in Rue du Havre. Victor stepped down outside the Printemps department store and soon discovered that the cause of the hold-up was a crowd of people in the middle of the road.

'Is it a demonstration?' he enquired of an omnibus driver who was pacing up and down alongside his vehicle, which was crammed with excited passengers.

'Just imagine – it's a milkman! Those fellows drive too fast. He was going top speed when he ran over that poor devil. He's a goner from the looks of it; there's blood everywhere.'

Victor turned round hurriedly and started elbowing his way

down the boulevard. He skirted a public urinal as well as a number of the flower and newspaper kiosks that had begun springing up of late, forcing pedestrians towards the big cafés. There were other obstacles in his path: shoe-shiners' boxes, discarded oyster shells from the oyster-sellers' stalls, cast-iron chairs and tables. And dotted here and there were sandwich boards vaunting the merits of throat pastilles and herbal teas, while passers-by crowded around the leaflet distributors and street vendors, causing the pedestrians to risk their lives by stepping off the pavement on to the road.

Relieved to have escaped the beady eye of the concierge, who was engaged in an animated conversation with a street sweeper, Victor slipped through the entrance to number 24 and raced up the stairs. He rang the bell to the fifth-floor apartment several times. Taking a deep breath, he slid one of the keys into the lock. It wouldn't budge. He tried another key and this time the latch clicked open.

He felt instantly aware of that particular silence of an empty house. He stood in the doorway waiting for his eyes to grow accustomed to the dark corridor, then plucked up his courage, set down his bag and tripod and lit the petrol lamp, resolving to make a thorough search of the apartment for clues as to Odette's whereabouts.

Nothing appeared to have been disturbed since his last visit. A maze of sheet music still lay scattered on the carpet at the feet of the baby grand, whose squat form reminded him of an animal waiting to pounce. As he drew closer he noticed that the porcelain jar he'd seen on the piano had been placed on some cushions on one of the two sofas, and the vases full of wilted flowers had migrated to the fireplace. He lifted the lamp level with his eyes. The velvet drape that had adorned the piano lay scrunched up on the floor. Somebody had evidently removed the porcelain monstrosities so that they could lift the piano lid and search the tuning pins and the sounding board. Who had been back here, Odette or Denise? He made his way towards the maid's quarters – a room barely bigger than a cupboard, with a bleak, chilly atmosphere. Odette had always been thrifty, cutting back on the heating and her servants' salaries until she'd ended up employing only one.

As he'd anticipated, the wardrobe was empty. The bed had been made, but the pillow case was missing. The washstand near the door and the jug and basin on the floor appeared to confirm Denise's story – unless of course she had placed them there deliberately.

He doubled back, entering Armand's bedroom. The strong, musty odour caught in his throat – the room hadn't been aired for weeks. He held his breath. That smell! Suddenly he was transported back twenty-three years in time to London, and the flat in Sloane Square where he'd spent his childhood. He recalled with amazing clarity a scene he thought he had buried deep in his memory.

His father scolding him, imposing and threatening, devoid of pity. And he, a little boy of seven, standing with bowed head, paralysed by a mixture of fear and loathing. What crime had he committed that justified him being locked in the cellar for hours? A mistake in one of his lessons, perhaps, or some illicit gesture? It was dark and lonely in the cellar. He'd be unable to bear it, he'd die. A silent appeal to Kenji, his father's assistant at the bookshop, had worked. Kenji had secretly given him a candle and a book of fairy tales. He was saved! Transported by the magical story of a Chinese empress turned into a dragon, the little boy was no longer the prisoner of a damp jail. With the white dragon Fang Wei-Yu at his side, he plumbed the depths of the ocean, fought the demons of Tiger Hill and rode the waves and clouds.

He heard a clock ticking and the distant hum of the boulevard below. The images from his past dissolved, leaving only a whiff of mildew. He opened the windows to get rid of the stale air and walked around the room. It contained dusty furniture and a billiard table piled high with hat boxes whose lids had been taken off and replaced askew.

On the floor in front of a pitch pine wardrobe lay two men's shirts with their sleeves entwined in an attitude of prayer. Having set down the lamp, which was beginning to sputter, he pulled open the wardrobe doors and found a jumble of clothing worthy of Carreau du Temple. Someone had been frantically searching for something here too. On his way out, he noticed two faded rectangles on the coppery-green wallpaper where two pictures had once hung.

He took a deep breath to master the revulsion Odette's bedroom inspired in him, and sought refuge in the bathroom whose plush ostentation he found pleasing. The memory of his former lover at the height of their affair pervaded this space where she used to spend hours in front of the mirror banishing every last wrinkle. The sight of the Farnèse cream purchased at La Reine des Abeilles stirred him, and he had visions of her face caked in the stuff. He was tempted for a moment to breathe in its scent, but stopped himself, instead making a mental inventory of the various beauty salves, blushers, make-up accessories and perfume bottles laid out on a round, marble-topped table beside the washbasin. Ranged along a shelf, a tumbler, toothbrush, coal-tar tooth powder and coloured soaps conjured up the image of an immaculate Odette adorned with chiffon, lace and ribbons that enhanced her blonde complexion. An inspection of the little cupboard where she kept her gloves and handkerchiefs revealed a disorder identical to the one in Armand's wardrobe.

In the bedroom he made an effort not to look at the bed, a ghost ship with sails unfurled, drifting towards the kingdom of the dead. The wardrobe would offer up more revelations. He was about to open it when a thought occurred to him and he went back into the bathroom.

He looked again at the expensive soaps, the ivory toothbrush and the tooth powder ranged under the mirror covered in black gauze. Had she eloped, it was conceivable that she might have left her toothbrush behind, but not her make-up. A woman like Odette, who took such care of her looks and her complexion, would never go anywhere, not even to a local restaurant, without her vanity case. No, the make-up shouldn't have been there.

He hesitated, torn between the urge to leave and an almost perverse desire to stay and pursue his investigation. He looked over at the ottoman where Odette used to sit browsing through the morning papers, at the palm tree swathed in black and the mahogany table that served as an altar dedicated to the memory of Armand de Valois. Suddenly he felt giddy and the room began to sway. The rosewood wardrobe loomed before him like an iceberg. After a few moments it stopped moving and he was finally able to penetrate its depths. The inside looked as if it had been hit by a tornado: the clothes rail on the left had collapsed under the weight of an army of black dresses and fur-trimmed coats on hangers and a row of books on a shelf on the right had been swept into a heap against the side panel of the wardrobe.

He stood staring at the clothes. God, what a morbid collection! He fished a heliotrope-scented chiffon negligee out of the black mound of shoes. A sudden memory surfaced of Odette, languorous after their love-making, but hastily covering up her nudity with that frilly gown, which had all the allure of a lampshade.

Feeling foolish, he turned his attention to the books. Above them the skull's empty eye sockets stared back at him. 'I didn't know Hamlet was playing here!' he quipped, trying to reassure himself as he pulled out a few of the battered, dog-eared volumes, nearly knocking himself out in the process.

His arms full, he collapsed on to the ottoman. Reading out the titles, he piled the books up beside him: *The Book of Prophecies*, *The Divinatory Sciences*, *The Occultist's Laws*, *Astral Body & Astral Plane*, *Psychic Phenomena*, *The Spiritualist's Doctrine*.

'For a woman who isn't fond of reading . . .' he murmured. 'Now, what have we here? *Photographs of the Astral Body*. That looks amusing. I must try it some time.'

He glanced through a booklet intriguingly entitled: *Account of a Table-turning Session on the Island of Jersey with Victor Hugo*, by Numa Winner. Odette hadn't read a word of the great

Hugo's prose, yet judging from the pencil marks in the booklet's margins she was passionately interested in the conversations he claimed to have had with poltergeists during his exile in Marine Terrace on Jersey.

He discarded the booklet and opened a box file labelled: *Satanism Under the Inquisition*. As he examined the engravings depicting the tortures reserved for heretics by the Holy Office, he became convinced that Odette had lost her mind. Faintly nauseous, he began replacing the books and the file in the wardrobe. His hand encountered an obstruction. He craned his neck, but he wasn't tall enough see what it was and went to fetch a chair from the sitting room.

Precariously balanced, he rummaged at the back of the shelf and pulled out a large envelope with the word *Private* written on it. His racing heart, sudden perspiration and another wave of nausea told him it was time to leave the apartment.

Now I know what women feel like when they have the vapours. As Kenji would say, 'The body suffers the mind's blows as the earth suffers those of the typhoon.' Unless I'm simply coming down with influenza.

He left the apartment with a feeling of relief, the envelope tucked under his jacket and his bag and tripod over his shoulder.

Sitting over of a glass of beer in the smoky bar of the Bibulus, Victor contemplated the still unopened envelope lying on the barrel serving as a table. A few swigs of beer gave him the courage he needed and he pulled out a dozen or so letters from Colombia tied with a ribbon and addressed to Madame de Valois, along with an appointments diary and a sheaf of papers. Four aspiring artists in overalls burst into the bar from the passage leading to the studio, amongst them Maurice Laumier. Victor hastily stuffed the papers back into the envelope and turned away from the counter where the four painters were emptying their tankards. He thought Laumier hadn't noticed him until he heard the man exclaim in a loud voice:

'This place is becoming gentrified. One day it'll be so thick with men of independent means that we shall be obliged to decamp, unless of course we show them what's what!'

The others laughed approvingly and shot sidelong glances at Victor, who feigned indifference. He had more important things on his mind. How was he going to explain Denise's disappearance to Tasha? The question was still plaguing him when at last he saw her. Ignoring Maurice's calls, she was making a beeline for him in her embroidered blouse and grey skirt, her red hair held up by two gilt hair combs.

Later, he promised himself, rising to his feet and offering his arm to the young woman who smiled at him as she adjusted her little hat adorned with flowers.

'See you tomorrow, Tasha. Get some sleep!' Maurice Laumier called out.

Since she had drifted off to sleep half an hour earlier, he'd been trying unsuccessfully to do likewise. He got up quietly, a cramp in his calf, and went into the room that served both as study and sitting room. He sat facing the roll-top desk, lit the Rochester lamp and glanced wearily at the engravings of Charles Fournier's phalanstery that his uncle Émile had left him. The universal harmony propounded by the Utopian had been left behind by the bandwagon of history; was this something to rejoice over or to deplore? He emptied out the contents of the envelope he had purloined from Odette's apartment. Over the course of the evening, which had started out in the restaurant of the Hotel Continental and ended in the bedroom, he couldn't stop thinking about Denise and how annoyed Tasha would be when she discovered what had happened, and about Odette's disappearance. He had done his best to hide his concerns and was certain he'd been successful, despite their having somewhat interfered with his enjoyment of the caresses they'd exchanged in bed.

His discomfort at his own duplicity quickly gave way to a feeling of renewed excitement about the investigation and, setting aside Armand's letters to his wife, he concentrated first on the black leather appointments diary, decorated with a tooled portrayal of General Boulanger astride a horse. At the top of each page Odette had written the date, beginning 1st October 1889. The entries were unremarkable. *Monday 6th: hairdresser . . . Wednesday: tea with A.D.B. . . .* Who was A.D.B.? *Friday 24th October: fitting with Maud . . . Monday 27th: Received package from Armand, hung Madonna on his bedroom wall . . . Tuesday 28th October: sent telegram to Armand . . .* He forced himself to read on through a list of trivia largely concerning visits to hairdressers and dressmakers. From 20th December onwards the entries related to the arrangements for the memorial, the ordering of a marble plaque and further meetings with different people. *20th December: appointment with Maître Arnaud . . . 22nd December: Turner . . . appointment with Zénobie three-thirty p.m. Pâtisserie Gloppe, Champs-Élysées . . . 28th:*

Père-Lachaise . . . 3rd January '90: A.D.B. . . . 7th January: Zénobie. 10th January: Église de la Madeleine, memorial mass for Armand . . . And from then on as regular as clockwork on Monday and Thursday afternoons, *Zénobie, Zénobie, Zénobie* up until March.

'Who was this *Zénobie?* A relative of Armand perhaps?' he wondered, closing the diary.

He scanned the papers: legal documents notarised by Maître Arnaud relating to Armand's will and apparently naming Odette as sole heir. There was also an official letter from the French Consulate in Colombia.

Tumaco, 22nd November 1889

Dear Madame,

It is our sad duty to inform you of the death of your husband Armand de Valois, geologist with the Inter-Oceanic Canal Company, who succumbed to yellow fever on 13th November 1889 in the village of Las Juntas. His body was laid to rest in the ground with all the respect due to him. We hereby return to you his papers and personal effects.

Please accept our deepest sympathy and sincere condolences.

There was another letter from Armand de Valois, written in October and containing some underlined passages.

Cali 8th October

My dear wife,

I am sending you the portrait of the Madonna we saw together at Lourdes in '86. It is very dear to me so please take great care of it. I want you to hang it up in my bedroom above my desk next to the portrait of the Archangel Saint Michel which Monsignor Carette left me. Send me a telegram as soon as you receive this letter telling me it has arrived safely. All is well here. I am heading for Panama, and will sail to France at the end of November. I shall be back in Paris in time to celebrate Christmas with you. Until then.

    Much love,
    Armand

What a cold letter! I wouldn't have credited dear Armand with such religious zeal, Victor thought.

He looked briefly at a third letter written by Odette.

29th July 1889

Dear Armand,
    How are you, my duck?

Oh, so she calls him by that silly nickname too, he observed, a little piqued.

    . . . I returned from Paris yesterday. I thoroughly enjoyed my stay at Houlgate . . .

He skimmed through the letter, ashamed of prying.

    . . . met some charming people, in particular the well-known English spiritualist Monsieur Numa Winner . . .

Numa Winner . . . The author of the booklet about the table-turning in Jersey?

    . . . he assured me that your troubles will soon be over [. . .]. Did I tell you that your bookseller M. Legris, from Rue des Saints-Pères [. . .] a loose woman who poses nude as an artist's model [. . .] he doesn't wear a top hat and has a Chinese servant?

'Marvellous', muttered Victor. 'Bah! It's fair enough, after all I left her – she's just getting her own back.'

It occurred to him that their separation might have caused her grief. Shrugging off the idea, he replaced the papers in the envelope, disappointed not to have discovered anything of real interest. He yawned. It would be better if he stopped trying to invent a plot based around some make-up left behind in a bathroom. Odette had run away with a lover and her maid had taken advantage of the situation to carry out a series of petty thefts. That was all there was to it.

Victor returned to the bedroom. He pulled the sheet back and was displeased to find Tasha stretched out in the middle of the bed. He tickled her, without success. Lying at the edge of the mattress, he felt her breath caress his neck and not for the first time found himself wondering how two such independent men as he and Kenji could have fallen under the spell of a woman.

It's more understandable in my case, but he seems so resilient, so indifferent to the weaker sex . . . However hard he tried to put it out of his mind, he couldn't help imagining his associate and adoptive father performing lascivious acts with a certain Iris. Slightly ashamed, he snuggled up to Tasha and found refuge in a fitful sleep.

CHAPTER FIVE

TWO scholars tightly buttoned into their black frock coats were examining works on genealogy and exchanging observations in hushed voices at the back of the bookshop. Victor stood holding a bundle of yellowing papers and conversing with a long-haired gentleman in his sixties, who was looking for documents relating to Marshall Lefebvre.[1] When the man took his leave, Victor accompanied him to the door and said goodbye politely.

'Joseph, please wrap this package properly, and deliver it immediately to Monsieur Victorien Sardou. Damn! The battle-axe,' he groaned, beating a retreat to the shelter of the office.

To his utter astonishment, Jojo, beaming, hurried over to greet the Comtesse de Salignac and her niece Valentine.

'Young man, have you received *Spirit of Stone* yet?'

As he rushed to her niece's side without answering, she addressed Victor frostily.

'Must one go on a waiting list in order to enjoy the privilege of finding you at home, Monsieur Legris?'

'I have been awfully busy of late,' he replied, with the utmost affability.

He was about to continue, when a woman of around forty, plump and cheerful and enveloped in the folds of a tartan cape, with a Maltese dog tucked under arm, burst into the bookshop.

'Olympe! I knew I'd find you here. Have you seen *L'Éclair?*' she cried, brandishing the latest issue.

Before the Comtesse had time to open her mouth, she read aloud:

Two university doctors have been examining the question of whether life can continue after a man has been guillotined. Whilst one insists that the moment of death definitely marks the end of thought, the other, having satisfied himself that a man's heart carries on beating for several seconds after decapitation, concludes that mental activity still occurs in the brain after it has been separated from the body.

'What do you say to that! Isn't it thrilling? Doesn't it put you in mind of our friend Adalberte's experiences?'

'Preposterous,' retorted Madame de Salignac, sniffing haughtily.

'Is Madame de Brix in the habit of frequenting the guillotine?' Victor was surprised.

Joseph, all agog, had posted himself next to Raphaëlle de Gouveline, hoping she would forget her paper so he could cut out the article.

'Since her son's death she's become obsessed with spiritualism. And when her husband disappeared Odette went the same way. I never made such fuss when mine gave up the ghost! Well, Monsieur Legris, I'm waiting!' said the Comtesse.

'Poor Odette! One can't blame her for finding it hard to bear such a loss! Nevertheless, I agree with you, Olympe; spending more than three months in deep mourning is perhaps excessive. We were supposed to meet last Sunday at Adalberte's – she's not very well at the moment, by the way, heart trouble – just us widows, we find a certain solace in evoking the memory of our dear departed, but Odette let us down. She probably decided to go and see that clairvoyant of hers at the last minute, that . . . oh, what is the name of that charlatan, I never can remember! I shall go over to Boulevard Haussmann at the end of the week. Do you have a message for her, Monsieur Legris? She's so lonely these days,' concluded Raphaëlle, looking meaningfully at Victor, who remained impassive.

'You'd do well to put off your visit, what with the Mid-Lent parades. One never know—' Madame de Salignac stopped mid-sentence, her eyes fixed on a point behind Victor's shoulder.

'Monsieur Legris, a young woman is asking for you,' whispered Raphaëlle de Gouveline.

He turned round. Tasha, her hair loose, was leaning over the banister. She waved to the little group before going back upstairs, followed closely by Victor.

'So that's the Russian hussy,' Raphaëlle de Gouveline sighed.

'Why men fall for such creatures is a mystery to me. Animals, my dear, all animals!'

Joseph took advantage of the diversion to take Valentine to one side.

'You spend an awful lot of time with your aunt; you must be very fond of her,' he whispered.

'It's her. She won't let me out of her sight,' she sighed, blushing. 'But I intend to go and see the new spring collection at the Grands Magasins du Louvre tomorrow. Alone,' she added meaningfully.

Joseph understood, but with one boss away and the other blissfully in love, it would be hard for him to get out.

Victor came back down the stairs and graciously handed a paperback volume to each of the women.

'Allow me to offer you these editions printed on Japan paper in the hope that you will forgive my absences.'

'*Spirit of Stone!* How terribly kind!' exclaimed Raphaëlle de Gouveline.

She leant over to Victor while the Comtesse was busy examining the book through her lorgnette: 'Between you and me, my dear man, I prefer Guy de Maupassant's novels to those of Georges Ohnet. They're so much racier, don't you think?'

'I am of the same opinion as you. Please convey my regards to Madame de Valois if you see her.'

'I shan't forget, my dear man, I shan't forget. Are you coming, Olympe?'

The Comtesse called out sharply to Valentine, who detached herself reluctantly from Joseph's side, and the three women left the shop, followed by the two scholars.

During his lunch break, Jojo climbed on to his library steps with his customary apple and newspaper – delighted at having been able to pinch Raphaëlle de Gouveline's copy of *L'Éclair*. Victor sat at his desk mechanically flicking through the orders list, preoccupied by the events of the previous day. Joseph let out a cry:

'Listen to this, boss!'

Corpse at St Nazaire continued . . . The cause of death of the unidentified body found on the cargo ship *Goéland* has finally been established. According to the pathologist who carried out the autopsy it was a murder. The man was approximately 5 feet 9 inches tall and aged between thirty-five and forty-five. He had dark-brown hair and a beard. His right femur being somewhat shorter than his left would have given him, when alive, a slight limp. The back of his skull was fractured in two places, suggesting heavy blows to the head resulting in almost instantaneous death. His body was undoubtedly pushed into the hold and then concealed. According to the pathologist, the attack occurred weeks, possibly months ago. Messieurs Lechacheur and Goron spent part of yesterday afternoon checking the lists of shipping entering and leaving St Nazaire harb—

'Enough!' Victor, at the end of his tether, exploded. 'I've allowed you to display those detective novels in the shop window, though they're hardly likely to attract any real bibliophiles, but please spare me your ghastly news items!'

Incensed by such a blatant display of hypocrisy, Joseph let his newspaper drop and stammered: 'But— but Monsieur Legris, that's unfair! You're the one who introduced me to that kind of literature and, as for the window display, it wasn't my idea – you suggested it just before Christmas! But, if that's how you feel, I'll dismantle it this minute!'

Victor couldn't help laughing.

'Forgive me, Joseph, I'm sorry. I've got a few things on my mind at the moment. Take no notice of me – I didn't mean a word I said.'

'So you say,' muttered Joseph, retrieving the scattered pages of his newspaper.

A headline caught his eye and he drew the page closer so he

could read it. Victor watched him, intrigued. He was scanning one of the articles, visibly distressed.

'Well, what is it?'

'Top right-hand page,' Joseph murmured, '"Woman drowned" . . .'

'"Woman drowned at Pont de Crimée".' Victor had snatched the paper and was reading in a low voice.

Early yesterday evening, a boatman by the name of Jean Bréchart, who was waiting to pass through the Pont de Crimée, pulled a young woman's body out of the river. All evidence points to the poor creature having committed suicide. The corpse was taken to the morgue where it is waiting to be identified. The drowned woman, blonde, approximately twenty years old and of slender build, was dressed in shabby clothing and wore a cheap bracelet on her right wrist with a pendant in the shape of a dog.

'It's Denise,' gasped Joseph.

Disconcerted, Victor tried to reassure him. 'Now what makes you think it's her? Why do you think she'd—'

'It's her, I tell you. We were at the funfair the day before yesterday, Sunday. That bracelet . . . I won it for her at the shooting gallery.'

'Hundreds of girls wear trinkets like that.'

'It says in the paper that she's blonde.'

'And there are thousands of young blondes in Paris, Joseph . . .'

But he was careful not to mention that only one had gone to a meeting at Pont de Crimée.

'Monsieur Legris, I want to be sure. I'm going to the morgue.'

'All right, I'll close the shop and go with you. I'll just tell Tasha . . .'

Despite the warmth of the stove, Joseph suddenly felt very cold.

The carriage ride took place in silence. Joseph was imagining Denise laughing aloud astride her wooden horse, pleased as punch when he presented her with the bracelet and hungrily devouring the pile of frites served up to them by his mother, Euphrosine Pignot. She was too full of life to have thrown herself off a bridge. Monsieur Legris was right: it wasn't her, it couldn't possibly be her . . . Victor, his head turned stubbornly towards the window, was trying hard to make sense of the young girl's desperate act. He could see only one explanation: guilt at some irreparable wrong. But how could a simple theft justify suicide? Was there another motive? He was beginning to feel seriously worried about Odette.

Behind the chevet of the Notre-Dame, a levy office, which looked like a Greek mausoleum, jutted out of the Seine at the tip of l'Île de la Cité. Victor had often crossed Pont Archevêché without paying attention to the morgue. He certainly never imagined he would one day have reason to enter the squat building. He recalled someone saying to him recently: 'People queue up to see drowned bodies like they do the latest fashions.' He was unsurprised, therefore, to discover a crowd standing outside the doors to the sinister establishment. Joseph, however, wasn't expecting to come across so many women, young and old. There were shop assistants, dressmakers on their way back to their workshops and mothers carrying brats. Navvies too, who had slipped away from their gantries, and children playing truant. Not to mention shifty individuals up to no good. Some were laughing and they were all jostling for position in the queue.

'Nice way to spend your free time,' Joseph grunted.

'Sharks are attracted to blood like a bear is to honey,' Victor replied, quoting one of Kenji's proverbs.

As they reached the main display room they had the impression they were walking into some kind of foul operating theatre, where the icy air reeked of chlorine. The sparse daylight filtering through the tiny, arched windows fell on the spectators thronging in front of the corpses. At first Victor and Joseph stood, unable to see anything and powerless to push through the crowd, party to a series of comments they could have done without:

'. . . they stick 'em in a cave where it's minus sixty and then bring 'em up 'ere where it's zero degrees. It's a paradise for corpses!'

'. . . it's not just drowned people, it's hanged ones too and victims of road accidents, it's a shame they keep the murder victims in the back room, though.'

'. . . nearly seven hundred last year, on account of the Universal Exposition attracting the crowds, so naturally there were more deaths.'

'A drunkard knocks at the door of the morgue at two in the morning. "What do you want?" cries the caretaker. "I've been on a bender since the day before yesterday and I haven't gone home. I was worried. I thought I might be here!"'

The joke, told by a big lad wearing a cap, was met by howls of laughter. Just then the crowd surged forward and Victor and Joseph found themselves in the front row of the spectators.

Stretched out on zinc-topped tables behind a glass partition, the pitiful corpses – most of them naked but preserved thanks to the refrigeration – were waiting to be claimed. Behind them on the walls hung the rags intended to help identify them.

A woman next to Joseph was sobbing and pointing at a man's corpse.

'It's Daniel! My God, it's him. He was looking for a job but no one would take him on. I never thought he'd . . .'

Her voice faded away and another, younger woman, who was supporting her, started shouting: 'Get back, get back, you vultures! Aren't you ashamed of this disgraceful exhibition?'

'Calm down, my dear,' said one of the workers, 'we have to attract the crowds if we want these corpses to be claimed by their families.'

As though propelled by some supernatural force, Joseph moved forward, his legs stiff. All of a sudden he froze, unable to breathe, his eyes fixed on a small body with tangled blonde hair beside which hung a black woollen dress, a waisted jacket and a shapeless bonnet. A mauve shawl, a few clothes, a crucifix and a mirror had also been laid out on the table.

'Denise . . .'

He recoiled, retching. One of the mortuary workers rushed over.

'Were you acquainted with this young woman?'

Not knowing quite why, Victor squeezed Joseph's shoulder hard as a way of telling him to keep quiet.

'No,' he declared.

'And yet I distinctly heard this gentleman say "Denise".'

'He thought it was our cousin Denise Elzévir – she's gone missing. Happily he was mistaken. The strain . . .'

Joseph, white as a sheet, was staring down at his shoes.

'It often happens,' the employee assured him.

'The poor girl, she looks so young.'

'Oh, we get all ages in here, young, old . . . It's poverty that drives them to it. But this one, I'm not so sure she's a suicide, she's got a nasty gash on the back of her head. The pathologist will be doing an autopsy to see whether she was dead before she went in the water. That's why we'd like her family to come forward as quickly as possible.'

'Where did they pull her out?'

'Pont de Crimée. Most of our corpses are washed up by the Seine. And it's more often men who choose to end it that way. Just last week there were seven of them.'

'Which explains all these people here . . .'

'Oh, this is nothing compared to what it can be like!'

Joseph, refusing to listen any more, made for the exit, eliciting a stream of abuse from people he bumped into on his way. Victor joined him in the square at the foot of Notre-Dame. Slumped on a bench, the young man was staring blankly at the strutting pigeons.

'When I think that I was talking and laughing with her about the Canal de l'Ourcq . . . What are we going to do, Monsieur?'

'For the moment we're going back to the bookshop.'

*

They had only just arrived when Tasha burst through the door. She marched over to Victor, who was pouring a glass of brandy for Joseph.

'You should have told me!'

'Told you what?'

'That my room's been flooded! Denise is a real little housewife. She's tidied everything away, including the buckets I expressly told her not to move, and the result is two ruined canvases!'

She held out her hand.

'The key I lent to your protégée, please.'

'I don't have it.'

'What do you mean you don't have it! Liar! I've just spoken to Madame Ladoucette and she said you told her yesterday that Denise had left the key under my doormat.'

'Tasha, let me explain . . .'

'There's nothing to explain. You were afraid I'd leave before the week was up, that's all. Once again you didn't trust me! And what's this, may I ask?'

She waved a piece of blue paper in his face, which he grabbed. It was a letter that had been sent by pneumatic tube.

'I found it on the floor by the head of the bed. Luckily, Madame Ladoucette has a master key or I wouldn't have been able to get in.'

Victor glanced through the letter.

Sunday evening.

Madame de Valois has furnished me with a reference for you and I have found you a post through an employment agency called 'The

*Good Servant'. Meet me on Monday at midday in front of the Church
of Saint-Jacques-Saint-Christophe, near Pont de Crimée. We shall see
to the formalities and I shall accompany you to your new place of work.
If it is to your liking, you may begin immediately. Bring your belongings with you and leave Mademoiselle Tasha's key under the doormat.*

V.L.

Victor stared at the initials, stupefied.

'I didn't send this letter . . .'

'You didn't!' exclaimed Tasha. 'But V.L. stands for Victor
Legris, doesn't it?'

'I don't understand it. I know nothing about it!'

'But you did promise to write Denise a reference; I heard
you. Isn't that right, Joseph? I was there when . . .'

Tasha turned towards Joseph who, head in his hands, had
just slumped on to the counter.

'What's the matter? Aren't you feeling well?'

'It's Denise, she's . . .' he began in a leaden voice and then,
sitting up straight, he addressed Victor:

'Are you certain you didn't write the letter, boss?'

'I'm not suffering from amnesia,' Victor replied testily.
'Somebody has assumed my identity.'

'If it wasn't you . . . then she was enticed there . . . But by
whom? Do you think she might have been . . . I am beginning
to fear the worst!'

'What on earth are you two talking about? What's happened
to Denise?' Tasha cried.

Victor was silent for a moment.

'She's dead.'

'What! How?'

'Drowned. There's only one thing for it, Joseph. We must go the agency.'

'You're not serious,' Tasha protested. 'He's as white as a sheet! He can barely stand—'

'I'm fine, thank you, Mademoiselle Tasha. Monsieur Victor's quite right. We've got to find out whether she went there, because if she did, it changes everything.'

'The poor girl drowned herself – there's nothing you can do about it. Suicide or accident, it's a matter for the police.'

Tasha looked anxiously at Victor, who was putting on his coat and hat while Joseph knocked back the last of his cognac.

'Could you look after the shop while we're out? Unless you've made other arrangements, of course,' Victor whispered in her ear, kissing her neck.

'Of course I can. But I have some advice for you . . .'

The door closed before Tasha could finish her sentence. She stood pensively twirling a lock of hair round her finger.

The carriage sped along Quai de la Loire towards the Bassin de la Villette, where the Seine broadened, forming a vast port for barges to unload their merchandise of sand, paving stones, flour, wheat and wood, all destined for the local factories. As it crossed the bascule bridge over the Canal de l'Ourcq, Joseph and Victor were able to glimpse the cast iron columns at either end that supported the heavy pulleys and chains. The mechanism was designed to lift the roadway to allow high-masted vessels to pass through. Neither man could prevent himself from imagining Denise's corpse being dragged through the murky waters below.

126

They skirted round the Church of Saint-Jacques-Saint-Christophe and down Rue de Crimée. The agency known as 'The Good Servant' occupied the first floor of a brick building in Impasse Émélie, near Cité Gosselin. On an enamelled plaque was a picture of a hand with the index finger pointing downwards to a sign saying:

The agency is on the second floor.

As they climbed the narrow, dark staircase they passed a young girl coming down clutching a piece of paper. Joseph felt a pang as he recalled Denise's account of her arrival in Paris.

Victor pushed down on the grimy door latch and the hubbub inside instantly went quiet as twenty or so curious women craned their necks at the visitors. Bareheaded, they were sitting on a wooden bench running along a whitewashed wall, patiently waiting to be registered. They were decked out in their finest flowered percale or striped calico dresses, and only the sharpest eye could have spotted in the half-light the darns in the threadbare fabric. They were telling one another in hushed tones about their hopes and fears, nervously glancing towards the office at the back of the room, where the proprietor, enthroned behind his desk, received them one at a time, jotting down details of their references on a register to be verified later by the police.

Meat, thought Joseph, remembering the expression Denise had used to describe these slaves in search of a master.

'I shall go and enquire,' Victor said.

While he walked over to the office, Joseph remained

standing, embarrassed by all the girls staring at him. Muffled giggles broke out on all sides and then a plump dark-haired girl invited him to sit between her and the girl next to her, a haggard blonde.

'Have you come for a job?' she asked, in a strong Provençal accent.

'Er . . . no. Just to make some enquiries.'

'It's my second agency this morning. The other one offered me a job as cook in an asylum for the deaf and dumb, twenty centimes an hour, ten hours a day. What with bread at forty centimes a kilo I said no thank you very much, and they said, "We don't want any truck with finicky girls like you." I had something to say about that: "My references don't say I'm a cook. I'm a maid, I am!" The morons!'

'That's right!' the blonde girl chimed in. 'If it weren't for us queuing at their counters, they wouldn't be behind them!'

'Where're you from?' the brunette asked, craning her neck.

'Up North. I worked nights packing beets. They take us women on because we're cleverer and more agile than the men. We put up with the rain and the mud better too, only they pay us half as much! I packed it in. I never saw my children and I couldn't make ends meet even though I scrimped and saved. It was too hard.'

She held out her cracked fingers, retracting them almost immediately when she spotted a snooty couple looking for a housemaid walking towards them. With an air of distaste, the woman sized them up from beneath her wide-brimmed hat and made a face. The office door opened and out stepped Victor. Joseph rose and doffed his hat.

'Ladies . . . I wish you luck,' he said in a low voice, before following his boss.

Out on the landing, the latter shook his head.

'He says he registered no one by the name of Denise Le Louarn.'

They returned to the canal and stopped halfway across the bridge, both tortured by the same thought. Victor pretended to take an interest in the view. To his right he could make out the Bassin in the fading light and beyond it the General Stores at the entrance to La Villette. To his left, the passing barges furrowed the water, red-roofed warehouses lined the quays and the iron structures of other bridges gradually vanished in the mist.

'I'll get the bastard who killed her,' said Joseph.

'There's no positive proof that it was a murder.'

'But we both think it was, don't we?'

Without answering, Victor started to walk back down Rue de Crimée towards Buttes-Charmont. After a few yards, they stopped and went into a tavern.

Joseph knocked back a glass of Mariani wine, his finger tracing mysterious symbols on the greasy table top.

'Why tell her to go to that agency where no one's ever heard of her? Think about it, boss. She receives the letter signed with your initials so she goes off unsuspecting to the meeting and she's found drowned with her skull cracked open. Whoever sent that letter knew a great deal. Read it again.'

Victor reached into his pocket for the crumpled piece of paper.

'You're right,' he agreed. 'The sender knows Tasha's name, he knows Denise is looking for a new position and he mentions a reference from Madame de Valois. Who could it be? A friend of the family, perhaps?'

'Or Madame de Valois herself! As Monsieur Lecoq[2] says, "One must not take things at face value." '

'Come now, Joseph. I'd like to agree with Émile Gaboriau that in matters of guesswork it pays to be bold, but there's no reason to think . . . No. I am seriously beginning to fear for the safety of Odette de Valois.'

'Has she come home yet?'

'How did you know she'd been away?'

'Denise told me she'd disappeared at the cemetery. She was terrified.'

Victor sipped his vermouth. 'No, Madame de Valois still hasn't returned. I went to her apartment yesterday evening to find the whole place had been turned upside down. What worries me is that Tasha's room has been ransacked too. I admit that up until a moment ago I suspected Denise of pulling the wool over our eyes to cover up some wrongdoing. But now . . . Whatever happens don't breathe a word of this to Tasha. I put everything back in its place.'

'What if there's a connection between Madame de Valois's disappearance and Denise's death?'

'What sort of connection?'

'Remember at the morgue, Denise's things were on display – you saw them as plainly as I did. Well, there was something missing: a picture of the Virgin Mary. I'm positive it wasn't there, and yet Denise was very fond of it. When I took her to

Rue Notre-Dame-de-Lorette on Saturday afternoon, she showed it to me and burst into tears and said Madame de Valois would be furious because it was the one she wanted to place in her husband's funerary chapel. Then she said, "I didn't steal it; I just borrowed it. I thought it was pretty so I changed it for the other one, the one of the Archangel Saint Michel." I didn't know what she was on about at the time, but now when I think of it . . .'

'Yes, she mentioned it to me when we were in the Temps Perdu, but I didn't attach any importance to it.'

Victor's mind was filled with murmurings and muddled images. His memory of the conversation in the café was all the more vague because he had only been half-listening to the girl's story. He frowned and tapped his glass. Joseph's face became a blur, replaced by two faded patches on a dark wall.

'That's it! They were hanging in Armand's bedroom.'

'What was that you said, boss?'

'Nothing, nothing.'

Anxious to keep certain pieces of information to himself, he began counting out the change for their drinks to try to put his assistant off the scent. But nothing would divert Joseph from his own thoughts.

'I remember now, boss, that picture, she called it *The Madonna in Blue*. Maybe that's what they were looking for in Madame de Valois's apartment and Tasha's room; it's probably valuable. What do you think?'

The 'Madonna' . . . the 'Madonna' . . . Victor had come across that word recently but he couldn't remember where . . .

His study! He was in his study with a bundle of papers in front of him. There was one . . . what was it? A letter! A letter with some sentences underlined . . .

He stood up, eager to follow Ariadne's thread to see where it would lead.

They sat opposite one another in the kitchen nibbling at Germaine's veal roulade. The carriage had dropped Joseph at his home on Rue Visconti. Now Victor regretted not having invited his assistant to dine with them, since his presence might have dissuaded Tasha from pestering him. Indeed, as soon as he had stepped through the door to the shop, she had started to complain about how long he'd been away. After apologising and confiding in her his concern following their visit to the agency, he had responded with an evasive gesture to her demand that he tell Denise's story to the police.

She picked at her fruit salad and finally threw down her spoon in exasperation.

'Promise me that you'll go.'

'Where?'

'Don't be obtuse.'

'Give me a little time. They probably wouldn't believe me anyway, or, if they did, they'd ask me endless questions.'

'I know exactly what you're up to. You're dying to get mixed up in another mystery and to flush out the criminal. Do you know what I think? You read too much! I don't want you to carry out any more private investigations – it's too dangerous. I nearly lost you last time; don't do it again.'

'You're behaving towards me the way you hate me behaving towards you,' he remarked, touched by her concern.

'It's not the same thing at all. When I do my painting, I'm not putting my life in danger. I refuse to be worried sick every time you're late!'

'I am so glad you care; it proves you love me. Would you pass the sugar, please?'

'And on top of that, you make fun of me! Very well! It's no use talking to someone who's deaf. I'm going to bed!'

He waited until he heard the bedroom door close, then hurried into the office, emptied out the contents of Odette's *Private* envelope and skimmed one of the letters.

Cali, 8th October 1889

My dear wife,
I am sending you the portrait of the Madonna we saw together at Lourdes in '86. It is very dear to me so please take great care of it.

Why had Armand underlined that sentence? He tried to remember what Joseph had said at the tavern: 'She showed me a painting. She called it *The Madonna in Blue*. It was the one her mistress wanted to leave in her husband's funerary chapel, but Denise changed it for the one of the Archangel Saint Michel.' He read on feverishly.

I want you to hang it up in my bedroom above my desk next to the portrait of the Archangel Saint Michel. [. . .] Send me a telegram as soon as you receive this letter telling me it has arrived safely.

That's why Armand was so keen on the painting. It's valuable!

I was a little surprised at his sudden show of religious fervour . . . Denise must have given Odette the Archangel Saint Michel so that she could keep *The Madonna in Blue*. The very Madonna that some unknown person is trying to find. I can see it all now. He enters Odette's apartment and searches for it in vain. Denise runs off terrified and he follows her, first here and then to Tasha's, where he encounters a problem: how to gain entry to the garret? He has an idea: to lure Denise out with all her belongings, which include *The Madonna in Blue*. To make it more credible, he sends her a letter signed V.L. on Sunday evening (I wonder how he found out about the reference?), arranging to meet her at Pont de Crimée, where he kills her. But why go to such extremes? Did she refuse to hand over the picture? Perhaps she left it behind at Rue Notre-Dame-de-Lorette? Yes, that must be right. Denise's killer must have found Tasha's key before he threw her body in the water. He goes to Rue Notre-Dame-de-Lorette and ransacks the room. Did he find *The Madonna in Blue*? I'll have to go back to Tasha's to find out . . . Who is this killer? He must know me because he signed my initials . . . But do I know him? The old man in the cemetery! The one who claimed to recognise me! I need to question him. I'll go to the Cour des Comptes.

Chewing on his penholder, he was carried away by his deductions. He had often been tempted to write detective novels and felt strangely as if he were the author of this plot.

I'm losing my grip. I must relax and write all this down.

He opened an unused order book and began to write:

Odette. Is there a connection between her disappearance and the death of her maid?

Bathroom: make-up left behind.

Bedroom: macabre décor, skull, esoteric literature. Why? Why would such a superficial, shallow woman, concerned only with appearances, fall under such an influence? Was she really mourning a husband for whom she felt neither affection nor desire? What had been going on since Armand's death?

He looked again at her appointments diary. The same name appeared every Monday and Thursday: Zénobie.

Zénobie. Find out who this person is and what role she played in Odette's life.

Exhausted, he put the papers back in the envelope one by one. As he was folding up Odette's letter to her husband, his eye lit on a sentence: . . . *met some charming people – in particular the well-known English spiritualist M. Numa Winner . . .*

Where else have I seen or heard that name? . . . It was Denise, in the Temps Perdu . . . What had she said? Come on, remember! YES! 'Madame de Brix took Madame to see a medium . . . Monsieur Numa . . .' There was something else . . . The book about the table-turning with Victor Hugo, the author's name was identical . . . Make a note of it.

See Adalberte de Brix. Find out Numa Winner's address.

Return to Odette's apartment: books.

Cour des Comptes: question . . . Père . . . Moscou.

He put the light out and sat motionless in his chair, suddenly overwhelmed by the image of Denise's body lying in the morgue.

CHAPTER SIX

HIS legs numb, Père Moscou levered himself painfully to his
feet by leaning against the wall, and almost went
sprawling into the middle of some dustbins. He had now spent
two nights in Rue des Saints-Pères, in a shed in the back yard of
one of the buildings. Ever since Barnabé had given him the card
left by Victor Legris at the Père-Lachaise the day before yesterday, he hadn't dared return home for fear of being set on by the
man who looked exactly like the one in the locket and who had
no doubt killed Josephine and dumped her body in his handcart.
He preferred to be the hunter not the hunted, so he was hanging
about in the quarter, even though he lacked the courage to
actually confront Victor.

His presence had not passed unnoticed. Madame Ballu, the
concierge of the building next to the bookshop, was beginning
to be alarmed at the sight of the white-haired old man prowling
about, enveloped in a frayed greatcoat, his pockets jingling as
though he was a branch of the Bank of France.

'For heaven's sake, there he is again. He pops up out of
nowhere, just when you least expect it, so he must be planning
some foul deed. Oh, that really is the limit – he's going to
relieve himself against my lamp-post!'

She charged up the street, seething, bucket in hand.

*

Victor jumped out of bed, alarmed at the noise outside. It sounded as if someone were being slaughtered. He ran over to the window and spotted Madame Ballu brandishing her pail above her head, menacing an old man who was shaking his fist at her. It was the fellow from the cemetery!

Congratulating himself for sleeping practically naked, he threw on his shirt, jacket, trousers and frock coat any old how. Tasha, watching him through her eyelashes, saw him struggle with the buttons on his spats, then cram his hat on sideways, snatch up his cane, and lean over her. She hastily closed her eyes. When she opened them again he was already on the stairs.

He dashed past Madame Ballu who, bristling with indignation, was calling on Madame Pignot to witness the fleeing old man.

'Can you believe it? I told him not to dirty my pavement and he treated me to a volley of abuse!'

Tasha lifted the curtain just in time to see Victor running towards Quai Malaquais. She tried to console herself with the thought that falling in love with a will-o'-the-wisp kept life from being dull. But she was unhappy and worried: what hornet's nest was he going to stir up this time?

A raging wind was churning the dark clouds that had built up over the Seine. Père Moscou kept looking over his shoulder. On Quai Malaquais the secondhand booksellers were dragging their handcarts in which they carried their boxes filled with books, and starting to fix them to the parapet. Several times Victor took advantage of these comings and goings to escape the old man's attention. At Quai Conti, he concealed himself by the corner of the police station and then behind a stationary carriage.

They both set off across Pont Neuf, which was already crowded with throngs of workers hurrying to their offices, housekeepers with shopping baskets over their arms, school-boys in grey smocks and vendors of *frites* or roast chestnuts carrying their stoves. Victor hid in the half-moon shadows cast by the stone benches, crouching down and pretending to be picking up his cane to wait, before hurrying to the next one. The equestrian statue of Vert-Galant provided him with cover while the old man shouted at a cyclist who was hurtling across Place Dauphine at high speed.

'Two-wheeled imbecile!' he bellowed.

They reached Place des Trois-Marie and then followed the windswept Quai de la Mégisserie. Shop assistants, their collars turned up, were having a last puff of their cigarettes before resigning themselves to taking up their positions behind the counters of the shops of La Belle Jardinière. The vendors of grain and birds and of hunting and fishing equipment were taking down the shutters from the fronts of their shops.

Moving between groups of people, Victor never lost sight of Père Moscou. They passed the Théâtre du Châtelet and were swallowed up in the merry-go-round of vehicles that were a permanent feature encircling the Palmier fountain. Caught up amongst the carts of vegetables on their way to Les Halles, the carriages, the tilburys, and the fire carts drawn by white horses, Victor thought that he had lost the old man. But there he was, a few yards further on, forging a path by hurling insults. They reached the pavement in front of the Opéra-Comique, crossed Avenue Victoria and Square de la Tour Saint-Jacques, where some bourgeois folk were reading their newspapers, and Rue de Rivoli. On arriving at Boulevard de Sébastopol, they turned off right almost immediately into Rue Pernelle.

Victor slowed down. He saw the old fellow disappear into a shop whose sign announced: *Secondhand Silver and Jewellery*. He hid behind a wagon left by the side of the gutter in order to watch what was going on inside.

He saw Père Moscou extract a locket from his pocket, open it with difficulty to remove a photograph and then hold it out to the shopkeeper, whose face was obscured by a pillar. Two coins were put into his open hand, and he hurriedly stowed them in the pocket of his greatcoat. He left the shop so quickly that Victor leapt back, banging his head on a hand cart. In spite of the pain, he had the presence of mind to duck. After a moment's reflection, the old man set off again. Victor wondered what to do. Should he follow him? Tired and cold as he was, he decided not to follow. He could always find Père Moscou at the Cour des Comptes. He went over to the shop window. In the midst of a jumble of watches, spoons, silver cups and snuff boxes, some wedding rings threaded on a rod and brooches displayed on velvet cushions shone like so many stars. As Victor watched, the shopkeeper added to these treasures a coral necklace, a mother of pearl pencil box, some yellow diamanté earrings and a locket in the shape of a heart. Not without nostalgia, Victor remembered having given a similar locket to Odette at the start of their relationship, when he was in the grip of his passion for her. He had taken her to a well-known jeweller on Place

Vendôme, and while she was looking at the jewels he had prayed that she would choose something reasonable. Luckily, instead of a ring or a bracelet, she had chosen a locket and chain and had insisted on having it engraved with the words: *To O. from V.* 'I'll put your photograph in it, my duck. That way, you'll always be with me.' He had asked: 'What if your husband wants to see what's inside it?' She had burst out laughing. 'Armand? No danger of that. We've had separate bedrooms for years.' He had pretended to believe her, since it suited him that way.

He was about to leave, but on the spur of the moment decided to push open the door of the shop. He had never given Tasha a present, other than some illustrated books. The pencil box, with its iridescent shimmer, would be perfect for her pencils and charcoals. The shopkeeper, a tall, gaunt man whose eyes, behind their thick lenses, were reminiscent of a fish, handed him the pencil box. Examining it up close, Victor discovered that it had a slight nick.

'What a pity,' he murmured.

He caught sight of two ivory combs.

'How much are they?'

'Twenty-five francs. Shall I wrap them for you?'

Victor paid, took the package and hesitated. Would Tasha accept a locket from him? 'She could slip my portrait into it,' he thought, amused.

'I'm interested in that locket, the one in the shape of a heart.'

The shopkeeper hastened to put it on the counter. Victor turned it over to look at the clasp.

'It's silver, you know.'

Victor opened the locket. Where you would normally put either a photo or a lock of hair, he read, engraved in small letters:

To O. from V.

His heart raced. He broke out in a sweat and felt weak. The contents of the shop seemed to be submerged in a sort of fog, like the fragments of a dream.

'Don't you like it, Monsieur?'

The voice seemed to come from a long way off. Odette! She was dead. He staggered sideways.

'Monsieur,' repeated the voice.

No, it was absurd. Odette must have sold the locket. But she couldn't have, she was so attached to it. Then she must have lost it, yes, that must be it, she'd lost it. His panic abated gradually and his breathing found its normal rhythm. Forms and colours came back to life.

The myopic beanpole was staring at him. Embarrassed at having lost his composure, Victor forced himself to smile.

'Yes, yes . . . It's very beautiful,' he managed to say in a strangled voice. 'Was it the old man with the white hair who sold it to you? I have to know, it's important.'

The solicitude of the shopkeeper vanished in an instant. He snatched up a packet of labels. 'Are you from the police?'

'No, not at all, I'm just asking . . .'

'In that case, I'm not obliged to answer you. I respect the privacy of my clients. Do you want it or not?'

'Allow me to insist; it's a matter of some importance. You

probably have a ledger which you note all your purchases in. If I could take a quick look . . .'

'Monsieur, my papers are all in order. If you have any doubts, you may register a complaint.'

'No, no, I'm not going to do that. I'll buy it from you. How much?'

'Thirty francs and it's worth every penny!' the shopkeeper shot back.

Victor took out his wallet, counted out forty francs and stared unblinkingly into the fish eyes until they looked down.

'Oh, all right,' murmured the shopkeeper, pocketing the notes, 'It's just that I don't want any trouble. Yes, it was the old chap who sold it to me, but, I assure you, that's the first time I've ever seen him.'

'I'm sure it is,' said Victor, leaving.

The street seemed threatening all of a sudden. How could a simple bauble have become in the space of a few short minutes such a source of anguish? Had the old fellow broken into Odette's apartment? Was he a thief . . . or worse? He pictured a withered old hand wrenching the chain from the neck of a corpse. My photo was in the locket – that's how he recognised me at Père-Lachaise! A cold wave of anger engulfed him. He was determined to nab the wretch. Furious, he strode away.

If Odette had sold her locket, wouldn't she have taken care to remove my photo first? Not necessarily, she's so absent-minded . . . Or . . . the clasp was undone . . . Perhaps there was nothing inside it when the old fellow picked up the locket. No, no that doesn't fit with him bolting when he bumped into me at the cemetery.

He was so absorbed in his internal monologue that he did not try to avoid the crowds pouring in from the *faubourgs*, shopping for clothes, hats or porcelain. In his mind he was constructing various scenarios. He was annoyed with himself for having paid so little attention to Denise's story, and distraught that his negligence had made the situation worse by allowing Odette's disappearance to go unremarked. Tasha was right; he would have to inform the police.

Père Moscou clutched the five-franc coins tightly. Two paltry little coins, it was chicken feed for such a beautiful piece. But even though he knew he'd been swindled, he was relieved to be rid of the locket. He fished Victor's photo out of the bottom of his pocket, tore it up and scattered the confetti in the gutter of Rue Saint-Martin, opposite the Saint-Merri Church. 'No need to keep his ugly mug; it's engraved on my mind!'

The crumbling old buildings were crammed together to form a dark tunnel in which there was a succession of wine merchants, and displays of coffee, dried fruit and boiled sweets. As he penetrated further into the network of narrow medieval alleys, the noise from the main arteries of the city began to fade. On Rue Taillepain, crumbling walls, propped up with staves, were pierced by dusty windows behind which scrap-iron and rags were heaped. The lodging houses of Rue Brisemiche, where he had lived before taking up residence at the Cour des Comptes, had not yet extinguished their lamps. *Lodgings Starting At 40 Centimes the Night, one franc for a room*, declared the signs. He remembered how he'd had to make himself scarce at dawn when the owner had violently pulled the cord slipped under his and his fellow dossers' heads and did not regret no longer living there. He waved a greeting to his old pal Bibi la Purée,[1] but he pretended not to see Moscou, having become more snobbish since he had started associating with the poets of the Latin Quarter. Barely glancing at Rue de Venise to his left, where in a clutter of haphazardly parked wagons the travelling florists had come to fill their carts with violets and mimosa, Moscou hurried towards Rue Rambuteau.

What about the ring? What am I going to do with that? Bah, I'll sell it to another fence, to confuse the trail. I had my head screwed on when I set up camp in Rue des Saints-Pères. The cut-throat in the locket, who is surely one and the same as that cursed A.D.V. who messed up my bivouac, couldn't track me down because I was where he least expected to find me, right under his nose!

The pavements of Rue Rambuteau were clogged with costermongers' carts where fruits and vegetables were heaped around copper-plated scales. Voluble women, plump and chubby-cheeked in clogs and aprons, with their fan of paper bags to hand, were hawking their wares, competing to see who could bawl the loudest:

'Fresh and sweet! Buy my Seville oranges! Hey, you there, old man, taste my oranges – you'll be in heaven!'

'He'd rather have my radishes. Try my radishes – you'll go straight to paradise!'

'Look at him – he's a misery! Eat my carrots – they'll make you happy!

Père Moscou, hurrying to escape their jibes, plunged unthinkingly into the haven of peace that Rue Archive seemed to offer. A hundred yards further on, he stopped, about to turn back and have the ring valued by the jewellers standing in a group outside the pawnshop with the dealers in pawnshop tickets. No, I can just ask Maman Briscot. She knows the right places to go, he decided.

Now he was passing through a quieter district. Behind the old façades were vast courtyards populated by toy-makers, studios and workshops making and selling bronze items. He passed between the town hall of the third arrondissement and Square du Temple where the statue of Béranger holding a closed book stared at him mockingly. The sight of the lime tree beside which, it was said, Louis XVI had made his son recite his lessons, inspired Moscou to make an emotional tribute to 'the conqueror of kings'. In a hoarse voice, he intoned:

Napoleon is emperor,
His brav'ry inspires us all!

He crossed Temple Market, the first floor of which was occupied by the famous 'Carreau du Temple' where all the rags that couldn't be sold on the ground floor were displayed. The rest of the market was spread over several pavilions where objects cast off by the rich were sold as new. Weary and in a hurry to reach his goal, Père Moscou staggered about amongst the stalls of shoes and frock coats, the mountains of petticoats and curtains and the sea of carpets, old decorations and quilts. The bazaar was giving him vertigo, reminding him of his devastated bivouac. Picturing the feathers littering the floor, he was appalled all over again.

They're going to kill me, and I can't go to the cops. The cops! Why not? I'll be housed and fed at the expense of the State, in the warmth, out of reach of Grouchy . . .

'I don't want that!' he barked at a young milliner who was offering him a shabby bowler hat.

'I'll let you have it for nothing at all, cross my heart and hope to die! You'll be handsome as a king!'

'Out of my way, Josephine!'

Finally he escaped the market and reached Rue de la Corderie, a little street that was narrow at either end and opened out in the middle in a triangle. Maman Briscot had a bar there and she would be able to advise him about the ring.

After asking for directions, Victor eventually hunted down the Bureau of Missing Persons in the heart of the labyrinth of the police headquarters, a department run by a certain Jules Bordenave. He explained what he wanted to a young functionary, whose hollow eyes and suppressed yawns suggested immense fatigue.

'I've made a note, Madame Odette de Valois. Are you family?'

'Er . . . no.'

'An in-law?'

Victor shook his head. The pen-pusher sighed.

'What exactly are you to this woman?'

'A friend.'

'A friend or a lover?' asked the young man, in a tired fashion.

'I'm a friend and I'm very worried about her; she hasn't been home since last Friday.'

'Is she married?'

'Yes, at least she's not married any more – she's a widow.'

'I see,' said the functionary, looking as if he might just keel over himself. 'When did her husband die?'

'In November or December; I can't remember. He died of yellow fever.'

'I see, I see, the canal . . .' grunted the young man, dipping his pen-holder in an inkwell and amusing himself by creating ripples of ink. 'And had he worked for the canal long?'

'Since September 1888. But what's that to do . . . ?'

'If I understand correctly, this lady . . . de Valois has lived alone since September 1888?'

'I've just told you so!' exploded Victor, whose patience was running out.

'My dear Monsieur,' retorted the functionary, tapping his pen dry, 'I don't doubt your good intentions, but you must see that we cannot set in train a search simply at the request of a friend. In a republic, everyone is free to come and go as they please. This lady has probably gone on a trip without telling you. These things happen all the time.'

Clearly pleased with his line of argument, the young man bent over a pile of papers.

'You're refusing to open an inquiry?'

'I repeat, dear Monsieur, you are neither her husband nor a member of her family. Do you know that in any one year we receive forty to fifty thousand requests for searches from families? Mostly from the provinces, because the majority of provincials who disappear take refuge here in Paris. We are completely snowed under . . .'

'You don't look as if you're doing anything at all! Goodbye, Monsieur, and thank you for nothing!' shouted Victor, banging the door angrily on his way out.

He only calmed down when he reached Passerelle des Arts. At Place de L'Institut, he bought the papers and leafed through them, searching for a mention of Denise's death. Nothing.

He went up to his apartment by the outside staircase. Tasha, dressed and ready to leave, was finishing a cup of coffee. She didn't ask any questions, letting him trip himself up with his own lies.

'You were fast asleep and I didn't want to wake you. I remembered that I had promised to go and see a collection of books at Quai Saint-Michel, at Père Didier's stall. He's a secondhand bookseller who specialises in the sale of posters, but from time to time he has old books . . .'

'And did you make a good purchase?'

'Actually, I didn't, they were all too damaged, but Père Didier invited me to Café des Cadrans, and there I bumped into some bookseller friends, so . . .'

'All's explained then. Well, I have to show some sketches to my editor. Will you be here this afternoon?'

'Yes, I should be.'

She went up to him, stood on tiptoe to smooth back a lock of hair that had fallen over his forehead and kissed him. 'Must run, see you later.'

After she had run down the staircase, Victor went down to the bookshop. Joseph was arranging the complete works of Restif de la Bretonne. 'These will never sell,' he said to Victor in a worried voice.

Victor made no mention of his recent absence, nor did he say anything about Denise. He scanned the shelves, took down a book, then another, took a sudden interest in a newly displayed Diderot, ran his finger over the bust of Molière and seemed satisfied that there was not a trace of dust there. After about ten minutes, he could stand it no longer and announced abruptly to Joseph: 'I'll be back in an hour. I've an errand to run.'

'All right, boss.'

The door bell had only just sounded when Tasha appeared from the back of the shop. 'Hurry, and keep out of sight.'

'What if he takes a cab?'

'You'll manage. Just don't lose him; all that matters to me is that nothing happens to him. Do you have money?'

'Don't fret, you can count on me. I won't let you down.'

Joseph shoved a cap on his mop of hair and hurried into the street after Victor, who was heading for the Seine.

Victor stood studying a building intently. Its gaping windows stood out clearly against the sky. The basement and the first storey were each composed of nineteen very tall arcades surrounded by Greek columns. The second floor formed an attic interspersed with nineteen bays. Two wings at the front jutted out on either side of the façade. The Cour des Comptes, which had once incorporated the Ministère du Commerce and of Travaux Publique would, in its current state, appeal to lovers of Ancient Greece: classical design and ruins invaded by vegetation. But to Victor, who was steeped in English culture, its sinister aspect invoked one of the haunted houses so beloved of Ann Radcliffe. The stone, reddened and blackened by the fire, the collapsed roof, the windows devoid of glass and a peculiar detail, the remains of a blind, groaning in the wind across one of the window frames, all conspired to create a fantastical and desolate picture.

'Bluebeard's Castle,' he said as he turned in the direction of Rue de Lille. He rang the concierge's bell. She half-opened the door and peered at him suspiciously, only consenting to open the door wide after she had read his visiting card. 'Please excuse the mess, I was just about to tidy up.'

'I'm looking for an old man with white hair. I wanted to thank him for putting flowers on my wife's grave at Père-Lachaise cemetery.'

'Ah, Père Moscou. I haven't seen him for ever such a while. He must be on a bender somewhere, but he'll come to his senses and come back – I know him.'

'If you show me where he lives, I'll leave him a tip.'

'Very sorry, Monsieur, I can't do that; he would be angry with me. Only last Sunday someone ransacked his room. Poor thing! He was in such a state when he discovered, he called me to help him. What a scene! More frightening than the sight of *The Raft of the Medusa* at the Louvre. A real shambles. His belongings, I tell you, they were strewn about everywhere, as if a whirlwind had blown through. The worst thing was the way he stared at everything, fixedly, as if he'd just seen a ghost, yes really as if he'd seen a ghost, though with what he does for a living, you'd think . . . But there was nothing supernatural about that business; I'd stake my life on it. I have to tell you that louts sometimes come to mess about with girls in the undergrowth, it's a real virgin's paradise back there, then they come here and amuse themselves by creating mayhem . . . I have reported it to the police, but I might as well not have bothered – they've bigger fish to fry. I'd keep your tip if I were you, otherwise he'll just drink it.'

She was about to shut the door when she hesitated. 'Wait! I've just remembered. It's Wednesday today – I know where you'll find him, if you still want to thank him. Today's his day for going to Carreau du Temple. He forages about there, buying things and selling them again, and meeting his pals. He usually goes to Maman Briscot's, on Rue de la Corderie, for some soup. *Briscot's Fine Fare* is written on the front. You could see if he's there.'

To Joseph's great displeasure, Victor hailed a cab on Quai d'Orsay.

Great, what on earth am I going to do now? Mademoiselle Tasha is going to be furious. Well, I won't shadow him any more, but I'll go and take a look round that pile of bricks. Lord love me, it's got more holes in it than a Gruyère cheese!

The shops were narrow and too dark for the secondhand dealers to show off the old togs to their best advantage, so they displayed them on boards supported by trestles, or sometimes even out on the pavement of Rue de la Corderie. Père Moscou had just spent some time haggling with a shopkeeper who was selling tattered military uniforms, rusted swords and old clothes he claimed had been worn by the Empress Eugénie, for a badly dented bugle. Pleased that he had driven a hard bargain, Père Moscou stowed the instrument in one of his pockets and went off to Maman Briscot's bar, which stood beside a shed where you could rent handcarts for five sous an hour.

Inside, the bar was low-ceilinged, very smoky and crammed with tables and benches. At some tables workmen played cards or battled over dominoes, whilst at others poor wretches were catching forty winks. An enormous cast-iron stove breathed its burning fumes over the customers busy tucking into onion soup, the house speciality. Maman Briscot, a well-endowed woman with frizzy grey hair who reigned supreme over this establishment, was circulating with a tray of steaming bowls.

She greeted Père Moscou with a booming, 'Hello there, Père-Lachaise! Come and sit down next to the fire. Do you want some soup?'

Without giving him the chance to reply, she set a bowl down in front of him. 'You brought some bread, I hope? You know I don't provide it here.'

'I can do without. What I need is a quarter-pint of red wine.'

'Right away, General.'

After gobbling the wine and the soup, Père Moscou drifted into a light doze and gave a start when the landlady shook him by the shoulder. 'Come on, Père-Lachaise, time to pay up and move on; everyone else has left.'

'I need your expert advice, my dear. I have a ring, a family heirloom that I want to flog . . .'

'Show me.'

She held the ring up to the light. 'I like it. Where did you pilfer this from, you old scoundrel?'

'It was left to me by a deceased relative.'

'Of course it was. I'll make you a proposition, something better than money. You can eat here, free, for a month. How about that?'

Victor, watching through the bar window, observed their interminable discussion, by the end of which, one month had become three. Relieved to have tracked down Père Moscou, he hid in the shed. He had to wait half an hour before the old man left the tavern, at precisely the moment Joseph leapt from a cab at the other end of the street.

Unaware that he was being watched, Père Moscou made his way back towards Carreau du Temple, followed at a distance by Victor, who was in turn being tailed by Joseph. In Pavillon Forêt-Noire, neither man noticed the rag merchants who tried to tempt them by calling out, 'I have a beautiful greatcoat! Look, Monsieur, this would look superb on you!'

Invigorated by his meal, Père Moscou greeted acquaintances as he passed and seemed to be looking for someone. He squeezed his way through a crowd grouped around a hawker and charged at a policeman. Planting himself in front of him, he began to cough violently, jabbering unintelligible words. Then he spotted a second policeman and repeated his coughing fit. Frozen to the spot in front of a display of chandeliers, Victor did not notice Joseph who was watching the whole scene from behind a mountain of mattresses. The two guardians of the peace had just called on an army officer to come to the rescue, when Victor, with his hat pulled well over his eyes, cautiously approached the quartet.

'What's going on?' asked the officer.

'What's going on is that this individual coughed right in my face, boss. I asked him what was wrong and he shouted, "I'm not talking to you!" Then he started on my colleague.'

'I could see straight away that this fellow was trouble,' his colleague went on. 'I went over to him and he practically spat on me. I ordered him to behave himself and he yelled, "Dirty dog, are you blind? Can't you see that I'm ill?" '

The officer scrutinised Père Moscou. 'Do you have anything to say in your defence?'

'Excuse me, Colonel, when you have lungs as congested as mine you just have to spit sometimes!'

'Is that sufficient reason to splutter your miasma over the forces of order?'

'With respect, Captain, the cough comes over me without warning. I can't swallow it!'

'But you could cover your mouth with your hand! What's more, you called the officers pigs, if I'm not mistaken.'

'Me, Major? As the Emperor is my witness, I never did that! I just said that I'm as sick as dog, there is a difference!'

'The Emperor, eh? You're making matters worse. Off to the police station with you. We'll sort your cough out for you.'

As Père Moscou appealed to the crowd, Victor just had time to dive for cover behind a pile of embroidered robes. 'See how unfairly they treat me? It's all Grouchy's fault! It was him who said "Dog, dirty dog!" and then he scarpered and I got the blame!'

Once he was safely in the hands of the coppers, he affected a tearful expression, which aroused the indignation of the bystanders. 'Poor man, he's definitely not right in the head and they're still arresting him – it's shameful. It's not his fault he has the flu,' said one stallholder.

There were whistles and boos and insults were hurled. Disconcerted, Joseph watched Victor mingle with the crowd thronging around Père Moscou. He remembered Monsieur Lecoq's credo: 'If you withdraw, you gain much more when you emerge from the shadows.' Deciding to apply this rule immediately, he slipped away.

Victor waited until the crowd of onlookers had dispersed before entering the police station. He made enquiries of an orderly who was wearing the sort of uniform usually reserved for the elderly.

'Don't worry about him; a night in the cells will calm him down. In any case, in his condition and with the weather we're expecting, he's better off in the warmth.'

Victor went back out, groaning inwardly, promising himself that he would come and fetch the old man at dawn. The sky was now leaden and small white dots were accumulating on the dirty pavements. He tucked his cane under his arm, thrust his hands into his pockets and went off, watched at a distance by a schoolboy lurking in a doorway.

'Terrible weather,' grumbled Joseph, wiping his shoes on the mat in front of Molière's bust.

'You lost him!' cried Tasha.

'He nearly saw me, so I thought it best to leave him to it, but if you insist, I'll go back . . .' retorted Joseph, piqued.

He turned as if to serve two young dandies who were leafing through the new books, but she caught him by the sleeve. 'Don't be cross, my little moujik. I'm really worried – please tell me what happened.'

Joseph did so, giving Tasha a blow-by-blow account. 'Don't worry, the boss isn't running any risks, and besides I'm there to protect him.'

'Thank you, Jojo, I know I can count on you. Remind him that we're meeting tonight at the Soleil d'Or.'

She hurried away. When the two dandies had paid for *Modern Masks* by Félicien Champsaur, Joseph settled himself on his stool, pulled *Le Siècle* from his pocket and looked to see if there was anything new about Denise. He found nothing, but one article caught his attention.

THE ST NAZAIRE CORPSE

Until recently, little progress had been made on the case of the unknown corpse of St Nazaire and the legendary reputation of Messieurs Goron and Lecacheur seemed set to be tarnished. But the day before yesterday, Inspector Lecacheur spotted a short report in *Quotidien de l'Ouest* of a wallet found by some dockers wedged behind a container in the hold of the cargo ship Goéland. The wallet, in very bad condition, contained papers that have been sent to the police for analysis.

Joseph cut out this snippet and had just stuck it into his notebook when Victor appeared.

'I'm happy to see you, boss; there aren't many customers because of the snow so there's nothing to distract me. I can't stop thinking about Denise . . .'

'I can't either, but it's hard to make sense of everything and . . .'

Their conversation was cut short by the arrival of a connoisseur of illustrated works on Lepidoptera. 'Mademoiselle Tasha will meet you at nine o'clock at the Soleil D'Or,' Joseph whispered to Victor.

The amber light of the street lamps of Boulevard Saint-Michel illuminated a bustling crowd of penniless students, teachers and bohemians of all types, drifting towards the café terraces where absinthe, that goddess of dreams and oblivion, could be imbibed. From there they ogled the ankles of the young women holding up their skirts to keep them from sweeping the trampled snow as they made their way to dinner, or hurried towards the omnibus stand near the ornamental fountain.

The Soleil d'Or, Number 1 on Place Saint-Michel, on the corner of the quay, was an ordinary brasserie that attracted a stream of bearded, long-haired and unfashionably dressed young men. Some had disreputable women, faces caked with powder, on their arms.

Victor followed them in. A staircase behind the counter led down to the basement decorated by Gauguin. Furnished with a piano, trestle tables and chairs, which were now piled with hats, the cellar smelt of cigars, pipes and cheap scent. On arrival, the artists rested their canvases against the walls and then ordered an aperitif from the sulky waiter leaning on the bar. Maurice Laumier, dressed in a wine-coloured velvet jacket, greeted them with a friendly slap on the back and invited them to sit down, always with the same joke, 'Take a pew, Cinna!'

Disgusted, Victor turned round and bumped into Tasha, looking charming in a pale green dress with a white lace collar and puff sleeves gathered at the cuffs. 'That's gorgeous. I haven't seen it before – you've never . . .'

'It belonged to my mother. I keep it for special occasions.'

He was hurt that she had never worn the dress for him. As if she could read his thoughts, she added, 'It's much too tight at the waist. I have to wear a corset and after half an hour I'm suffocating. Come nearer to the piano. Would you like a glass of champagne? It's Maurice's treat. *Na ̩dorovia*,' she said, raising her glass.

He could barely bring himself to swallow a mouthful of a drink offered by Laumier. A man who looked like a second-rate actor, draped in a cape full of holes and wearing a sombrero at a rakish angle, and giving off a pungent odour, greeted them obsequiously and asked for a coin or two for poor Paul and a cigarette for himself. Victor gave him what he wanted.

'Who's that?' he murmured when the pseudo-hidalgo had departed.

'A famous pianist.'

'Really?'

'Didn't you see his teeth? One black, one white, one black, one white . . .'

'Very funny!' he cried. 'Seriously, who is he?'

'That old tramp doused in all the perfumes of Arabia rejoices in the name of Bibi la Purée.'

'Which poor Paul was he referring to?'

'Verlaine. Bibi la Purée has set himself up as his secretary, in fact all he does is drink up Verlaine's dregs and act as messenger to his mistresses. He also sometimes poses for the painters of Montmartre.'

'Verlaine,' murmured Victor. 'A great poet, perhaps a genius. A pity he's destroying his health in the drinking dens. *J'ai la fureur d'aimer. Mon cœur si faible est fou . . .*'

'I didn't know you liked poetry! I thought you were only interested in crime novels.'

'You've known me for less than a year! Do you think you know every—'

'Ah! I must introduce you to my new friend. Mademoiselle Ninon Delarme, Monsieur Victor Legris,' she said, cutting across his recrimination.

Victor kissed the gloved hand extended by a young woman whose dark-brown hair was escaping from a sable fur hat. When he straightened up, he found himself looking at a low-cut neckline revealing a small, round bosom. Next, he took in a moist mouth and almond-shaped eyes outlined in black.

'Delighted to make your acquaintance,' he murmured.

'Follow me,' said Tasha, 'I'll show you the canvases I'm thinking of exhibiting.'

'Who came up with the idea of this exhibition? Laumier?'

'No, it was Léon Deschamps, the editor of the magazine *La Plume*. Two Saturdays each month he also invites poets to come along and give a reading of their work in public.'

As soon as Tasha had led Victor away, Maurice made a beeline for Ninon. 'Don't tell me – let me guess! You've come to see me!' he exclaimed, putting his arms round her waist.

With an animated gesture, Ninon spread out a silk fan, aware that the eyes of all the men were on her. Victor, charmed, was not immune from the general infatuation. Tasha invited them to join her.

'Maurice, I have four canvases here. I'll bring five more at the beginning of the week.'

'That's annoying; we won't be able to decide how to hang everything if we don't have . . . Let me see that.'

He made a face as he looked at one of the paintings. 'More roofs of Paris! You know perfectly well that I don't like them. Why didn't you choose your male nudes?'

He stepped back to judge the overall effect of the canvases. 'They lack virility.'

'Surely virility, which is the characteristic of men, would be inappropriate for women, who would worry about growing a moustache?' suggested Ninon.

Tasha burst out laughing. 'Don't worry, Ninon, I'm used to that word, the only word that impresses men – it reassures them.'

Out of the corner of her eye, she glanced at Victor who judged it prudent to accelerate the retreat he had embarked on when Laumier had mentioned the male nudes. But Maurice, taking up the gauntlet good-naturedly, held him back by the arm. 'My dear Legris, how can we take women seriously? What have they ever created? Has there ever been a great female genius? And I hope you're not going to put forward Sappho or Madame Vigée-Le Brun!'[2]

Ninon smiled sweetly and batted the ball back in a honeyed tone: 'How many male geniuses would history have counted had men spent two-thirds of their existence peeling potatoes and washing nappies?'

'My dear child, please don't tell me that your daily activities are confined to those two things!' protested Laumier.

'Where did you meet that girl?' Victor whispered in Tasha's ear.

'We met yesterday afternoon at Bibulus. She helped me carry my canvases to the framer. You were at the morgue, otherwise . . . She wants to pose for me, but I turned her down.'

'Why?'

'I wouldn't be able to pay her. No, no, I know what you're going to suggest, but it's out of the question and, besides, female nudes . . .'

'Shame.'

'What do you mean?'

'I would have asked permission to be present at the sittings.'

'Oh, you! Look, you can apply to Maurice; he's already got her in his clutches. Go and wait for me downstairs – I'm just coming.'

He sat down at a table in the room downstairs where sullen bachelors were gorging themselves on sausages. He unfolded one of the dailies, skimmed through the articles, which were largely devoted to Chancellor Bismarck's resignation and the news in brief, but there was nothing new.

'My dear, don't believe anything printed there – it's all made up!'

'Don't speak ill of the press; we need them to publicise our work.'

He turned round to find the brunette and the redhead, each as attractive as the other, seated next to him.

'Tasha has told me about you. Bookseller, photographer, gallant lover, amateur detective. That's a lot for one man!'

'Well, as for the amateur detective, Tasha is exaggerating,' observed Victor.

'Hypocrite!' cried Tasha. 'Admit that you love involving yourself in what doesn't concern you; last summer you risked your life on a case!'

'I did become involved in that case, but not because I wanted to . . .'

'Stop squabbling,' said Ninon, 'and enlighten me. Tasha claims that you're a devotee of crime novels. Don't you find them a bit dull? I've read two or three and they all seemed to be written according to the same formula: good triumphs over evil, the murderer is interrogated, judged, executed and, hey presto, society can sleep soundly again.'

'They're much more than that,' replied Victor. 'Honest people are fascinated by crime. The authors of these books lead us along routes we don't dare venture down in real life, but which we delight in exploring in our imaginations.'

'Really? Perhaps I spoke too hastily. I must admit that I'm more interested in the interaction of men and women. You'll have to initiate me, Monsieur Legris. I'm counting on you,' she said, pressing Victor's hand for longer than was necessary before taking her leave.

Victor watched her going out of the brasserie.

'A panther,' he murmured.

'Has Denise been identified by a relative?' asked Tasha.

'No.'

'What have you decided to do?'

'Give me two more days.'

'I'll give you two and no more, you understand? I've no desire to share my life with a high-wire artiste who could crash to the ground at any moment.'

'You really want to share my life?'

'What do you think we're doing?'

On the way back, he abruptly held out the ivory combs he had bought on Rue Pernelle. Touched by this gesture, she kissed him and held him tight against her shoulder. She couldn't bring herself to tell him that she had a horror of things that came from dead animals, that for her they evoked suffering and death. Deep in his pocket, Victor fingered Odette's locket, that frozen little heart and keeper of a secret that he would have to reveal to her. It was still snowing.

Madame Pignot piled up the plates and cutlery on the draining board in the kitchen. 'Have you had enough to eat, my pet?'

'Yes, Maman.'

Armed with her poker, she lifted the cast-iron lid of the stove and threw in a lump of coal, then pulled back the curtain from the window.

'Still falling, falling, really vile weather. If this goes on, I'll stay at home tomorrow.'

'And you'd be right to, Maman. At your age you have to look after yourself.'

'Don't worry, I'm strong. Your poor father used to say, "Euphrosine, you're as strong as an ox." '

'I'm going into Papa's study.'

'Don't go to bed too late, my pet.'

Joseph shut himself in and put the petrol lamp in the middle of the table, which was littered with a confusion of cartidges, broken shells, pointed Prussian artillery helmets and relics collected by his bookseller father who had been in the National Guard during the war of 1870. Adjoining the tiny ground floor apartment he shared with his mother, the little study sheltered his entire inheritance: old books, prints, magazines, piles of newspapers carefully sorted into years. It was his kingdom. It was here he planned out his stories, drafted his novel, sorted through his press cuttings and thought about Valentine de Salignac.

This evening he was feeling low. He sat down and gloomily considered the newspapers spread out in front of him. Denise was only a short news item amongst other miscellaneous snippets; it was as if her death counted for nothing. He would have liked to work on his novel but his heart wasn't in it. He closed the school exercise book with *Blood and Love* on the cover and, opening his brand new notebook wrote *Lady Vanishes from Père-Lachaise, March 1890* at the top of the first page. For a moment he chewed the end of his pen, then made up his mind and started writing:

Go back to Cour des Comptes. The boss is hiding something from me. Why was he tailing that old man?

He gazed at the photograph pinned up on the wall. A twenty-year-old Madame Pignot and a rotund secondhand bookseller were smiling at him, leaning against the parapet of Quai Voltaire.

'You're right, Papa, you should never throw in the towel; when you really want to do something you find a way. I've decided I'm going to apply myself wholeheartedly to this case; you would be proud of me.'

CHAPTER 7

A WARM sun, worthy of spring was melting the snow. But far from feeling relieved by this sudden improvement, Joseph felt outraged. It seemed wrong that the weather should be clement when the *Éclair* announced on page 4:

DROWNING AT PONT DE CRIMÉE

An autopsy has shown that the unidentified young girl found in the Canal de l'Ourcq three days ago had been knocked out before being thrown in the water. Was she killed by a prowler or was this a crime of passion?

He cut out the paragraph and stuck it into the new notebook he had prepared the night before. Then he browsed through the other dailies, seizing on *Le Passe-partout*, which also mentioned Denise.

The young girl found in the Canal de l'Ourcq had been savagely beaten before she went into the water. Her identity remains unknown. It is time the police devoted more effort to guaranteeing the safety of our citizens . . .

He placed this article after the first one. A door banged overhead. Hastily tidying away the newspapers and notebook, Joseph threw on his jacket and took up his pen as Tasha came down the stairs.

'Isn't the boss with you?' he asked, dusting the desk.

'He left very early, saying he had a meeting with a client. I'm sure he's lying; he had that worried look . . .'

'Don't tell me, I know. He raises his eyebrows a little and gets two big creases right across his forehead. You'd swear that he was going to bite.'

She couldn't help laughing as he pulled a face like a sulky dog.

'I think he's hooked on sleuthing again, and I don't like it,' she murmured.

'And she thinks that I do?' Joseph said to himself. 'The boss promised to include me in his investigations but he was just fobbing me off! A bit of trust would be nice.' A wave of rancour swept over him, hitting him in the pit of the stomach. He shook his duster angrily over the bust of Molière.

'Well, if he's going to cast me aside, he'll see what I can do on my own. I'm going to be ill, starting this afternoon. In five years' good and loyal service I've never been off sick, so now . . . He'd better not accuse me of not pulling my weight! This will teach him, no more running off across town leaving me with sole responsibility for the shop, and this way Mademoiselle Tasha won't have to worry any more.'

He was muttering to himself, waving his duster and lifting up books only to slam them noisily down again.

'What's wrong, my little moujik?'

'What's wrong is that I caught cold yesterday, chasing after Monsieur Legris. I'm feeling under the weather, I'm ill, that's what's wrong!'

He was going to continue when his attention was caught by

a carriage stopping in front of the bookshop. He went over to the window. 'Well, well! Mademoiselle Tasha, come and see what's blown our way!'

Victor was furious. He left the police station, tapping the ground with his cane – he had arrived too late! Père Moscou had been set free twenty minutes earlier than normal, because his cell was urgently needed to house five people accused of burgling an apartment. He consulted his watch: five past nine. He would have to go back to the bookshop or Tasha would bend his ear again. He took the time to buy the new edition of *Le Siècle* and unfolded it just as he was passing a bistro on Rue du Vertbois.

Slumped against the bistro stove, Père Moscou was gleefully tucking into his black pudding with apple, and between mouthfuls regaling his audience of shop girls and drunkards with anecdotes of his night at the police station in the company of prostitutes.

'One of them, who was past her best and was as wide as a house, said that during the Prussian siege she had been so hungry that she'd had to survive on rats and Jerusalem artichoke and that ever since she'd eaten enough for four. I raise my glass to her!'

He took a swig of wine. 'She called herself Madame Sans-Gêne, like Bonaparte's friend. Oh, how he loved women; he was mad about his Josephine . . . Damnation!'

That name, which he had given to the dead woman, had reminded him of something. He could picture the exact place where he had buried the body, with the two uprooted and replanted lilac bushes. His wine went down the wrong way and he almost choked. A girl banged him cheerfully on the back, and he rose to his feet in a sudden panic. 'Got to go back to the courtyard to collect my things so that I can disappear somewhere, otherwise I'll be done for.' He took three uncertain steps towards the door, to an *oh* of disappointment, whereupon he sat down again and everyone applauded.

'I'm not an idiot!' he thundered.

'No, you're a pig, you drink and you blame it on me!' shouted a drunken voice.

'You're just waiting for that, aren't you, Grouchy! You're waiting for me to show my face, then you'll take me unawares! I'm not an idiot, but I'll make you look like one! I'll just slip home quietly when it's dark – you won't see me, at night everyone looks alike.'

'But you're as round as a barrel!' bawled the voice

'To the slaughter!' yelled Père Moscou. 'While I'm waiting I'll just settle down here, nice and warm with a good bottle of wine. And if anyone objects to that . . .'

He half stood up then fell back on his stool trumpeting: 'We'll breach their flank, talley-ho!'

Victor stood stock still in the middle of the pavement in front of the large hotel in the Magasins Réunis building, indifferent to the passers-by who cursed and jostled him. He heard nothing and saw only the words running across the top of the page.

MURDER AT THE CANAL DE L'OURQ

The young girl fished out of the Canal de l'Ourcq had been hit over the head before being thrown into the water.

He let himself sink down on a bench, the newspaper slipping from his grasp.

Quick, think. My deductions are ill-founded. The day I went to Tasha's to talk to Denise, Madame Ladoucette told me that she had gone to the employment agency at seven in the morning. I went up at ten o'clock and found it in a terrible state, so Tasha's room was searched *before* the murder, not *afterwards*, let's say between seven thirty and my arrival.

Staring unseeingly at a starving dog who was scavenging in a rubbish bin, Victor decided that Joseph was right to invoke the methods of his hero Gaboriau: 'Easy puzzles are of no interest – let's leave them to the children. What I need are unsolvable enigmas, so that I can solve them . . .' Adopting the method of Monsieur Lecoq, I need to identify with the criminal, what would I do in his place? Let's see, the letter has enticed Denise out of Tasha's room, you're lying in wait near the building, you watch her. She comes out. She doesn't have *The Madonna in Blue*. You're taken by surprise. You follow her to make certain. No, she doesn't have it. Her little cloth bundle couldn't possibly contain a flat, rectangular object thirty by forty centimetres. She must have left it upstairs. It's early, you've more than enough time to make it to the meeting place you've fixed with her. You go back to number 60, manage to cross the courtyard without exciting the attention of the concierges. You go up. The key is indeed under the mat. The coast is clear. You search everywhere, systematically. In vain. Yet you're certain Denise didn't have the picture with her. You hurry to the Church of Saint-Jacques-Saint-Christophe. You're angry. Denise is there. You threaten her: what has she done with the picture? Where has she hidden it? She takes fright, denies having it – if she's accused of theft, she'll lose everything. You grab her bundle and she flees, but you catch her and hit her savagely. She falls: she's dead. No witnesses. You throw her into the water. You scrabble through her belongings . . . Nothing, the wench misled you, you're empty-handed . . .

He got up briskly. The murderer didn't recover *The Madonna in Blue*, he's still looking for it! And if he's still looking . . . I have to make certain.

He hurried to find a cab rank.

Disappointed, he ran down the stairs and was about to cross the courtyard when he stopped himself just in time and lit a cigarette, to give Helga Becker the time to leave on her bicycle. He had inspected everything again and looked at each picture, no *Madonna in Blue*. He knocked at the concierge's lodge and the door was opened by Madame Ladoucette, brandishing a broom. 'Oh, it's you, Monsieur Legris! You know the saga of the key that you started is getting on my nerves. Mademoiselle Tasha was furious, I'm telling you.'

'Yes, yes, it's all sorted out. Do you remember how many bags the maid was carrying when she left the building?'

'Why? Has she stolen something?'

'No, I'm not suggesting anything like that. I just wanted to know if she had inadvertently taken a long, flat package, like a large book or picture.'

'A long, flat package? No, I didn't notice. She only had her bundle, you know, a square of material knotted at each corner. And she wouldn't have taken one of Mademoiselle Tasha's canvases would she? If she did, I wash my hands of her. That's what happens when you lend your house to other people; it's nothing but bother.'

'You're right, Madame Ladoucette. I'm going to have the locks changed.'

Victor pushed open the bookshop door. Tasha sat in front of the counter looking through a study of Rembrandt.

'Are you still here? Where's Joseph?' he asked.

'I sent him home, he's ill.'

'Ill?'

'Yes, I hope he hasn't caught influenza.'

'He hasn't been ill once in the last five years; it's surprising.'

'Talking of surprises, Monsieur Mori is amongst us.'

Appalled, he looked towards the stairs. 'Did he see you?'

'Of course, I'm not invisible.'

'What did you say to him?'

'I said to him, "Hello, Monsieur Mori, did you have a good journey?"'

173

'And what did he say?'

'The sea was choppy, but, yes, I did have a good journey.'

'You're making fun of me.'

She stared at him mockingly for a moment. 'You're obsessed by what he thinks. You have to stop feeling guilty towards him, you're thirty years old, more than four times the age of reason. I suppose you're going to ask me to move out?'

'How can you think that of me? I'm the one who asked you to come here. There's no question of you having to leave, this is your home! Move out, good heavens, what do you take me for? A . . . I don't care what Kenji thinks!' he cried.

She went up to him and laid her finger on his lips. 'Calm down. In any case, I have to go back to prepare the last canvases for the framer, the exhibition opens . . .'

He seized her arm. 'I forbid it!'

'You forbid me to exhibit?' she shot back coldly, freeing herself.

'I forbid you to return to your garret until I've changed the locks. Denise took the key with her, and she's been . . . You can surely wait until tomorrow, can't you?'

Since he seemed genuinely worried, she softened. 'You're wrong to think that I'm at home here, and neither am I exactly sharing your home: we're both sharing . . . his. But it's agreed, I'll stay another day. I'm going to Bibulus. See you this evening.'

She went out, giving him a little wave through the window. He wasn't going to risk losing her through cowardice. He decided to confront Kenji immediately.

He found him writing a letter, dressed in a maroon smoking jacket with white spots, and grey pinstripe trousers.

'British elegance!' exclaimed Victor, shaking his hand. Without wanting to admit it, he was pleased to have him back.

'I brought you a printed velvet waistcoat, over there, the package on the sideboard, and for Jojo there's a purple silk tie. He's not well.'

'So Tasha told me,' said Victor, unfolding the waistcoat. 'It's magnificent! Thank you.'

He was relieved that he had already mentioned the young woman's name, now he would have to press on. But with one of his habitual changes of tack, Kenji steered the conversation in another direction. 'No doubt you're surprised to see me back in the fold so soon? I was able to wrap up affairs in London, so there was no need to prolong my stay, and besides there was a fog you could cut with a knife.'

Poor Iris! thought Victor, recalling the beautiful, childlike girl he had seen in a photograph. He only devotes the minimum of time to her. It can't be fun loving a man who keeps his emotions so completely in check.

Determined to broach the subject, he launched in: 'And you must have been surprised to find Tasha here?'

Showing no more emotion than if he were a stone, Kenji signed his initials at the bottom of the letter, which he carefully folded, and contented himself with replying, 'Yes.'

'Well, there's a simple explanation. I . . . she . . .'

A dull fear swept over him, as if he were eight years old again, had stolen some biscuits and was trying to blame the dog. If he told the truth, he risked souring the harmonious relationship he, whose father had been a tyrant, enjoyed with his adoptive father who was full of solicitude but too perfect.

'She was asked to leave her garret by her landlady . . . Mademoiselle Helga Becker, she wanted to put up a cousin from the provinces.'

'Does she have the right to turn out a tenant who has paid her rent?'

'She gave it back. Tasha is only staying for a few days. She's looking for a studio.'

Kenji gave a little smile, showing that he was not taken in, and began to address an envelope. *Miss Iris Abbott,* Victor could make out, by reading upside down. He felt irritated at being made to feel like a schoolboy caught out in a flagrant lie. The far-off tinkling of the door bell came to his rescue.

'I'll go down. There's no one there to greet the customers.'

'I'll join you shortly,' said Kenji.

A man sporting a bowler hat and monocle was advancing purposefully on the counter. 'Good morning, Monsieur. Would you have *The Illustrated Jewish France* by Édouard Drumont?[1] I've looked everywhere for that book; all the editions are out of print.'

'Why do you want to read it?' Victor demanded, becoming angry.

'Well, to inform myself, Monsieur, to learn . . .'

'I only sell authors whom I admire, and not those who preach hate and distort the truth, among whom Monsieur Drumont can pride himself on being the leader of the pack. Good day, Monsieur.'

'And you claim to be a bookseller!' exclaimed the man with the monocle. 'You may as well call yourself a grocer!'

The bell jangled under the violence of the man's exit.

Soothed by having vented his spleen, Victor lent his elbows on the counter. A voice from upstairs declared: 'There are as many fools on the earth as there are fish in the sea.'

Victor smiled. Kenji could not stand moral baseness and confronted it with a withering humour that largely made up for his arrogance on other occasions.

He glanced through *Le Passe-partout* and found an article devoted to the Gouffé affair, which recounted the tribulations of two French policemen in New York and San Francisco on the trail of one Michel Eyraud, suspected murderer of the porter whose body was found in Millery, concealed in a trunk. The article was written by Isidore Gouvier. That name evoked the solid form of the perspicacious and phlegmatic reporter whom Victor had met the previous June during the Universal Exposition. Gouvier had previously worked at police head-quarters; he would be able to give him invaluable advice.

He went upstairs to tell Kenji, who had put on a frock coat and was in the process of knotting his tie.

'I have to go out, but I won't be long.'

'I'm coming,' said Kenji. 'Could you buy me *Le Figaro*? And post that letter for me?'

Victor picked up the envelope, touched by this show of trust. Perhaps he had been hasty in his judgement of Kenji, perhaps he would come to accept Tasha's continued presence.

And will I accept Iris's?

At the far end of the back room studio of Bibulus, a new model was posing on a podium. To her surprise, Tasha recognised

Ninon Delarme, dressed only in long black gloves. With legs crossed, back arched and her breasts jutting forward, she was like a pagan divinity ruling over a secret brotherhood, waving not incense sticks, but paintbrushes. Sitting right at the front, Maurice Laumier interrupted his work at regular intervals to go and correct her pose, turning her torso or putting one of her arms behind her head. He was so absorbed in his task that he was oblivious to the ribald comments being tossed between the artists.

Tasha wandered amongst the easels. Laumier's picture seemed uninteresting to her. She recognised the style of painting that he favoured and which recalled at once the stylised drawing of Ingres, the flatness of Gauguin and the technique of partitioning, giving the effect of a stained-glass window. She felt increasingly alienated by that type of composition and thought of the works of Renoir and Monet, which she loved so much, with their exploration of light. Maurice Laumier seemed to be dedicated to darkness.

He hadn't noticed her; nothing could distract him from the rectangular canvas which was the focus of his attention. She half-closed her eyes and even in the artificial darkness which she conjured up, his efforts seemed unconvincing.

He's so full of theories, he's making 'works of art'. I need to work towards an ideal, I want to express my intimate thoughts and I'd better get on with it, time presses.

She took out her drawing pad and sketched a caricature of Laumier.

'My dear, rescue me, I need someone to talk whilst I'm doing my contortionist's act! Otherwise I'll go mad.'

Tasha made an effort to come back to earth. She couldn't help smiling at the sight of Ninon frozen into a grotesque postion. She glanced again at Laumier's picture and felt a fit of giggles coming on. She tried to disguise it as coughing but in the end gave free vent to her laughter. Ninon herself chuckled and cried out in a tremulous voice: 'He's using me like modelling clay! I've had enough of this! I'm tired, cold and hungry!'

Laumier, his hair in disarray and gaze fixed firmly on her, implored her not to move: 'Please, my angel!'

'I've got pins and needles – I have to move about. Let's go, Tasha . . .'

Ignoring the outcry of the painters, she jumped down from the podium, wrapped herself in a pearl-grey satin peignoir and went into the little room where her clothes were tucked away.

'Come on, Ninon, you can't be serious! We only started an hour ago!' protested Laumier.

'One hour! One hour of torture! It's too much. Believe me, if I don't eat something, I'll faint.'

She gestured dramatically. Laumier gave in with a smile. 'But promise you'll hurry.'

'We girls are going off to have lunch, then, my friend, I will be back, I promise.'

'You girls? That'll take all day!' cried one of the artists as they went off arm in arm.

Seated in a modest restaurant on Rue Tholozé, the women laughed at the memory of the painters' indignation.

'Thank you for introducing me to Maurice,' said Ninon,

cutting her lamb chop. 'He's very handsome and rather sweet.'

'Introducing you? He practically threw himself at you. I had nothing to do with it.'

She was fascinated by the freedom with which Ninon, who was taking a second helping of mashed potato, expressed her opinions.

'What were you doing before now?' asked Tasha.

'Before? The past isn't relevant any more – the only thing that counts is today. My dear, there are two things I can't do without, men and money. They are indispensable to my happiness. Without money, you can't live as you please.'

'But men are often an impediment to our independence, don't you think?'

'You just have to manage them, to make use of them, as they make use of us. They're objects, beautiful objects to use for the satisfaction of our desires, but burdensome as soon as they try to control us. Are you shocked?'

'Well, no . . . yes. And love? What do you think about that?'

'Love? An invention of men to make us bend to their will. Believe me, Tasha, love or not, without money, a woman is at the mercy of men.'

'I don't agree, and anyway if you have an artistic passion, money takes second place.'

'Does it? Why shouldn't art be renumerated? Love is, often.'

'Yes, but only prostitutes . . .'

'By prostitutes, you mean those amoral women, scorned by right-thinking people? But does prostitution not exist in every walk of life? Doesn't the artist sell himself when he makes money out of his talent? And the actor when he interprets someone else's text? The journalist when he writes what everyone wants to hear? Even the bookseller, when he exchanges works he hasn't written, for coin of the realm?'

'Are you referring to Victor?'

'Victor the Vanquisher, that trips off the tongue. But be careful, his victory over you might cost you dear.'

'No, Ninon, you won't convince me. I love waking up beside him and having him hold me in his arms.'

'I like waking up beside a man too. As long as he gets up and goes away.'

'Stop it, you're undermining my sense of morality!'

'That would be a good thing. Besides, it would be perfectly immoral if you kept your bookseller all to yourself.'

'Watch out, Ninon, I'm jealous!' Tasha said, laughing. She stopped short. Jealous, like Victor? She added, 'If you want to seduce a bookseller, I would advise you to go after his business associate, Kenji Mori, instead.'

'Is he Japanese?'

'Yes. He avoids women.'

'Does he prefer men?'

'No, no, he has a crush on a London girl.'

'You're making me curious. Is he glamorous?'

'He possesses a certain charm, if you like your men crabby and over the hill.'

'I love a challenge. I wager that I can have your misogynist eating out of my hand! I've never had an Oriental man before. Nor an amateur detective either,' she remarked, winking at Tasha. 'And what was the mystery that Victor the Vanquisher solved?'

'It was last year — there was a series of murders at the

Universal Exposition. He put a stop to them. You must have heard about them. They were all over the front pages.'

'I was in Spain last year. But heavens, may it rest in peace, my past is dead and buried. I'll get the bill. It's time to take up my pose again,' said Ninon, pushing back her chair. 'Aren't you going to finish your meal?'

Tasha did not respond. She had found the chop rather tasteless. She would have given anything for some salted pickles and *ʒakouskis* washed down with a glass of *kvas*.

Victor followed Rue Croix-des-Petits-Champs. He had not been back to this district since Tasha had left her job as caricaturist for *Le Passe-partout*. It felt strange to be here again. And yet it also seemed as if they had met only yesterday.

'Buy my fresh endives!' sang a market gardener as he passed by. He reached Galerie Véro-Dodat and leant against the gate, beyond which a succession of courtyards led to the offices of the newspaper. A boy with a satchel on his back was spitting into a puddle to make ripples, and a little girl was playing with a rag doll. She would throw her into the air, then catch her again, cradling her in her arms as if to comfort her. Another little girl was gathering dandelions from between the paving stones. When was the last time I gave Tasha a bunch of flowers? As he was about to push open the gate, he caught sight of a familiar figure coming towards him and thought better of it. The woman, under the straw hat adorned with yellow acacia, was a picture of fashion. She was beautifully corseted, emphasising her slender waist whilst accentuating her curves. She knew how to present herself to her best advantage . . . Eudoxie Allard the secretary-accountant for *Le Passe-partout;* it was her, without a shadow of doubt. Since the day she had set her cap at him, he had resolved never to find himself alone with this succubus. He hastily turned back to face an old half-torn publicity notice, which he forced himself to read slowly.

Dancing at Le Moulin Rouge
Place Blanche
Every evening
Gala evenings Wednesdays and Saturdays

Eudoxie Allard shimmied past, trailing an exotic fragrance in her wake. He resolved to move once he was certain that she was out of sight; but then it occurred to him that she might return before he'd had time to invite Isidore Gouvier out for a drink. He gave up on his mission and went instead to have lunch at Le Café Oriental at the corner of Rue des Petits-Champs and Avenue de l'Opéra.

'Why don't I go over to Odette's? Boulevard Haussman is just a stone's throw away . . .' he said to himself as he sipped his coffee. 'Perhaps she's come home.' But he did not really believe that, and the mere thought of bumping into that Hyacinthe . . . He paid the bill and went back up towards the post office on Rue du Louvre.

Pleased at having wrangled a day of freedom, Joseph paced up and down the study, considering the best way of conducting his investigation. Denise had definitely been murdered, and he was convinced that the *The Madonna in Blue* had provided the motive for the murder. That old tramp that the boss had taken such pains to follow was probably also involved in the tragedy. He decided to go and explore the Cour des Comptes. Like a character from a Jules Verne novel preparing to set off on a perilous expedition, he assembled his equipment: a muffler, cap, a tweed jacket (a present from Monsieur Mori), and brown leather boots. Since he did not own a Ruhmkorff lamp,[2] he made do with candles and matches, which he put deep into his pockets along with his notebook and pencil. He wrote a quick note to his mother, pinned it up near the sink and departed, feeling proudly that Monsieur Lecoq would have approved. 'I must have a challenge to show my strength, I must have an obstacle so that I can overcome it,' he sang as he walked briskly along the quays where at this late hour, strollers were few and far between.

'Here's the paper you asked for.' Victor put *Le Figaro* on the catalogue-strewn desk.

'You must have got it straight from the printer – it smells of ink,' remarked Kenji, ostentatiously looking at his watch. He got up and began to read, leaning against the counter.

Victor watched him with curiosity. This was a new development; Kenji rarely bought a paper other than when he wanted to keep abreast of literary news. Had he looked over Kenji's shoulder he would have been even more surprised.

It will be a real nuisance if I don't find a studio to rent in the next day or so, thought Kenji, scouring the list of apartments to let. He feared he would not be able to stand Tasha's presence long, although he did recognise her kindness and tact. He refused to admit that she was anything more than a fling for Victor. He had conceived a clear picture of the ideal companion for his adoptive son: submissive, reserved, devoted to assuring his domestic comfort, preoccupied with the upkeep of his house and bookshop, and cultivated without being involved in artistic creation. Tasha met none of these criteria. Although he was trying to keep his countenance, Kenji feared that Tasha would sow discord between Victor and himself.

He had to interrupt his search to greet Anatole France and bring him a chair. With a nonchalant air Victor prepared to grab *Le Figaro* and find out what was of such interest to Kenji. But Kenji quickly slipped the paper into a drawer. Piqued, Victor bowed to the writer and retreated to his apartment.

He picked up a skirt, shawl and some hairpins, strewn by Tasha across the rooms like so many little stones that led to the unmade bed, impregnated with her *benjoin* perfume, the same Oriental fragrance that reigned over her bohemian domain in Rue Notre-Dame-de-Lorette. He thought of how he had been through the attic with a fine-tooth comb, even inspecting the guttering. But without success. He had not been able to lay his hand on *The Madonna in Blue*.

Discouraged, he flopped down on the bed and buried himself in the perfumed sheets.

The delicious aroma of hotpot tickled Joseph's nostrils and

fought its way down to his stomach. Madame de Valladier answered his questions while skimming her salt pork.

'Are you sure he's not there?' asked Joseph, a hand on his belly.

'Absolutely. I'm a bit worried about it. Especially because, the day he went to Carreau du Temple, he dashed home for a moment, saying that he was at his wits' end.'

'Well, they must have kept him.'

'Kept him? Who's that?'

'The coppers. Yesterday he caused a rumpus at the market, and the police arrested him. But, don't worry, they will release him. My compliments, Madame.'

He left the concierge's lodge after bowing to Madame de Valladier. *What a charming young man. I wish I'd dared to invite him in for supper!*

Now that he knew there was no risk that the old man would take him by surprise, Joseph walked from Rue de Lille as far as Rue de Bellechase and from there reached Quai d'Orsay. It was not too difficult for him to grab hold of the branches of a maple tree that hung over the wall on to the pavement. Then he had to slide all the way down the trunk, landing in the middle of a clump of blackberry bushes and grazing his hands. The light of the street-lamps was sufficiently bright for him to make out the gutted carcass of the building. Several times his feet got caught up in tendrils of ground ivy and he cursed the annoying creeper, while congratulating himself on having come in his boots. He went up a flight of steps and crossed a square room denuded of its parquet. He caught sight of the moon between enormous iron girders twisted by the fire, which had ravaged the building.

More excited than if he were exploring in the Amazon, he boldly entered a passage of archways overgrown with weeds. When I've conquered your territory, Père Moscou, I'll name it after me. I'll christen it . . . let's see . . . Pignot Isle, the jewel of the Islands of . . . of . . . Saints-Pères!

These comforting thoughts helped him to forget the aroma of the salt pork. He stopped at the bottom of a monumental staircase, telling himself that it was time to light a candle. To his amazement, he discovered faces, animated by the flickering flame, regarding him. A woman urged him to silence, a finger on her lips. Opposite her a semi-naked warrior was untying some horses from branches, their tails swishing and their hooves pawing the ground. He went cautiously over the crossbeams covered with boards, his head turning to left and right towards the high walls covered with the cracked frescoes, whose titles were barely visible in their tarnished casings: *Meditation . . . Law, Force and Order . . . War . . . Peace protects the arts and works of the Earth . . .* He remembered Théophile Gautier saying of the painter Théodore Chassériau: 'He's an Indian influenced by Ancient Greece.' But, rather than Antiquity, these allegories awakened in Joseph memories of a childish universe of fairy tales, devoured at the back of his father's study, a supply of apples to hand.

He ventured along a porters' corridor, an interminable arched and vaulted passage bordered by cracked walls, and littered with metal debris and undergrowth. He hauled himself up on to a terrace open to the sky from where, like an alpinist at the top of a mountain, he could see the roofs of the neighbouring houses, the white walls of the barracks on Rue de Poitiers, the great plane trees in the courtyard of a townhouse, their branches dotted with nests. On the horizon the clouds pursued the moon. Leaning forwards he made out a curtain of creepers tumbling down into the courtyard. He was overtaken by dizziness and only just managed to keep his balance.

'Whoa, it won't help if I fall over the edge!'

He lay down flat on his stomach and directed the light of his candle downwards. He could vaguely make out a corridor in which there was an opening covered by a faded hanging that was flapping in the breeze.

'I'll wager that that's Ali-Moscou's cave! I've got to get down to the ground floor – come on, move yourself!'

Joseph pulled back the hanging to reveal Pignot Isle, whose messy aspect strangely resembled his own little study in Rue Visconti. Joseph whistled through his teeth.

'That there can be such marvels, right here in Paris! This room is as exotic as old Hugo's sacred elephant. Look at all those trinkets! Bits of military uniform, and medals . . . Oh and books! Let's have a look. Jules Verne *The Underground City*, I haven't read that one. Ali-Moscou, you've secured yourself a magic cave. I'm sure you don't pay rent for it. I'm going to explore further.'

He made a tour of the room looking for clues, but amongst all the bric-a-brac he didn't know what to focus on. His candle went out and he lit another, and it was then that he saw the inscription, etched above a mountain of quilts:

He took out his notebook.

Sweating profusely in his greatcoat, Père Moscou paced along Quai d'Orsay, tormented by total indecision.

Damned weather, it's always changing; Christmas in the morning, then spring by the evening. What in God's name am I going to do? I'm famished. I would go straight to Maguelonne's but I fear that Grouchy is lying in wait to spy on me in the dark – it would be just like that dirty dog – well, that'll be the end of me!

He thought mournfully of Madame de Valladier's cooking, warming and flavoursome. No doubt a soup would be simmering on the stove, an excellent thick pea soup, which sticks to your insides and leads you gently into the arms of Morpheus. He went towards Rue de Poitiers, but fear was gripping him again. He stopped near a lamp-post. He would dearly have loved to come across a police patrol.

These coppers! The less they do the more they have to rest. Now they'll be tucked up at their station, leading the life of Riley and playing cards. When honest people need them, not a sausage, nothing! But there's no one here, not a cab, not a body in sight!

He was relieved to see a figure wrapped up in shawls half-hidden in an alcove and went over to her. 'Please could—'

A woman's voice shrieked, 'What's going on? Can't a soul have a moment's peace?'

Leaning on a cane, she moved off, muttering.

'Oi, no need to be frightened, I just wanted to . . . Damnation, wait!'

The woman had disappeared. Confused, Père Moscou stood still, his arms dangling. I can't go on pounding the pavement all night. I know! Back there, beside my muse, I'll have shelter. And tomorrow, at crack of dawn, I'll go and check that I really did dig Josephine's grave under the big plane tree. I'll put clematis and then lilac on the top, even if it hasn't flowered yet, it will still give her pleasure. Come on Moscou, pow, pow, pow, after all it's not Berezina!

He bent double to get into his secret entrance, a crevice concealed by an acacia bush, which led straight into the Cour des Comptes. To give himself courage he sang loudly:

> Mother Fanchon, wipe your tears away, I've come to
> comfort you.
> I've covered myself in glory and only lost an eye . . .

Alerted by the din that Père Moscou was making, Joseph blew out his candle and tried to find a hiding place close to the monumental staircase.

With his lantern in hand, Père Moscou climbed the stairs. A strangled cry shattered the silence. Joseph jumped, his heart beating wildly.

'It's only me, old fruit! Don't you recognise your old friend? You should be ashamed, giving me a fright like that!' burst out

Père Moscou. He resumed his ascent, holding on to the handrail. Finally he reached the Oceanid with the bare breasts, and stared at her fixedly. 'So my beauty, all well?'

The gaze of the Oceanid, liquid like stagnant water, refused to acknowledge the intruder.

'Why are you looking at me like that? It's me, Moscou, your mate!'

A velvety silence enveloped him, so thick he could hear his blood pounding in his veins. He remained still, sensing a presence. There was a furtive movement to his left, and then a flashing light exploded in his skull. He glimpsed the serene face of the Oceanid as he toppled over the handrail.

Joseph was jolted by a metallic vibration followed by a dull thud. Instinctively he dived down and crawled as far as a niche at the foot of the staircase. The moon emerged from behind the clouds, playing hide and seek between the broken beams of the first floor. Joseph could make out a shadow bending over an immobile form. He retreated further into his niche, crunching over some old plaster, and the shadow straightened up suddenly. Joseph hunched up, holding his breath. The shadow took a few steps forwards, then raced away. Frozen to the spot, incapable even of taking a gulp of air, Joseph waited, all his senses alert, before stealing out of his hiding place towards the imprecise shape which looked like a sack.

When he realised what it was, he could not repress a cry, 'No, No!' he pleaded. 'For pity's sake . . .'

Père Moscou, his eyes wide open, his lips pulled back in a mute cry, stared without seeing.

Joseph knelt down and bent over the body. His fingers

brushed the old man's greatcoat. He encountered a warm sticky substance. Dead! The old man was dead! His skull crushed. Horrified and nauseous, Joseph frantically rubbed his hand against the floor, in the grip of the kind of terror that makes you want to wake up in bed, telling yourself, 'It's all right – it was only a dream.'

When he finally succeeded in controlling his trembling, he forced himself to look again at the corpse of the old man. A little round object in the palm of his hand caught the light of the moon. Joseph had to brace himself several times before daring to take it from the old man and stow it in his pocket. Then everything happened so rapidly that he could barely take it in. He was suddenly aware that someone was spying on him. He wasn't sure how he knew, but he definitely felt he was being watched. His legs reacted before he had time to think. They carried him across the corridor and the square room; he climbed over a pile of debris, but skidded, tumbled down the steps of the entrance and collapsed, waiting for the blow that would finish him off.

He lifted his head, his vision clouded. Spirals of mist were rising from the ground. There was not a sound nor any sign of life. He got painfully to his feet. 'I have to go back there. I can't just leave the poor old man.'

A branch cracked. He listened, straining to hear the least sound. 'If only the boss were here! . . . No, I don't need anyone else: it's going to be all right, it'll be all right.'

Pulled between terror and excitement, he relit his candle,

turned round and sped back along the corridor, then stopped abruptly a few feet from the staircase.

'My God,' he breathed.

Père Moscou had evaporated.

He shook his head, incredulous. Where the lifeless body had been a few moments earlier there was now nothing but a whitish object. A handkerchief? No, a pair of gloves.

CHAPTER 8

Frrom behind his newspaper Kenji observed Victor, who was cataloguing the works of Buffon.

'I am going to ask Dr Reynaud if he'll go and examine Joseph. His mother came round early this morning while you were still asleep. He has a high temperature.'

'Don't trouble yourself, Monsieur Mori, I'll take care of it,' said Tasha, who had just come downstairs.

'You are too kind,' Kenji mumbled.

She walked over to Victor and planted a kiss on the corner of his mouth, her eyes fixed on Kenji who remained impassive, holding her gaze unflinchingly while Victor feigned a sudden interest in anatomical illustrations of Neuroptera.

'See you this evening,' said Tasha softly, tousling his hair.

The moment she'd left Kenji folded away his newspaper.

'I have some good news. I've found somewhere for your friend to live. You did tell me she had been asked to vacate her lodgings?'

'Er . . . yes.'

'In any event it's all arranged. I went to see an old print works that would be ideal for a painter. The rent is reasonable; naturally it needs some work done on it.'

'She'll never leave her neighbourhood!' Victor protested in an exasperated voice.

'It's only a stone's throw from her old house, 36a Rue Fontaine.'

'I think I'll go and see how Joseph's doing,' muttered Victor, pushing his chair back violently.

In his irritation he put his jacket on inside out.

Immobilised under three eiderdowns, Joseph recognised Tasha standing next to Dr Reynaud, who was just leaving. Madame Pignot wrung her hands and invoked all the saints in Heaven.

'Jesus, Mary and Joseph! I knew no good would come of it! When I heard him come home after midnight last night, I thought to myself: "It's not like my boy to stay out at all hours without letting his mother know; he's up to something!" Well, I was right – just look at him now! He's dying! Dying I tell you! He's going to end up like his poor father, and they'll shut me away in the Salpêtrière Hospital with all the nutters!'

'Now, don't upset yourself. You heard what Dr Reynaud said, it's only a chill. A few fumigations, some hot soup and a sachet of *cérébrine* and he'll be as right as rain.'

'Traipsing around at night in this weather! And he had the cheek to say: "Don't worry, Maman, I'm searching for clues." Searching for hussies more like!'

'He's twenty. It's the age for falling in love.'

'Not my Joseph. He only loves me! Cupping glasses! What if I cup him?'

'No, Maman, not the cupping glasses!' Joseph wailed, sitting up in bed.

'And who's going to make his soup for him? Jesus, Mary and Joseph, I've got to go to work!'

'Have no fear, Madame Pignot, Germaine will see to it and in the meantime Mademoiselle Tasha and I shall keep him company,' said Victor, who had just walked in.

'I'm not sure if . . .'

'Please go now Maman, I've got to speak to the boss,' implored Joseph.

'Would you like some help, Madame Pignot?' Tasha enquired from the doorway.

'No, I'll be all right,' muttered the costermonger. 'Just make sure he gets cream in his soup!' she barked, and then she went out and trundled away strapped to her cart.

'Has she gone?' Joseph asked.

Victor nodded and handed Tasha a set of keys.

'You have a new lock.'

'I thought you were joking!'

'Read this.'

He handed her a newspaper dating from the previous day and she read the article circled with a pencil.

'*Bojemoï!* How terrible! The poor girl! Why? Has this anything to do with your friend Odette de Valois?'

'Madame de Valois has disappeared and the concierge doesn't know where she went . . . Tasha, your key wasn't among Denise's belongings. I'm worried, that's why I . . .'

He drew her close and put his arms around her.

'You should have told me about it,' she whispered.

'Whatever for! You've enough on your plate already with your exhibition.'

'I'm really sorry. Promise me you'll go to the police today.'

'I've already been and they're up to their eyes,' he assured her, remembering the exhausted employee at the Bureau of Missing Persons.

'I forbid you to carry out the investigation for them! I care too much about you.'

'So do I. Women! Always fretting over trifles! Go on, off with you now or you'll be late.'

She hurried out and he watched her cross the courtyard. He hadn't lied to her, but he'd made no promises either.

Joseph, propped up against the pillows, attempted to smooth down his hair with a damp flannel.

'Do me a favour and open the window, boss. I'm suffocating in here.'

'Most certainly not. What's that smell?'

'Maman burnt some eucalyptus cigarettes in a saucer before the doctor arrived.'

'Do you mind if I light one of mine?'

'Not at all. Listen, boss, I have to tell you, something awful happened yesterday. I went to the Cour des Comptes and . . . Old Père Moscou, he's dead, murdered.' The words came tumbling out.

Victor's face went blank; he felt completely numb. The match burnt down to his fingers and he let out a cry and sank on to the bed.

'Dead? What do you mean dead?'

'I mean dead. Someone pushed him from the first floor, only then his body disappeared. I haven't said anything to the police, not a word, but it's been on my mind ever since and I'm afraid whoever did it followed me . . .'

'Did you see it happen?'

'I heard a thud and saw a figure leaning over the body.'

'And you expect me to believe that the body just vanished?'

'On my honour, boss, I'm telling you the truth!'

Indignant, Joseph struggled to get up, but Victor held him down.

'What made you go there in the first place? Have you taken leave of your senses? Answer me, for crying out loud!' he shouted, angrily shaking the boy.

'Ow! You're hurting me, boss! And it's all your fault, anyway!'

Victor, taken aback by the vehemence of his assistant, relented.

'Very well, start again, but try to be clear.'

'It's because of you, boss. Mademoiselle Tasha asked me to follow you. She was afraid you might walk into trouble – she knows you well enough! I saw you tailing some old fellow and that set me thinking. I realised you weren't putting me in the picture, so I decided to show you what I'm capable of.'

'Well done, you succeeded! Carry on.'

So Tasha has me followed, thought Victor, not knowing whether to be pleased or annoyed.

Adopting the manner of a primadonna about to sing her grand aria, Joseph requested a glass of water, a slice of apple and a puff on Victor's cigarette before recounting his adventure. It gave him immense pleasure to have his boss hanging on his every word.

'. . . and when I reached the staircase the old man's body had gone. I looked everywhere for him. I said to myself: "Jojo, what've you got yourself mixed up in now?" I was sure the murderer was watching me. Have you ever had the feeling you're being watched, but when you look round there's no one there?'

'Perhaps that's all it was – a feeling.'

'No, boss, I'm certain. I'm not crazy. I told myself: "He doesn't know where you live, so you've got to lose him at all costs." I crossed the Seine and walked as far as the Grands Boulevards. There were people everywhere, and it was brightly lit, so I walked around until midnight, then took a carriage home.'

'Perhaps the old man staged his death,' Victor suggested.

'I had . . . blood on my fingers. Whoever did it threw him over the handrail and then made him disappear, a veritable conjuring trick. Why exactly were you following him, boss?'

Joseph shuddered, and Victor suppressed a smile.

'Stop looking at me as if I were the murderer! Père Moscou worked at Père-Lachaise cemetery and I thought he might have seen Madame de Valois and Denise last week.'

'Of course,' murmured Joseph. 'I've been doing some thinking myself. Tuesday morning, when the battleaxes came into the shop, I heard Madame de Gouveline mention a clairvoyant whose name she couldn't remember. Well, it put me in mind of what Denise told me at the funfair. She was convinced there was an evil force at large in your old lov— I mean friend's apartment. According to her, this clairvoyant who Madame de Valois was seeing had given the place the evil eye. Well, it's a start isn't it?'

'I don't know.'

'We shouldn't ignore any clues. Denise was really scared. She didn't even want Madame Topaz to read her palm, and when I suggested we go and see the re-enactments of famous crimes she insisted on waiting outside, but I'm glad I went in because it's an impressive show and—'

'Stick to the point.'

'I have a clue that could help us find this clairvoyant. Denise told me that the building where she lives is near one of the panoramas and it has statues of nude women on the front. She also said they'd been up to the second floor. If I wasn't feeling so rotten I'd follow it up right now.'

'You just stay put and take your medicine! I need you back at the bookshop.'

Joseph rummaged under his pillows and pulled out his notebook containing the mysterious sentence which he'd seen scrawled on Père Moscou's wall: *WHERE HAVE YOU HIDDEN THEM? A.D.V.*, and showed it to Victor.

'I wonder what it means,' Victor pondered. Could it be Latin? '*Ad vitam*, for life? *Ad valorem*, according to worth?'

'Attention Danger Vengeance?' suggested Joseph.

'It could mean anything or nothing. What's more it might have been there for years.'

He remembered Odette's locket, and what Madame Valladier had told him, that Père Moscou's room had been ransacked, which meant 'somebody' was searching for something.

'Another thing, boss. Where the old man's corpse should have been I found these.' Joseph looked like the cat that had got the cream as he produced his *pièce de résistance*.

'A pair of gloves! So what? Where could that possibly lead?'

'It's a clue, boss, you must never—'

'Ignore any clue, I know. I'm going back to the shop. Look after yourself and I'll have some soup brought over. And later on we'll decide what we're going to do. I'll keep you informed of any developments.'

'Is that a promise, boss? You won't ditch me, will you? I've proved to you I have a brain in my head.'

As soon as Victor had gone, he jumped out of bed and went to put the gloves at the back of the little study between two spiked helmets.

The canvases, framed in pale wood, were heavy. Tasha and Ninon breathed a sigh of relief as they reached the sixth floor.

'The Promised Land,' Tasha sighed, producing her new set of keys.

As soon as they had set the paintings down inside, she bolted the door.

'Victor told me not to let anyone in. I feel like Little Red Riding Hood. Boo! I'm scared! The big bad wolf is coming to get me!'

'Well, it looks like your Victor has vanquished us! We must rise up!' cried Ninon.

'I agree! Men have been our masters for too long!'

'Now we must become their mistresses!'

They fell about in fits of laughter, one collapsing on a chair, the other on the bed. Tasha hadn't felt this close to anyone since she'd left Russia. Ninon reminded her of her sister Ruhlea and also her best friend Doucia, although her free ways were no match for their sweet natures.

'If it weren't for you, I'd have had to make three trips to the framer, and with his wandering hands . . . *Spassibo!*'

'Don't mention it! You can offer me a drink, though.'

'I only have water.'

When Tasha returned holding the jug and glass, she found Ninon examining the nude canvas of Victor.

'What a handsome man! He looks good enough to eat . . .'

'Ninon! Isn't Maurice enough for you?'

'He'll do until I find something better, though his clumsy lovemaking scarcely satisfies me.'

'Do you never feel love?'

'Hardly ever – why should I bow down before bucks who worship their own virility? I'd rather have them trembling in my presence and be the one in command: "I'll have you, but not you!" Tell me, are you going to exhibit this oil painting? It's very good.'

'You're not serious! Victor would die!'

'I can see no reason for him to be ashamed; on the contrary!'

'Well, I'm taking it away and then maybe you'll stop thinking about him.'

Tasha removed the canvas from the easel and hid it behind one of the framed paintings propped against the wall. She chose two other canvases, one of some pale yellow – almost white –

pears in a fruit bowl, and another of a basket of oranges tinged
with blue, and handed them to Ninon.

'What do you think?'

'Well . . . still lifes aren't really my . . .'

'I'm moving towards this type of composition because
it allows me to work on my own and to study form and
light more deeply . . . Maurice doesn't want them in the
Soleil d'Or. He only reluctantly agreed to exhibit my Paris
rooftops.'

'Have you painted any female nudes?'

Startled, Tasha gazed at Ninon, whose sensuous, faintly
provocative smile was disconcerting.

'Yes, at the studio, as a compulsory subject. I have a
preference for male models.'

'You don't know what you're missing. A woman's body is
beautiful and should sell. I'll pose for you if you change your
mind.'

Tasha blushed.

'I mean what I say. I'll pose for you whenever you want, free
of charge and . . . I'll keep still.'

Tasha's mounting unease was swiftly dispelled. She had
been converted. Why refuse? At least if she failed Ninon
wouldn't laugh at her.

'All right. After the exhibition.'

On their way down, they met Helga Becker coming up the
stairs. She was terribly excited and carrying a long roll of paper
under her arm.

'Isn't it lovely? I only had to give it a little tug and it came
off all by itself. I already have more than fifteen in my

collection,' she explained as she spread the advertising poster out on the landing.

They looked on, amused, at a young woman dressed in a boater and culottes scattering a gaggle of geese as she rode through them on her bicycle. Against a bright, canary yellow background the words, *Take the Royal Route with Royal Bicycles* were printed in large blue lettering.

Out in Rue Notre-Dame-de-Lorette, the patch of bare wall bearing witness to Helga Becker's petty larceny revealed an old, half-torn electoral poster. A Gaul armed with an axe and a strident Marianne wearing a crested hat announced the general election of 22nd September 1889. Tasha recognised the work of the illustrator and lithographer Adolphe Willette.[1] She went closer and read:

Ad. WILLETTE

ANTISEMITIC CANDIDATE

IX Arrondissement 2nd electoral constituency

VOTERS

The Jews stand tall because

We are on our knees! . . .

IT IS TIME TO RISE UP!

JUDAISM is the true enemy!

The poster was soiled with brown streaks. All of a sudden Tasha was overcome by grief. She could still see the bloodied face of the man lying in front of the house on Rue Voronov. To have escaped that, and . . . She remembered the explosion of hatred, the screaming, the soldiers on horseback armed with sabres . . . Windows smashing, furniture splintering . . . Millions of swirling flakes – not snow, but feathers from the slit-open mattresses . . .

She leant against the wall, waiting for her emotions to subside.

'Tasha! What are you doing? Are you coming? Laumier's going to complain.'

She must put it behind her! She was in France now, in Paris . . . The notice was curling at the edges. She ripped it off the wall and tore it to pieces.

However intently he stared at it, Constable's watercolour of the verdant English countryside failed to soothe Victor. Had Père Moscou really been murdered, or had he staged his own exit? What part had he played in Odette's disappearance? He'd been in possession of her locket, but did this mean he had been party to kidnapping . . . Or murder? He banished the thought. Then it came to him in a flash: ADV! Armand de Valois!

He searched through the pile of papers on his desk and re-read the letter from the French Consulate in Colombia. There was no conclusive evidence that the body buried at Las Juntas was Armand's. Had anyone identified him? What if he were still alive? What if Odette and he were in league together . . . ? But why? And then there was the picture, *The Madonna in Blue*, which had appeared to be so dear to Armand's heart. Had it cost Denise her life . . . and Père Moscou's too?

He now had two clues to follow up: the famous Numa and the clairvoyant Joseph had mentioned. He decided to pay a visit to Adalberte de Brix to try and learn more, and then to question Raphaëlle de Gouveline.

He scoured the contents of Odette's *Private* envelope one more time, and went through her appointments diary page by page. *Zénobie* – the ubiquitous name intrigued him. He read the entry for 22nd December 1889: *Turner* . . . Appointment with *Zénobie. Three thirty p.m. Pâtisserie Gloppe* . . .

Annoyed, he pushed the diary and it fell to the floor. A letter became dislodged from a hidden pocket in the cover. He picked it up. It was dated 18th December 1889. He read it aloud:

Dear Madame,

We do not know each other and up until a few days ago I was unaware of your existence.

You may be ill-disposed to trust my good intentions, but if this is the case I beg you to set aside all your prejudices and to believe in me. For I possess the heaven-sent gift of being able to speak with the dead. Several weeks ago one such appeared to me. He told me his name was Armand de Valois, and that he has been unable to find peace since his death in a far-off land. When alive, he resided in Boulevard Haussmann with his spouse. I took the liberty of making enquiries and traced your address. I am writing to you in the hope that you are indeed the person with whom he wishes to communicate through me. Please believe me, Madame, when I tell you that I would not normally proceed in this way, but given the circumstances I did not hesitate. Meet me on 22nd December at Gloppe's, the pâtisserie on the Champs-Élysées. I will wait for you there, Thursday at three thirty. I shall sit at a table near the counter, wearing a lilac hat.

Yours faithfully,
Zénobie

What on earth is all that about!

He put the papers and diary back into the envelope, slipped it into his coat pocket and went downstairs to join Kenji.

'How is Joseph?'

'Just a chill. Nothing serious.'

'You look exhausted.'

'I have a headache coming on. I'm going to take the air.'

He was just leaving when Kenji called out.

'We have an appointment at seven this evening to visit the studio.'

'The studio?' Victor repeated blankly.

'Rue Fontaine.'

'Oh yes, of course.'

He should have known. Kenji was as stubborn as a mule! He hailed a carriage.

Adalberte de Brix's townhouse had a white façade with wooden shutters and was situated at number 22 Rue Barbet-de-Jouy, a stone's throw from Les Invalides. As soon as Victor rang the bell, the housekeeper, Madame Hubert, popped up at the small round window next to the carriage entrance. Her eyes were red and she held a handkerchief to her mouth as she led Victor silently to the plush reception room, where he found himself in the company of people speaking in hushed tones. Blanche de Cambrésis was there, as well as the Duc de Frioul, Raphaëlle de Gouveline, Olympe de Salignac, her niece Valentine, a military man festooned with medals, Mathilde de Flavignol and a priest in a cassock and roman collar. They all wore solemn expressions on their faces. When the hand-kissings and greetings had been exchanged, Raphaëlle de Gouveline pulled Victor aside.

'Ah! My friend, it is a terrible thing. Who told you?'

'What has happened?'

'Then you don't know? Poor Adalberte suffered a stroke yesterday evening. I came at once and sat up all night with her. She has lost the power of speech, she, who was such a talkative woman! All who knew her, including her relatives, were convinced she would live to be a hundred – she's buried three husbands – and now her life is hanging on a thread; her heart could fail at any moment. Excuse me.'

Weeping, she went over to Mathilde de Flavignol. A maid carrying a tray of empty glasses walked past Victor and he followed her into the anteroom.

'May I introduce myself? My name is Victor Legris.'

'Honoured, sir. Mine is Sidonie Taillade.'

She set down her tray and did a little curtsey looking up at him with her round face and *retroussé* nose.

'How did it happen?'

'It was just before Madame's bedtime. Gratien, the valet, handed me a letter which Madame Hubert had just given to him. So naturally I took it to Madame, who said to leave it on the dressing table and to prepare her verbena tea. When I came back she was lying on the carpet stiff as a rod. I thought she was dead! Gratien laid her out on the bed before going to fetch the doctor, who came and examined her and said she'd suffered a hemi something . . . some funny word for a stroke.'

'What did the letter say?'

'Why sir! I would never take such a liberty . . . In all my four years of loyal . . .'

'May I look at it, please?'

'Yes . . . I don't see why not.'

'I would be extremely obliged to you, Mademoiselle.'

Sidonie moved quickly. Never had a gentleman addressed her so politely in order to solicit a favour. She was back in a flash.

'I don't know whether I'm at liberty to . . .'

'You are now,' Victor said, pressing a coin into her hand discreetly.

Madame Hubert called out to Sidonie, who glanced at Victor with tears of gratitude in her eyes before disappearing again. He took advantage of her absence to take the letter out and slip it in his pocket and when the maid came back he handed her the empty envelope.

'I thought perhaps the letter contained a piece of bad news that might account for Madame de Brix's attack, but it seems not. You may put it back where it was. One more thing. Have you heard mention of a certain Monsieur Numa Winner?'

'The Englishman who fancies himself as a fakir! Madame should never have taken part in those black magic séances what with her heart condition, but she couldn't keep away!'

'Do you know where he lives?'

'I went with Madame on several occasions, though I never saw anything as I always waited outside. Number 134, Rue d'Assas.'

Victor ended the conversation when he saw Raphaëlle de Gouveline and Blanche de Cambrésis approaching.

'Monsieur Legris,' Raphaëlle called out, 'I've been racking my brains to try and remember the name of that clairvoyant and I've got it!'

'The clairvoyant?'

'Yes, Odette's clairvoyant. You remember, the other day at the bookshop . . . His name is Zénobie. Do you know how it came back to me? Thanks to the palm tree I just had delivered. An association of ideas you see. Palm tree . . . Palmyre . . . Zénobie, queen of Palmyre!'

'In which case she's a woman.'

'Not necessarily. These people often choose female sobriquets with an Eastern or mythical ring. Zaïda, Cassandra, Sybille, Doniazade . . . A man, a woman, what difference does it make?'

'And . . . the address?'

'Odette kept very quiet about it. She only ever mentioned a letter she'd received from this person with some important information about her dead husband.'

'Are you interested in the occult sciences, Monsieur Legris?' enquired Blanche de Cambrésis.

'Simply curious, my dear Madame.'

He skirted round the sitting room to avoid taking his leave, only to find Valentine de Salignac, pale and clutching her parasol, waiting for him in the hallway under a gigantic panel by Louise Abbéma.[2]

'Monsieur Legris, I . . . I ordered a book from Monsieur Joseph and I haven't been able to . . .'

'Joseph isn't well.'

'Not well! Is it serious?'

'No, no, just a touch of bronchitis. He'll soon be better. My compliments, Mademoiselle.'

He bowed, grinning. She watched him walk away, relieved to know the reason Joseph hadn't been to meet her at the Grands Magasins du Louvre.

Victor's amusement was shortlived. In Rue de Babylon he read the letter.

> *He who forced entry into the other world*
> *Will soon plunge into the abyss*
> *Unless he is silent and buries with him*
> *Death's secret mystery.*
> *You've succeeded, I shall NEVER return.*
> *Be silent, be silent, BE SILENT!*
> *Your son.*

'Monsieur is not receiving visitors today,' a prim butler told Victor.

Victor's use of Madame de Brix's name and his insistence on the urgency of the matter gained him entry. He produced his visiting card and was shown to a small sitting room the walls of which were lined with books and paintings. He admired the choice of pastels by Odilon Redon, hand-coloured engravings by William Blake and etchings by Victor Hugo – all with mystical themes. A fleeting glimpse of the complete works of Swift bound in red morocco was enough to make his mouth water, and he was sorry not to have more time to examine the books.

A tall man with long white hair limped into the room on crutches. He smiled at Victor, who felt he was being weighed up and categorised by his host at a glance.

'You take the rocking chair, I'll take this armchair,' said Numa Winner, tapping his left thigh. 'I'm in plaster from my ankle to my knee. So you're a bookseller, are you? A noble profession. What will you have to drink?'

'Nothing, thank you.'

Numa Winner, ignoring the refusal, hobbled over to the bookcase and pulled out two heavy volumes that concealed a bottle and two glasses.

'I hide this from Léon, my butler. He fusses over my liver like an old mother hen. Try it – it's an excellent cognac, twelve years old. I assume you have come for a consultation. You'll need to arrange an appointment with my secretary.'

'That is not the reason for my visit. I should like your opinion about a letter that may have caused Madame de Brix's stroke.'

'Adalberte! When?'

'Yesterday evening.'

Numa Winner lowered himself carefully into the armchair.

'That's dreadful, poor Adalberte . . . A letter you say?'

Victor stood up and showed him the letter. After he'd read it, Numa handed it back and sat looking pensive.

'Shocking. There's wickedness at work here.'

'Would you mind taking a look at this too?' Victor asked, his eyes fixed on the other man.

He passed him the letter arranging the meeting with Odette at Gloppe's.

'Zénobie,' murmured Numa.

'Is the name familiar to you?'

'Well . . .' Numa began in a croaky voice he seemed continually about to clear.

'You must know each other in your profession,' insisted Victor.

'My dear sir, I do not possess a directory of clairvoyants; there are new recruits all the time. Where did these letters come from?'

'Why don't you read my mind and find out!'

'Come now, Monsieur Legris, I find it hard to believe that you see clairvoyants as wizards with owls perched on their shoulders, a crystal ball or tarot pack in front of them and but one aim in mind – to take their customers' money. I confess to being as incapable of reading your thoughts as I am of seeing into the future.'

'What a shame; you could have avoided breaking your leg.'

'Even if I could have predicted this silly fall – something of a tautology wouldn't you say? – I wouldn't have been able to stop it happening sooner or later. And, anyway, isn't the unpredictability of life part of its charm? My God, how tedious if we could map out everything we did in advance!'

'When did it happen?'

'Three weeks ago, as I was stepping out of a carriage. You didn't answer my question. Who wrote these letters?'

'I have no idea. The one signed Zénobie was sent to a friend of mine, Madame de Valois, who has gone missing. I have no news of her.'

These words appeared to have no immediate effect on Numa, indeed nothing in his manner indicated that he had even heard them. He continued sipping his cognac. Victor studied the impassive expression on his face. Finally Numa spoke:

'Madame de Valois came to see me at Houlgate. It was Madame de Brix who introduced us. Six months later Madame de Brix mentioned to me a medium by the name of Zénobie. She asked my advice and I warned her to be careful. Then she told me that Madame de Valois had been contacted by this Zénobie, this would-be guardian of secrets. Madame de Brix tried in vain to dissuade your friend from giving any credence to the woman's unlikely stories. Swindles involving the death notices are quite widespread nowadays. In the last few years a veritable rash of mediums and false clairvoyants has sprung up, feeding the credulous with falsehoods and then fleecing them. Wise men, cabbalists, occultists, braggers of every hue abound in all strata of society.'

'And naturally you belong to a different category.'

Numa smiled.

'Precisely. No incense, no incantations, no dim lighting. I have no time for charlatans who take advantage of the gullibility of people in distress. Being a medium is a gift one is born with and should not be exploited for gain.'

'And how do you make a living?'

'I run a scientific review, *The Scientific News*, based in London. I am also a member of the counterpart to your Académie des Sciences. You see, Monsieur Legris, good mediums are as rare as great artists, and they fall into two categories: the physical and the psychological. I belong to the latter. I work by clairaudience, which means I have the gift of hearing disembodied voices inaudible to the ordinary ear. I interpret messages and convey them through my own voice.'

'Madame de Brix told me that her deceased son spoke to her

through you. Forgive me for saying so, but I find it impossible to believe in such nonsense.'

'Most people deny things that defy their senses, or what is known as their "common sense". Shall I tell you why I agreed to speak to you? The instant I stepped into this room I sensed you were not alone. There was a couple with you. I caught a brief glimpse of him – a rare occurrence for me – an elderly, balding man with hunched shoulders. He is offering his arm to a younger woman holding a spray of what looks like . . . it looks like laurel.'

Numa had gone silent, his stare fixed. Victor leant forward, fascinated in spite of himself.

'What significance, if any, does . . .'

'Cut the thread.' Numa spoke clearly, in a voice that had lost all trace of hoarseness.

Victor jumped.

'His death has freed us, you and me. My love. I have found him. You'll understand. You must . . . follow your instinct. You can be reborn if you break the chain. Harmony. Soon . . . Soon . . .'

Numa relaxed, and cracked his joints. He looked drained of all vitality.

'They've gone.'

'Who were they?'

'I don't know.'

'I'm sorry, but I'm not taken in.'

'The facts are plain and yet you doubt them. I have no interest in trying to convince you, Monsieur Legris. Indeed I would gain nothing from it. There is no rational explanation for spiritual phenomena. As regards the reason for your visit, I have only one piece of advice: tread carefully; this is a dangerous game.'

He lifted his glass to his lips and closed his eyes, a sign that the interview was over.

Victor walked back up Avenue de l'Observatoire where strings of cyclists were vying with the omnibuses. When he reached the Bullier music hall, a word Numa had uttered during his trance came back to him in a flash. 'Laurel.' He felt a rush of blood to his head. He tried to recall the part about Apollo's lovers in the Greek myths; the God was on the point of embracing a nymph he'd been pursuing with his attentions when she changed into a laurel bush. Her name was Daphne. Like my mother, he thought.

He continued to stroll, deeply troubled. Had he been in the presence of a true medium?

He bumped into an old lady who was feeding the sparrows and turned round. And Uncle Émile? How could Numa have known he was bald and relished the word 'harmony'? No! I refuse to believe it.

He hailed a cabman who was dropping off his fare on Rue de Chartreux.

'I want to make a tour of the panoramas.'³

'*All* the panoramas?' the cabman inquired, sensing he was on to a good thing. ·

'All of them.'

A building with caryatids on it shouldn't be too hard to

find, he thought to himself as he sat down on the worn seat.

The cabman, a big fellow with a face like a bull, preferred to begin with the most strenuous part of the journey, on account of his old mare. And so he took his fare to the top of Rue Lepic in Montmartre where, behind the scaffolding of the Sacré-Coeur under construction, was the Jerusalem panorama, on the corner of Rue Chevalier-de-la-Barre and Rue Lamarck. Victor looked around him at the allotments and rickety houses – all devoid of architectural adornments.

'On to the next!' he called out to the cabman, who was intrigued by this peculiar sightseer.

'I suggest you visit the Centenary Panorama.'

'Where is it?'

'Jardin des Tuileries.'

'No. Are there any others close by?'

'I should say so!'

The Champs-Élysées alone boasted three panoramas, and the cabman applauded Victor's decision to skip the rather sorry affair on the hill as it would give him more time for the Battle of Reichshoffen, on Rue de Berri.

'No caryatids,' Victor observed.

'He's a funny bird,' grumbled the cabman, cracking his whip.

But neither the diorama depicting the 1870 siege of Paris, situated opposite the Cirque d'Été, nor the brand new construction next door to it, built by Charles Garnier to house the panorama of Jerusalem in the time of Herod, found favour with his fare.

'Well, there's only one more I can think of!' the cabman called out, 'and that's the Bastille.'

'I only hope it's the right one,' Victor said to himself, feeling discouraged.

After a rather long ride they arrived at the Colonne de Juillet and continued down Boulevard de la Contrescarpe, flanked by warehouses, which ended near the Seine at Place Mazas. In the middle of this islet planted with trees stood the panorama of Paris in 1789.

Victor decided to get out and have a stroll around the neighbourhood, and he paid his fare, supplementing it with a substantial tip.

'There was I thinking you were funny in the head, sir, but you picked the right one! The paintings are spectacular and the storming of the Bastille feels so lifelike it's as if you were there! You can even hear birds singing. But the star attraction is the torture chamber. It's only wax figures, but there's plenty to feast your eyes on – beheadings, water torture, burnings, the rack, garrotting, the whole kit and caboodle! Gee up Zéphyrine!'

Feeling slightly sick, Victor strolled out along Avenue Ledru-Rollin past some naked façades and a paving-stone ware-house. He retraced his steps and turned into Boulevard Diderot. He had scarcely walked a few yards when a cornice buttressed by a pair of busty torsos almost caused him to cry out 'Victory.'

Once more he had to use his imagination to hoodwink a

concierge. 'I shall compile an anthology of tall stories,' he promised himself.

'The Comtesse de Salignac has asked me to deliver a message to the tenant on the second floor.'

'You're too late. Monsieur and Madame Turner have gone.'

Victor's heart started pounding. Turner was the name jotted down next to Zénobie in Odette's diary!

'When did they leave?'

'Yesterday morning.'

'When will they be back?'

'They won't. They gave their notice.'

'Perhaps they left a forwarding address? This is a delicate matter. I've been asked to ascertain their whereabouts, discreetly. Madame, the Contesse, lent them a large sum of money, and she wishes to avoid a scandal.'

'Sorry. That's all I can tell you. The Turners were an odd couple, very stiff and starchy. They moved here in December. Very few belongings and no servants – which didn't stop them leaving the apartment clean as a whistle. They received no letters or visits – apart from a woman dressed in mourning who came once or twice a week. They left in a great hurry – a family matter, the woman told me. Her husband went on ahead the evening before. She paid up until June without any fuss – well, it's only fair; we're already in March. The apartment is for rent. You must have seen the sign on the second-floor balcony.'

'Could you describe the Turners to me?'

'He used a stick and limped, but without really limping.'

'What do you mean?'

'Well, he had a very slight limp, hardly noticeable, only I've got a good eye.'

'Did you ever speak to him?'

'Only to say good morning and good evening. I couldn't have seen him more than five or six times in all. It was mostly her I saw.'

'Was he short, tall, fair, dark?'

'He wore his hat pulled down over his face, so I can't say if he was fair or dark . . .'

'What about the woman?'

'A pretty blonde, with a slim waist and a nice frontage . . .'

'I'd like to visit the apartment; I happen to have an aunt who is looking for a place to rent.'

He ferreted around in all four rooms, opening the windows to look at the view, frowning at the wallpaper and criticising the kitchen; in short doing everything he could to irritate the concierge, and when he sensed the man was about to have a fit, he asked him to go back downstairs and leave him alone in the apartment so that he might get the feel of the place and make his decision.

He hastily looked in the cupboards and wardrobes and in the two desks. All empty. He pulled out the drawers of a dresser and when he was pushing them back felt the top one stick. He pulled it right out and placed it on the floor, and fished out a crumpled piece of paper, which he scarcely had time to stuff into his pocket before the concierge reappeared.

'I don't think it'll be suitable after all – too many negative vibrations,' he told the man who, as soon as Victor's back was turned, tapped his forefinger against his temple.

Out in the street, he smoothed out his find. It was a piece of headed paper:

HOTEL ROSALIE
Owner Señora P. Caicedo, Proprietor
CALI

Victor sat beside the Bassin de l'Arsenal, comtemplating Odette's envelope marked *Private* that rested on his knees. The spidery handwriting danced before his eyes and he closed them for a moment, pretending that the city had disappeared and that he was floating in space. Inner landscapes appeared to him, as tangible as the real world. The pieces of the jigsaw were gradually falling into place. He opened the envelope. He already knew what it contained, but he wanted to make sure. There it was – the letter sent by Odette from Paris on 29th July 1889 to her dear husband, *Monsieur Armand de Valois, Geologist with the Inter-Oceanic Canal Company, care of Señora Caicedo, Hotel Rosalie, Cali, Colombia.*

He compared the address with the one on the headed paper he'd found at the Turners': 'Caicedo . . . Hotel Rosalie . . . Cali . . .' The words rang in his ears and he was plagued by a new set of questions. Was Monsieur Turner Armand de Valois? Nothing could be easier than faking one's own death. Had someone been buried in his place? Over the past ten years two-thirds of the twenty thousand or so French people who landed in Panama had succumbed to yellow fever – not to mention all the other nationalities. Procuring a corpse wouldn't present too much of a problem. Moreover, the concierge had stressed that

Turner walked with a limp, and Odette had once confided to him that her husband wore a lift in his shoe to rectify this congenital defect.

He put the papers away and glanced up at the pneumatic clock: it was six thirty.

Victor was early. He sauntered along the Rue Fontaine, stopping to read a music programme – *Concerts des Incohérents* – in the window of a brasserie owned by a certain Carpentier. He examined himself in the glass, tamed a rebellious lock of hair and straightened his hat. Arriving at 36a, he crossed a courtyard where an acacia tree was growing and nearly collided with Kenji.

'We're free to look around on our own. I have the key.'

The place was an old print works and full of rusty presses, cartons and boxes. Victor made an effort to imagine it all cleaned up and repainted, without the clutter, and what he saw was a vast studio with the not inconsiderable luxury of running water. There was an alcove blocked off by a machine for polishing lithographic stones that could be transformed into a bedroom. He liked the place, and thinking about it made him forget his worries. The low rent dispelled any lingering doubts he might have had. The question now was how to go about convincing Tasha? The simplest way would be to let her continue living at Rue Notre-Dame-de-Lorette while he renovated it, and then give her a surprise. Pleased with this solution, which didn't commit him to any immediate action, he tried to open a window but the catch came away in his hand. Kenji watched him with dismay, worried by his silence.

'You look troubled.' He was tempted to come out with an appropriate Eastern proverb: 'When the cuckoo builds his nest, his chant will become a melody,' but decided it was best to keep quiet.

'I was thinking about the work that needs to be done. We must make sure there are no leaks in the roof.'

Kenji's face lit up; there was still every reason to be hopeful. Naturally, it would be some time before Victor's young friend could move in there, but he was determined, he could wait. Buoyant, he looked towards the alcove and said: 'Don't you think this recess would make a nice kitchen?'

Slowly and deliberately Tasha slipped out of her underwear. Unable to contain himself, Victor slid his hands under her camisole.

'I love you, let me help,' he whispered.

She played along, allowing him to strip her naked. He led her over to the bed, where she pressed her body tightly against his.

He couldn't wait. He must try to sell her the idea of the studio now or he'd never have the courage.

'I visited a place today. A room for just the two of us. It's big – you could paint there.'

'You did what?'

He felt her body tense, but he went on calmly, running his fingers gently over her breasts.

'The rent is very reasonable; you could easily afford it. I'll take care of the furnishings . . . Are you upset?'

'How big is big?' she murmured.

Victor woke up in the middle of the night, anxious about the investigation. Tasha was asleep, her arms hugging a pillow. He dragged on his underwear. She groaned and he leant over and brushed her cheek with his lips. She had given in – they would visit the studio the next day.

He sat at his desk and lit the lamp. He wanted to carry out a little experiment in graphology. He unfolded the letter Denise had received, smoothing it down with his hand, and beside it he placed the letter signed by Zénobie and the anonymous note received by Madame de Brix.

He would examine, for instance, how all the Ts were crossed. He wasn't imagining it! They were all crossed with the same downward flourish! The Ns looked like Us and the As like little porticos, and the writing slanted heavily to the left.

All three messages had been penned by the same hand.

CHAPTER 9

A GRASS snake was warming itself, coiled on a smooth stone, when two black monsters with pointed noses trampled the grass around its safe haven, causing it to slither into a bush.

The shoes hesitated and stopped. A shrill voice rang out: 'I saw a snake!'

'You're imagining things, Elisa. This is Paris, not Senegal!'

The shoes trudged off again. They belonged to a boy of barely sixteen wearing sideburns and a peaked cap to make him look tougher. A young slip of a girl with a scared expression on her face was stumbling behind him.

'How'll we find our way out of here?' she asked, tugging at her skirt, which had caught on some brambles.

'I know this place like the back of my hand – it's a first-rate hideout when the coppers are about. There's an old geezer kips here, but he's always in his cups so . . .'

'Ferdinand! An animal!'

'It's only a tomcat, come on.'

He dragged her over to a crumbling wall where a recess was concealed by a tangle of clematis tumbling from a projection above.

'It couldn't be better! A real little love nest!'

He pulled off his jacket and laid it out on the grass. The girl shrank back.

'You're mad! It's all wet!'

He grabbed her face and crushed his mouth against hers as hard as he could to prove his manliness. After a few seconds she pulled away.

'You're hurting me,' she said, in a plaintive tone.

Exasperated, he pushed her away.

'Make up your mind, will you! Do you want to or not? You said you did.'

'I know, it's just . . . I'm scared, all right?'

'You're scared of everything! Snakes, cats, bushes!'

'It hurts the first time, and . . . what if I get big?'

He scoffed.

'You're not big now, that's for sure! Flat as a pancake. Why I wouldn't be surprised if there was nothing under that blouse of yours. Seeing as it's like that, I'm off. There's plenty of others, that Jenny for instance, she wouldn't say no, and at least she's got some padding!'

He snatched his jacket and slung it over his shoulder.

'Don't leave me here, Ferdinand. Don't you love me any more?'

Glowering, he aimed a kick at a stone, which went flying.

'Love isn't just canoodling.'

'Do you promise you'll be gentle?' she murmured, nestling up to his chest.

He spread out his jacket again and pushed the girl to the ground, smothering her in kisses as he grappled with the buttons on her blouse. They were rolling around, out of breath, when the boy's foot struck something protruding from the ground. He let out a howl.

'What was that?'

He tugged furiously at the object that had scratched his ankle and fell over backwards contemplating his haul with astonishment. It was an umbrella. The girl shrieked with laughter.

'Oh, so it's funny, is it?'

'That's a first-class brolly that is. See the handle, it could be ivory. Do you reckon I can keep it? Well, do you? Are you deaf or what, Ferdinand?'

The boy was frozen, his face twisted in horror and disbelief. Slowly, the girl looked down to the place he was staring at, right next to her, beneath a lilac bush. It took a few seconds for the scream that began in her throat to reach her mouth.

The five pinkish dots with pearly white edges in the middle of a green pool were not flowers.

The golden rays had managed to filter through the grime-encrusted window panes to cast a shimmering, stippled light on the floor. Like a Seurat painting, thought Tasha, as she walked around the studio. At first, she had been put off by the state of the place, but now she had begun to picture it in her mind's eye she was feeling very excited. My easel can go here, a plinth for the model there, and a drawing board over there. And later on the engraving materials in that corner. I wonder whether the press still works.

She stopped in front of the stone sink. A tap was dripping. Running water! No more need to make fifty trips to the pump in the corridor!

'And in the alcove a double mattress, the biggest we can find.

Farewell, bed of nails, rest in peace, your day is done!' exclaimed Victor.

'Hey! Not so fast! I'm not made of money, you know!'

'I told you I'd pay for the furniture, and any work that needs doing, naturally. I'd love to install a water closet. I realise it's a minor consideration, but . . .'

As he outlined his plans, she recalled her previous lover Hans, a painter from Berlin. She had ended the affair not just because he was married, but because of his meddling in her artistic career. Should she distance herself from Victor now simply because he was trying to make life easier for her? He'd shown great generosity in allowing her to enjoy her independence, and so far had never tried to influence her style of painting. What danger could there be in accepting an arrangement that was clearly beneficial to her? She had insisted on paying the rent, but gouache was so expensive. Even if she cut back on food and clothes, would she be able to afford everything?

'Well?'

'I think the answer's . . . yes!'

He gave her a long, drawn-out kiss.

'You'll paint your masterpiece here,' he whispered.

'Not before time. My poor canvases will soon be covered in mould. I've discovered a new leak.'

'This can't go on – not with all this rain. Listen, I have an idea.'

'Not another one! You're beginning to make me nervous.'

'Why not store your canvases at my place? Since you're leaving the attic anyway, we can stick them in the dining room for the moment. I'll move that mammoth table out of the way.'

'But . . . what about Kenji?'

'Kenji couldn't care less how I arrange the furniture in my apartment. We could do it today. The shop will be closed in the afternoon because of the Mid-Lent processions. If you agree, I'll hire Madame Pignot's cart.'

She chewed her thumbnail. Was he trying to force her hand?

'But this apartment is not nearly ready to move into yet.'

'You can come and see your paintings whenever you like, and it'll give you a good excuse to come and see me.'

'Oh, you!' she exclaimed, planting a kiss on his cheek.

The carnival was in full swing. After making a series of detours, the carriage finally came to a halt, hemmed in by a masked parade on the corner of Boulevards Saint-German and Saint-Michel.

'Can't go any further with all these Shrovetiders,' the cabman grumbled.

'This'll be fine,' said Victor.

They pushed their way through an oncoming procession of princes and paupers as unruly as an end-of-year student pageant. It was impossible for any vehicle to pass. Crowds of rowdy youths were letting off steam, dancing and singing. Tasha and Victor were sprinkled with confetti and swept along by the human tide until they reached the Soleil d'Or where they made a dash for the doorway, laughing.

'Are you fleeing the Mid-Lent processions?'

Ninon greeted them in the basement, dressed in her usual mid-length gloves and a cherry-red dress that showed off her curvaceous figure to advantage. Maurice Laumier was barking out contradicting orders to a couple of wretched apprentices who didn't know whether they were coming or going.

'No, no, no! It's crooked! Lift it on the left! Not too much! Now the right, the right! Oh, for crying out loud!'

The two apprentices, precariously balanced on a couple of stools, were trying their best to hang a picture measuring ten foot by twenty. They almost dropped it.

Laumier threw up his arms in despair, shouting, 'What did I do to deserve you two idiots? You're wrecking *my* exhibition!'

He kicked some chairs, stepped on an open box of nails, upturning it, and let out a great roar followed by a barrage of abuse as he hopped up and down on one leg.

'He's one of life's worriers,' Ninon remarked. 'He's been like this since yesterday. Come on, Tasha, I'll treat you to an anisette – it'll give you a lift. Have I your permission to abduct her, Monsieur Legris?'

Without waiting for a reply, she led Tasha away.

'I really can't stand that dauber any longer! Do you know what he had the nerve to say to me last night when I left to go home at midnight! "We spend so little time together, my minx, I suggest you disguise yourself as a will o' the wisp; you'd be a runaway success at the carnival." It's over! Finished! I've had enough. I'm free to model for you as of now if you like.'

Tasha felt her throat tighten and she took a deep breath.

'No. I mean yes, once I'm settled in. I need to ask you a favour. Victor has offered to store my canvases at Rue des

Saints-Pères, because – my room is practically covered in toadstools. Could you help us move them this afternoon?'

'With pleasure. Anything to get away from brush-boy over there,' she said, pointing at Maurice Laumier who had calmed down and was busy putting his shoe back on.

He stood up and limped cautiously the length of the piano.

'Don't bother commiserating!' he berated the two cowering apprentices. 'Would you deign to continue trying to hang that picture? Well! If it isn't Monsieur Legris! You've joined the party I see.'

Victor nodded. He was studying one of Tasha's paintings, a view of Paris at daybreak. An orangey sun emerging from the mist lit up the grey rooftops that bristled with chimney stacks like masts arising from the night.

'We could call it *Landscape as Seen by a Myopic Person Without Glasses*,' said Laumier, in a mocking voice.

'I think she's captured the quality of our sky superbly, with a singularity and poetry I admire,' retorted Victor, making an effort to hide his irritation.

'Sheer woolliness! She'd do better to practise proper drawing instead of inflicting her wishy-washy visions on us.'

'Doesn't Paul Gauguin, whose work you admire, insist on the importance of painting from memory as opposed to real life?'

'I've elaborated my own theory. Real life takes priority over memory, but drawing comes first, second and third – which is why nothing can replace studio work.'

'Then you'll be glad to know that Tasha will soon have a studio of her own.'

Maurice Laumier looked him up and down, sneering.

'A kept woman, eh? So she finally got what she wanted. Are you planning to introduce her to photography too?'

'If she wishes. Speaking of photography, do you know what Ingres said about it? "Photography is important, though one must never admit it."'

Kenji's eye lit first upon the extravagant wide-brimmed veiled hat, topped by a riot of violets and cherries and worn tilted back. His gaze moved downwards to the short, black cape and the crimson dress of a splendid brunette who approached him, preceded by a spicy *Cuir de Russie* perfume.

'Are you Monsieur Kenji Mori?' she asked matter-of-factly.

He bowed, mesmerised.

'Delighted to meet you. My name is Ninon Delarme. Perhaps Tasha mentioned me to you?'

He shook his head, dumbstruck.

'She didn't? What an oversight. On the other hand, she spoke highly to me of your knowledge and refinement in matters of culture. She admires you a great deal.'

Kenji, stunned, opened his mouth and managed to murmur: 'I had no idea.'

'You were born in Japan and have travelled in the East. You're just the man I'm looking for.'

'I . . . Would you like to sit down?'

'No. Standing is more intimate. I like to feel a current passing between me and my interlocutor,' she said softly, lifting her veil.

Without seeming to have moved at all, she suddenly felt so

close that Kenji found himself fervently hoping a customer wouldn't walk in.

'Monsieur Mori, you see before you a woman in distress. Since Tasha has revealed nothing about me, allow me to tell you that in spite of all appearances to the contrary I possess no fortune worth speaking of, and am thus obliged to earn my living. I work for an art review and have been commissioned to write an article on the subject of Japanese etchings. Do you own any?'

'Why yes, of course!' He exclaimed, his eyes shining. 'I have some Hokusai, Utamaro and Kiyonaga all dating from between the late eighteenth and early nineteenth – the finest period.'

'You're my saviour! I was beginning to despair of tracking down any erotic etchings!'

Kenji's expression froze.

'Have I said something wrong? Isn't carnal love the subject of your etchings?'

'Er . . . no. The artists I mentioned painted many different themes, but . . .'

'You mean you have none of that genre? What a bore. I shall never succeed now. You were my last hope!'

'To tell you the truth I do have a few examples that might interest you, only . . .'

'Only what?'

'I am afraid of offending your modesty. Here in the West, graphic depictions of the intimate act are deemed obscene, an effrontery, whereas in the East eroticism is considered an art, and . . .'

'I share your point of view, Monsieur Mori. I am not only a journalist, I am a model. I pose naked.'

If it hadn't been for her candid manner, Kenji might have thought this was a practical joke designed to unsettle him.

'Is it yes then? I promised to lend Tasha and Monsieur Legris a hand this afternoon. I assume you are going too – it would give us a chance to meet again.'

'I . . . ? Going where?' he stammered.

'Why, to Tasha's apartment to help move her canvases here. And afterwards you can devote some of your time to showing me your treasures. Please say you will, Monsieur Mori!'

'Of course. Shall we say . . . this evening at seven thirty after the . . . the move. Come in through the main building, my rooms are on the first floor.'

'Oh what a relief! You're an angel! I must go and change into my climbing gear – it's no mean feat reaching Tasha's roost!'

She blew him a kiss that left him gasping like a fish out of water.

Hitched to the cart, Victor made his way along Rue Jacob and into Rue des Saints-Pères. Madame Pignot, forced to take the day off because of the carnival, had finally agreed to let him borrow it. He was approaching number 18 when he saw a woman in a large, flowered hat with a veil leave the shop and wave to Kenji in a friendly manner before heading off in the direction of the quay. Victor parked the cart in the main courtyard of the building.

No sooner had he opened the door than a pungent fragrance tickled his nostrils, causing him to sneeze loudly.

'Have you been using disinfectant?' he asked Kenji, who was standing, transfixed, beside the counter.

'Do you not like this perfume?'

'Whoever wears it probably wants to remain incognito,' he said under his breath, his handkerchief pressed to his nose.

All this toing and froing had made him hungry and he was hoping Germaine had surpassed herself.

'Have you eaten yet?'

'No,' replied Kenji, with a distant look.

Some pretty customer's tickled his fancy, thought Victor, sitting down to duck *à l'orange*.

Kenji joined him.

'Have you anything planned for this afternoon? The Duc de Frioul is exhibiting his collection of incunabula,' he said nonchalantly as he served himself a wing.

'I offered to help Tasha bring her canvases here; it's too damp in her room.'

'In that case I'll help you.'

'You!'

Victor froze, his napkin halfway to his mouth.

'Yes, me! I'm not a complete wreck!'

When they finally reached Rue des Saints-Pères, they were exhausted. The mild weather, a dream for the carnival, was a nightmare for the two men dragging their heavy load through the streets, hampered by advertising floats and a steady flow of processions.

'Don't the men make a pretty tableau!' exclaimed Ninon.

'If I had your talent I'd paint them and call it *Sweet Revenge*.'

'You're too hard on them. They've gone to a lot of trouble. Kenji has risen greatly in my esteem.'

They were walking behind the cart, bareheaded, and dressed in long, colourful chemises that made them look like gypsy women.

'Don't delude yourself; he's only here because of me. He thinks I'm a journalist passionate about Oriental art.'

Tasha burst into peals of laughter.

'Shh! Don't give me away,' whispered Ninon as they arrived at the entrance to number 18.

Madame Ballu stood, hands on hips, and watched disapprovingly as they unloaded the cart.

'Where are you going with all that? Not up my nice stairs I've just polished, I hope!'

Without replying, they picked up a canvas each and crossed the courtyard in single file. Ninon opened the hallway door, but it slipped out of her grasp and slammed shut on her hand. Kenji and Victor rushed over.

'Did you hurt yourself?'

Ninon, unflustered, had not lost her composure; she seemed insensitive to pain.

'It's nothing. My glove cushioned the impact. I expect I'll come out of it with little more than a bruise.'

'You must run your finger under the cold tap immediately. Come with me,' said Kenji.

He asked her to follow him to the bathroom.

'Let me have a look.'

'What zeal, my dear man! I should inform you that although

I may pose in my birthday suit I never undress in front of a man. Wait for me outside. What a splendid bathtub! It must be heavenly to relax in after exerting oneself!'

She shut the door firmly, leaving Kenji standing in the doorway confused and frustrated.

Victor and Tasha propped the armfuls of frames they had carried up against the wall in the dining room.

'Your friend has clearly had an effect on Kenji. I've rarely seen him so solicitous with a woman. Let's hope she doesn't eat him alive.'

'He's big enough to defend himself.'

She looked around the room at the furniture piled to one side to make way for the deluge of canvases, then examined the nude of Victor with a critical eye.

'I'd like to do another one with more light in it. Will you pose for me again?'

'I will if you stop recriminating every time I do anything for you,' he said, sliding the canvas under the sideboard.

'Why are you hiding it? Are you ashamed?'

'I don't want my anatomy on show for all the world to see.'

'Mine is on permanent exhibition,' she retorted, pointing to a small picture on the wall.

'Yes, but it's so much prettier.'

'Hypocrite!'

She fell silent as Ninon and Kenji came in. After they'd finished emptying the cart they went to the kitchen to drink lemonade.

'What would you all say to a bite to eat? I'll take you to Foyot's,' Kenji suggested.

'Today! But it'll be packed with the carnival on,' Tasha protested. 'You all go without me. I must get back to the Soleil d'Or.'

'I promised Madame Pignot I'd return her cart as soon as we'd finished. I'll look in on Joseph at the same time, and then I have some letters to write.'

'What about you, Mademoiselle Ninon?'

'I'm terribly sorry, Monsieur Mori. I have just enough time to stop off at home and change before a very important meeting at seven thirty.'

'Get your *Passe-partout!* Latest! St Nazaire corpse identified!' a paperboy barked at the top of his voice.

Victor stationed the cart next to the curb and signalled to the boy. He leant against a lamp-post reading the article.

CORPSE IDENTIFIED

St. Nazaire corpse identified. The body appears to be that of a Monsieur Lewis Ives, an American citizen who, as the ticket found in his wallet indicates, boarded the ocean liner *La-Fayette*, which regularly makes the crossing between France and Central America, on 26th November 1889. In the wake of inquiries made at the appropriate consular authority it has been confirmed that before becoming a prospector Monsieur Ives was employed as a foreman at the inter-oceanic canal works in Panama. Monsieur Ives's last place of residence was Cali, Colombia, care of Señora Caicedo, owner of the Hotel Rosalie. It is regrettable . . .

Victor couldn't believe his eyes. He reread the passage several times. The significance of his discovery made him dizzy. The Hotel Rosalie again: Armand's address and the one on the headed paper he'd found at the apartment of the mysterious Turners . . .

Oblivious to the Javanese, Pusses in Boots, Pierrots and Colombines that were flooding the streets, he stood, trying to recall another news item Joseph had mentioned to him recently.

Joseph awoke in a sweat. His senses dulled by the fever and the sachet of cérébrine, he was only half aware of the distant hubbub of the city. A troupe passed by his window chanting a popular song.

He wanted to ask his mother for a glass of water, but remembered she'd gone to borrow some mustard powder from Madame Ballu.

Then he saw the intruder.

All he could make out in the gloomy light filtering through the thick curtain was a hazy, slow-moving shadow, wearing a hood and cloak that gave it a ghostly appearance.

'Who's there?' he asked in a muffled voice.

There was no reply from the shadow, which continued moving in the direction of the bed where he lay, petrified.

'Say something,' he implored.

Scared out of his wits, Joseph watched the pale, silent figure gliding inexorably towards him. It was Père Moscou coming to get him! Imagining death's gnarled fingers already closing round his throat he struggled to extricate himself from the sheets, kicked off the eiderdowns and ended up prostrate on the floor.

'Jesus, Mary and Joseph! Whatever's the matter, pet?'

Euphrosine Pignot rushed to his side.

'Has . . . has he gone?'

'Has who gone?'

'The ghost!'

'There's no one here, pet; you were having a nightmare. It's the fever. Now get back into bed and I'll make you a nice mustard poultice.'

He was about to object when there was a knock at the door. He slid back underneath the eiderdowns.

'How's the patient? Where is he?'

'I'm here, boss. Please, tell her not to make me a—'

'You keep an eye on him, Monsieur Legris,' his mother called out from the kitchen. 'I went in there just now and found him lying on the floor!'

'Joseph, quick, show me your press cuttings about the St Nazaire corpse – it's very important!'

'Why? It has no bearing on our case.'

'Don't argue!'

'That's a bit rich! The other day you sent me packing. There's no knowing with you . . . All right, all right.'

He retrieved his notebook from under the pillow. Victor leafed through it and slumped on to a chair. Without saying a word, he pointed to the evening edition of *Le Passe-partout*.

'Oh! How nice of you. I asked Maman to buy it for me, but she forgot.'

'Look at this,' Victor told him.

Joseph read the article.

'So, his name was Lewis Ives, was it? A cracking mystery; I'll use it in my book – I mean it would make a good story. Inspector Lecacheur came up trumps in the end, didn't he, boss?'

Victor tried to remain unruffled, and took his time before replying calmly: 'The St Nazaire corpse isn't Lewis Ives, it's Armand de Valois.'

Joseph gasped.

'Armand de Valois? But that's impossible – he died of yellow fever in Panama, and . . . Crikey! ADV: Armand de Valois! Of course! Why didn't I think of that? But how can you be so sure, boss?'

'A minor detail put me on the trail. Now listen carefully: "The man was approximately five feet nine inches tall and aged between thirty-five and forty-five. He had dark-brown hair and a beard. His right femur being somewhat shorter than his left would have given him, when alive, a slight limp . . ."'

'I don't get it boss.'

'Armand de Valois walked with a limp.'

'No! Are you sure?'

'Positive. Madame de Valois nicknamed him "old hop along". But the disability was almost undetectable, except to the keenest eye.'

Excited by this revelation, Joseph sat up in bed.

'If the St Nazaire corpse really is Armand, then whoever killed Denise and Père Moscou wants to make it look as though he's still alive.'

'It's possible, but why?'

'To pin the crimes on him, of course!'

'Nonsense! Why go to all that trouble? Armand de Valois is officially dead and buried in Colombia. That's what everyone believes.'

'I'm trying to think . . . How about this for a theory: A.D.V. is alive and well. He has assumed the identity of some other poor fellow with a limp, that Lewis Ives for instance, so that he can be free to perpetrate his crimes. Who'd suspect someone who is dead?'

'But he wrote his initials on Père Moscou's wall. Only a complete idiot would do such a thing! No, it's too involved.'

Victor stood up and paced around the room, his hands behind his back.

'We're looking at it from the wrong angle,' Joseph said. 'The long and the short of it is all we have are theories. And theories don't prove anything.'

'Not so fast. There's something else. I'd have told you sooner only you weren't well enough. Thanks to you I found the building where the clairvoyant lived, near a panorama at the Bastille. There, I established that Armand de Valois and Lewis Ives lodged at the same hotel in Cali, and that they were both connected to this clairvoyant. Denise was right.'

Joseph tapped the paper, chanting: 'I knew it, I knew it, I knew it!'

He stopped dead and put his finger on a sentence in the newspaper that had caught his eye. Just then, Madame Pignot came in carrying a steaming tray.

'It's ready, pet! A lovely mustard poultice; it'll do you the world of good!'

'Crikey, Maman, you made me lose my train of thought!

What do you want? Oh no, not again! Help, boss!' he shrieked in a falsetto.

'Forgive me for saying so, Madame Pignot, but I doubt very much this is the appropriate treatment.'

'On the contrary, Monsieur Legris, it works wonders for a fever. With all due respect, you know nothing about such things. Lift up your shirt, you!'

Joseph obeyed, emitting squealing noises that became loud bellows as the burning hot poultice came into contact with his skin.

'You keep still. You're just like your father! He's always been a cry baby has my poor pet,' Madame Pignot observed. 'Well, I must get on. I've got to stack my baskets. I've an early start tomorrow . . . Oh, my poor aching back!'

'I will help you,' said Victor, throwing Joseph a conniving glance.

As soon as they were out of sight, Joseph peeled off the poultice and hid it under the pillow. He felt so relieved that he began to hum, blissfully: *Marie Turnerad coiffed the toffs* . . . Suddenly he broke off, his mind awash with images of his walk with Denise on Boulevard des Capucines, and the train of thought his mother had interrupted came racing back. Where had he heard or seen that name before, perhaps printed in a newspaper? Memories of the fair flashed through his mind, and the showman's cry: 'Step right up, ladies and gentlemen, and see for yourselves, the re-enactment of . . .' He felt the blood pounding in his cheeks.

'Blimey! I've got it!' he yelled.

'What's going on? Are you all right, my pet?'

Alarmed, Madame Pignot rushed in, closely followed by Victor. Joseph just had time to dive under the eiderdowns.

'It's nothing, Maman. I'm in pain. Ouch it burns! It really hurts! . . . There, are you satisfied? Now go away, will you, please. I need to talk to the boss about work.'

Madame Pignot went out, muttering to herself. 'It's not going to kill you . . . and what doesn't kill you makes you stronger.'

'Boss, at the back of one of the shelves in the study there's a stack of newspapers classified by year. Bring me the pile for 1879!'

Not knowing where this would lead, Victor did as Joseph asked. He stood in the doorway to the study for a moment to accustom his eyes to the dim light seeping in from the skylight.

Pressed up against the wall, near the door to the courtyard, the intruder followed Victor's progress, watching his every move from behind the slits of the hood and trembling with each step he took. A hand slowly reached out for a pair of gloves lying between two spiked helmets. Just as it was about to seize them, Victor tripped over a pile of books and losing his balance grabbed on to the back of a chair. The hand stopped in mid-air, gripping one of the gloves as the other fell to the floor.

'Would you like a candle, Monsieur Legris?' Joseph called out.

'No, I'm almost there.'

The intruder slipped out into the courtyard a few seconds before Victor stepped over the glove without seeing it and reached the shelves.

*

244

Crouched scrabbling through the strewn papers on his bed like a dog digging for a bone, Joseph finally found the headline he was searching for:

CAICEDONNI AFFAIR. MARIE TURNERAD CLEARED

'That's the one! I wasn't imagining things! I don't know where it'll lead, but I know I'm on to something!'

'Are you going to explain yourself?'

Joseph put his thumb over the last three letters of the name CAICEDONNI.

What does that say, boss?'

'Caicedo . . . Well, I'll be damned!'

Victor snatched the newspaper,

'Caicedonni . . . Caicedo . . . Turnerad . . . Turner,' he mumbled.

He stood up suddenly and strode out through the door, leaving Joseph squatting on the bed, staring after him.

Victor crossed the interconnecting courtyards at the far end of which stood the editorial offices of *Le Passe-partout* – a decrepit two-storey building with an adjoining print works and engraving workshop. He crossed the typesetting room where a man was manipulating the linotype. He inhaled the smell of ink and dust with pleasure. The noise was deafening. A chubby man with bulging eyes, his bowler hat tipped back on his head and sucking on the stub of an unlit cigar, was supervising the typesetter as he closed the foundry proof. Victor tapped his shoulder.

'Well, look who it is! Long time no see! How's life treating you, Monsieur Legris?' boomed Isidore Gouvier, chewing on his cigar. 'Follow me. We can't hear ourselves think in here.'

He led Victor up to the first floor into a cramped and cluttered office. He had not changed at all since they last met some months earlier, with his perennial brown suit, unflappable air and pouting bottom lip. The man's ungainliness, his deliberately ponderous way of speaking and his kindly manner made him seem more like an uneducated peasant than the first-class professional he was.

'How goes *Le Passe-partout*?' Victor enquired.

'To tell the truth, things couldn't be better. We narrowly avoided financial catastrophe thanks to the promotional inserts. We're even hiring new staff. Our circulation is increasing daily, and it takes more and more people just to keep the paper running. We're in a bit of a panic because Eudoxie Allard just left us – she's kicking her legs in the air for Zidler at the Moulin Rouge. Apparently she always had a secret passion for dancing. A fat lot of good it does us! And how is the little Maroussia? I saw her caricatures in *Gil Blas*. What a talent! I wish I could say the same for her successor. What brings you here, Monsieur Legris?'

'I need your help, Isidore. I'm looking for information about a trial that took place some ten years ago. The Caicedonni affair. Does it ring a bell?'

'I'll say it does. I was working for the secret police then. We strongly suspected the victim's mistress, a strip of a girl, pretty as a picture. But we had no proof and she was cleared. Why this interest in the case, Monsieur Legris? If I may be so bold . . . '

'I'm writing a detective novel.'

'Well, well! It's fast becoming a popular genre. And how do you think I can be of help?'

'I'd hoped to talk to one or two people who might be able to tell me something about Marie Turnerad.'

'Easy. I'll look in my files. Are you on the telephone?'

'Yes, at the bookshop, 18 Rue des Saints-Pères.'

'I'll ring you there tomorrow.'

He accompanied Victor downstairs.

'You'll have to excuse me, I've ordered a carriage. Shall I drop you somewhere? We could talk on the way.'

They hurried out into Rue Jean-Jacques Rousseau.

'Cour des Comptes, Quai d'Orsay!' Isidore called to the cabman.

It took Victor a second to register the name of their destination.

'Cour des Comptes?' he repeated, in what he hoped was a nonchalant manner.

'Yes. They've just exhumed a body there. You'll read about it in the paper. I'm going back to interview our good Inspector Lecacheur, who's in charge of the investigation. The nation's copper has developed a sudden interest in archaeology – he's busy digging.'

'A man's been murdered?'

'A woman. Two kids were rolling in the grass when they came across an umbrella. Attached to it was the hand of a blonde woman still in her prime, thirty or thereabouts according to the pathologist. The kids got the fright of their lives; they'll not be going cavorting in the outdoors again in a hurry! I happened to be at police headquarters when the news came through. An hour later I was on the scene. It wasn't a pretty sight, I can tell you. She had received a violent blow to the back of the head. I reckon she's grande bourgeoise, her clothes are a dead giveaway: astrakhan coat and a dress from La Religieuse, a shop in Rue Tronchet specialising in mourning dress. We'll soon find out who she is when we look through their accounts. She was married, wore a wedding ring. Just to put my mind at rest I paid a visit to the Bureau of Missing Persons. An employee there by the name of Bordenave Jules remembers a fellow coming in, saying he was concerned about a lady friend of his whose husband had died in Panama. Since he wasn't a relation, Bordenave sent him packing. Those pen-pushers should be made to dig up potatoes for the rest of their days, useless creatures! If he'd done his job properly, we'd have this chap, no doubt the woman's lover and possibly her murderer: "I loved her so much I had to kill her!" Cracking title, don't you think?'

'I'll get out here,' Victor said in a hoarse voice as Pont Royal came into view.

'Come back and see me some time and we'll talk about the old days. Give my love to Tasha and tell her she's a traitor. By the way, Monsieur Legris! I'm looking for a secretary who knows how to type and keep her mouth shut. You don't happen to know anyone fitting that description do you?'

Victor's eyes filled with tears as he walked along the quayside as though in a trance. He felt a profound sense of fatigue, and despite the mild weather he was shivering. Odette was dead, laid out within those ruined walls. Why? He needed to speak to Lecacheur urgently, to tell him Père Moscou was certainly the murderer. He slowed down, ready to cross the bridge. Across the Seine he could make out the imposing outline of the abandoned building. Never before had the Cour des Comptes reminded him quite so much of Bluebeard's castle. 'Don't! You may regret it,' an inner voice whispered. He imagined Lecacheur looking at him quizzically. He won't believe your story it doesn't hold water, like Joseph said, all you have are theories.

Having managed to rein in his emotions, he found himself walking up Rue du Louvre. Jostled by the crowd, he ended up in the middle of a thicket of masks and false noses. The streets were thronging, the cafés stormed and all the seats taken. In Place des Victoires he stumbled upon a parade of Harlequins and Punches followed by carriages decked with flowers and full of washerwomen showering the frenzied hordes with streamers and jeering at them. Behind them came the floats carrying the orchestras that were to play dance music that evening at Place de l'Opéra.

Victor, his head spinning, couldn't see a way out. Suddenly he was hemmed in by a troupe of beggars from the city's seamiest quarter. They danced round him in an infernal circle, some dressed to look like pilgrims, others pretending to be epileptics – using soap to make them froth at the mouth, tricksters rattling their loaded die and cripples hobbling on crutches.

'He who wears no disguise is obliged to pay the price! Spare us some change, sir, spare us some change!'

They only let him go after he'd thrown them a handful of coins.

Tasha looked at the clock again. She had refused dinner at the Soleil d'Or because she was supposed to be spending the evening with Victor. And here she was still waiting after more than an hour while Germaine's lovingly prepared dish of hare in morel sauce went cold. The telephone rang. She waited, thinking Kenji might answer, and then assuming he hadn't heard it went down, leaving the door ajar to light her way on the stairs.

'Tasha? It's me. I'm dreadfully sorry. The streets are so crowded that the carriages are blocked.'

'Where are you ringing from?'

'From a café on Rue de Rivoli.'

'I'll wait for you. Gouvier telephoned. He wants you to meet him at the Jean Nicot at ten o'clock tomorrow morning.'

She walked slowly back up the stairs, deep in thought. She was pensive. What was he roaming the city for when he had said he had letters to write? Why was he meeting Isidore? She suspected him of continuing his investigation, but what could she do about it? There was nothing more deadly than an ultimatum where love was concerned. She stopped on the landing. Was she imagining things or was that laughter coming from Kenji's apartment? She heard a woman's voice call out: 'Make sure the water's nice and hot!'

And then the sound of the bathtub filling up.

CHAPTER 10

THE rain had been falling all morning and the Jean Nicot was filled with typographers and journalists. Installed at the far end of the bar, cigar in hand, Isidore Gouvier was sipping a glass of cognac. Victor hung his dripping raincoat over the back of a chair and ordered a coffee.

'Sorry to have made you come out in this weather, Monsieur Legris. I tried to ring earlier to save you from getting wet, but no one answered.'

'The bookshop is closed – my associate has taken the day off.

He'd had the pleasure of glimpsing Kenji that morning, dressed in a pinstripe suit and looking up at the sky with consternation before running, boater in hand, over to his carriage. Victor suspected him of having a tryst with the woman who wore *Cuir de Russie* perfume at a restaurant on the banks of the Marne River. If this were true, their romance was in danger of becoming waterlogged.

'My files didn't bear much fruit, I'm afraid. Here, I've written down the name and address of one of Marie Turnerad's character witnesses during the trial. I can't guarantee she still lives there or even that she's alive. I warn you, it's in the back of beyond.'

'Thank you – it's something at least. By the way, has the body at the Cour des Comptes been identified yet?'

'No. The corpse is in rather bad shape. The worms have had a field day with it – fertile ground around there. Not a pretty sight. But there's more. They've dug up a second body. An old man who'd lived there for years, a certain Père Moscou. His skull was smashed in too, more recently it seems. The cops are scratching their heads over it. This should be of interest to you, Monsieur Legris. It'd make a good opening to your murder mystery.'

'Oh, I prefer to draw on crimes that have already been solved,' Victor blurted out, rather too quickly.

His hands were shaking and he placed them on his thighs. Gouvier watched him closely.

'You're upset, Monsieur Legris. There's no need to be ashamed; I still find it hard to stomach and I've been in the business thirty years. You need a pick me up. Waiter, two cognacs!'

Shattered by Odette's death, Victor had spent part of the night imagining various scenarios, all leading to one conclusion: that Joseph had been duped, Père Moscou was still alive, he had murdered Odette and then decided to disappear. Unfortunately, with the news of Moscou's death this theory had collapsed.

'I must leave you, Monsieur Legris, duty calls. Good luck until I see you next. Keep me informed.'

Gouvier shouldered his way through the groups of people. The moment he opened the door the rain clouds evaporated and the sun glistened on the pavements.

'Sun's out. Back to work!' shouted the journalist.

The Louvre-Belleville omnibus bounced nonchalantly along, pulled by three bays. Its twenty-eight seats were all occupied and people were standing on the stairs. Relegated to the upper deck and flanked by a large lady loaded with baskets and a bearded man with hiccups, Victor felt as if he were venturing into the heart of a foreign country, for the modest fee of fifteen centimes.

Rows of old houses, their upper floors overhanging the pavements, gave way to an area of wasteland where a donkey was grazing, a goatherd watched over his flock and a dairy farm advertised its milk straight from the 'American prairies', a vast expanse of bare grass between Rue de Bellevue and Rue Manin where the gypsum quarries had been.

The thousands of labourers, employees and artisans wending their way to work in the centre of Paris had been replaced by a bevy of housewives wearing shawls, their string bags crammed with vegetables fiercely bargained for at the stalls. Children clattered behind the heavy vehicle in their clogs, shouting with glee as if the circus had come to town. A little girl tripped over a paving stone and a white puddle spilled out of her tin cup, instantly lapped up by a dog.

The horses stopped at 25 Rue de Belleville.

'End of the line!' cried the conductor.

'Yes, but I'm not home yet,' grumbled the large woman as she gathered all her baskets. 'When're they going to give us that flipping funicular they promised?'

'They promise us the moon, and what do we get? Nothing!' cried the bearded man between hiccups. 'Hey! Stop pushing, will you!'

Victor made his way down the stairs. Someone jostled him and he turned round and saw a schoolboy hurrying away.

All along the narrow asphalt path that ran between the fronts of the houses, women and old men sat on chairs con-versing as they peeled potatoes, knitted or played cards. The calls of the different door-to-door merchants overlapped: 'Twopence a pint for my cockles!' 'Chickweed for your birdies!' 'Rabbit skins, clothes for sale!' The gardens, courtyards and wells gave the area a village atmosphere, and as Victor searched for Rue Ramponeau, where Gouvier's witness Francine Blavette lived, he regretted that Tasha wasn't with him. She would have loved it. He promised himself he'd come back and take some photographs before the little houses were mown down to make way for the funicular. Baudelaire had understood when he said: 'The nature of a town changes more quickly, alas, than the human heart!'

Not only was Madame Blavette the picture of health, she was also at home which, she announced to Victor, was lucky for him since at this time of day she would normally be out promenading, in cavalier fashion.

'Pardon the expression but you see I visit a lot of theatre people; if I'd had any talent, my dream would have been to play all four musketeers. Female roles don't interest me.'

She invited him in to her two cramped rooms on the third floor at the end of a corridor in which some chickens were clucking. Shortish, plump and attractive, she was approaching forty and had a strong Burgundy accent. As soon as Victor said the name Marie Turnerad she opened up like a tap.

'She lived downstairs with her grandmother, a sweet woman who wrecked her eyes embroidering place mats to sell in the markets. I saw Marie grow up. Lord, was she pretty! Whatever she lacked in social standing she more than made up for with her looks! She had that certain something that attracted men, if you know what I mean. Rosalie, her granny, soon realised it – the girl was already turning heads when she was twelve. She needed keeping an eye on, which is why Rosalie was quick to apprentice her to a friend who ran a milliner's shop over at Batignolles.'

'Anatole! Anatole in a hole!' a tinny voice screeched from the adjoining room.

'Put a sock in it, Mélingue!' shouted Madame Blavette.

When Victor looked perplexed, she explained: 'It's a mynah bird. I named him after Gustave Mélingue,[1] who began his career with us before working with Frédérick Lemaître and triumphing in Paris where he made a fortune in his role . . .'

'Anatole, in a hole!' repeated the mynah bird.

'Shut your trap, Mélingue! My neighbour taught him that ditty – a comedian who's on at the Tambourin in Montmartre with Madame Mirka and Alfreda. I'm just thankful they haven't taught him their latest old chestnut, "I've got a bird in my corset"!'

'Are you an actress?'

'You must be joking! I've been working at Cour Lesage at Théâtre de Belleville for the last twenty years, usherette first then box office. If you haven't already you must come and see *Les Misérables*.'

'Rabbit! Rabbit!'

'Pipe down, chatterbox, or I'll pull your feathers out!'

'So, Marie Turnerad worked at Bat . . . At a milliner's shop?'

'She didn't last long there. She caught the eye of a conjurer who took her on. They did their act on the Grands Boulevards. But they fell out and the girl went to do the shampooing at Lenthéric's. And then she had the misfortune of meeting Dante Caicedonni, an actor. Oh, not one of the greats, just cameo roles. He started off as a prompter. They met here, in this house. I ironed his shirts for him and she came up one day to borrow some sugar.'

'He was murdered, wasn't he?'

'I'm coming to that. It was love at first sight, though I never understood what she saw in him, apart from his Florentine beauty – and it must be said he was a handsome devil – but he was a gambler. The girl paid for his bed and board, all out of her wages, and he had expensive tastes, did Dante. He had to look spruce so he could seduce the society ladies. Oh, he lived the high life all right, with all his gallivanting! He received his lovers at a boarding house on Boulevard Saint-Michel – we learnt that later. The same went for his debts – Marie paid them all off so she and her grandmother had nothing left, if I told you . . .'

'Later. Do you mean after he died?'

'He was found stabbed. They immediately suspected Marie because they discovered a bloody handkerchief with her initials, *MT*, embroidered on it near Dante's body. She was arrested, but denied the charge. Unluckily for her, on the same day as the murder she cut herself with a razor and had to have the tip of her finger amputated. The police looked no further, maintaining that she must've done it when she wielded the murder weapon. But she had a good lawyer and the coppers had no solid evidence. And Dante hung around with a band of lowlifes all of whom had reasons to want to him dead. Witnesses, including myself and the magician, were called, to testify to Marie's good character and devotion. In the end she was so young and pretty the jury disregarded the prosecution's summing up and acquitted her. The week she was released Rosalie died, the excitement was too much for her heart . . . So Marie packed her belongings in a bundle. We were crying as we said goodbye. "I can't stay here, Francine, there are too many memories. It tears my soul . . ."'

'Anatole! Anatole, in a . . .'

Without saying a word, Madame Blavette stood up and went over to close the door.

'Did you ever see her again?' Victor asked.

'Never.'

'Do you know what became of her?'

'She went back to that conjurer of hers. They got an act together, which played for a few months, and then just like that they decided to try their luck in America. Marie sent me a note saying she'd write. I'm still waiting. No, I don't know what became of her. It's been a long time – ten years, or more.'

'What was the name of the illusionist?'

'Médéric Delcourt. He used to play at the Théâtre Robert Houdin[2], 8 Boulevard des Italiens. Funnily enough, one of my neighbours took her son there recently. The company changed hands two years ago and now they're putting on shows using automatons, quite entertaining, they say. She showed me the programme and I saw the name Baptiste Delcourt. Perhaps he's a relation . . .'

Victor thanked Madame Blavette effusively and promised to

send her a signed copy of his book, *Notorious Crimes*, as soon as it was published.

His jaunt to Belleville had left him hungry, but he had no time to waste. Having staunched his appetite with a couple of croissants dunked in coffee, he made his way to the Grands Boulevards, feeling like a peasant whisked away from his quiet village and plonked in the heart of the great metropolis. The clatter of clogs on the wooden sidewalks, the cries of the cabmen and street vendors bawling out the latest popular songs – a myriad sounds assaulted his ears, and at the tables outside the cafés the idlers sat watching the passers-by stroll in front of shop windows and theatres.

He stood for a moment under the awning of the Théâtre Robert Houdin. There was a matinee on the billing, and a quick glance at the nearest clock told him he had an hour and a half before it began. He climbed the two flights of stairs to the box office. A young man in shirtsleeves was whistling and pinning up a poster.

'We're not open yet,' he said.

'I know. I'd like to speak to Monsieur Delcourt, Monsieur Baptiste Delcourt.'

'Is he expecting you?'

'No. I'm writing a book about magic and I was hoping to interview him.'

'You'll need to speak to the manager, Monsieur Georges Méliès, about that. I don't know if Monsieur Delcourt will agree to see you – he's rehearsing in that room over there.'

Victor entered a dark hall. A screen flickered and came alive. A train chugged by and a dove took flight, then a level crossing lifted a goat up in the air.

'An ingenious use of plates of coloured glass, giving the impression of movement,' Victor reflected.

'What in God's name are you doing in here?' a voice protested from the back of the room.

Someone pulled aside a curtain and Victor squinted, dazzled by the light. He saw a grey-haired man standing next to a tripod with a magician's lantern attached to it.

'I'm looking for Monsieur Baptiste Delcourt.'

'I am he.'

'Madame Blavette sent me. I'm writing a book on the ten most notorious murder trials of the last ten years and I wanted to devote a chapter to the Marie Turnerad affair. The man she emigrated to America with was called Médéric Delcourt. Is he a relative of yours?'

'Médéric the Great was my stage name twelve years ago. Now it's Baptiste. Listen, Monsieur whatever-your-name-is, that's all in the past now. I've suffered too much to want to rake it up again.'

'I understand. Forgive me; I was being untruthful just now. I'm not really writing a book. My name is Victor Legris and I urgently need to speak to Marie. She's here in Paris. I can tell you no more, but I need your help. She's in grave danger. I must know more about her past in order to be able to protect her.'

'Are you a policeman?'

'No, I assure you I'm not. Why?'

'Because I don't believe a word of your tall story – it sounds like something out of a penny dreadful. In grave danger, you say? So what! If you're her latest conquest, then I pity you. Half an hour is all I can spare, sir. Come along, you can buy me a drink.'

Baptiste Delcourt was probably in his fifties. His straight grey hair fell in front of his glasses and his cheeks were hollowed with deep lines. He rested his elbows on the table and recounted his story, slowly and with great difficulty.

'You only love like that once in a lifetime; I'm sure you haven't the faintest idea what I'm talking about. As soon as I set eyes on her I knew I was lost. I should have run a mile, but I wasn't strong enough. She became my assistant. I hardly dared look at her, let alone touch her. But one day I couldn't help myself and I kissed her. Oh, I didn't try to force her. She pushed me away, said I was too old. And it was true: I was old enough to be her father. She left and went to work for a hairdresser. Every spare moment I had, I spent standing outside the salon trying to catch a glimpse of her through the window. I would wait for her to come out. And then Dante came along, and the murder. Do you know about all that?'

'More or less.'

'I wrote and sent gifts to her before and after the trial. I testified to her good character. When they released her, she agreed to come and work with me again. She had nowhere else to turn; her grandmother was dead. I showed her the ropes – the woman sawn in half, the magic wand, the bottomless wardrobe,

260

all the usual tricks. She was a fast learner. I taught her the secrets of the quick-change artist too. Our show enjoyed a modest success and an impresario offered us a tour in the United States. You can imagine how keen Marie was to leave the country that had ruined her life, and she urged me to accept. And there was money in it too. We sailed in October 1880 on board *L'Amerique*, coincidentally on the same boat as Sarah Bernhardt, who was also going on tour. President Lincoln's wife was there too, and we would occasionally cross paths – an unforgettable experience. But the real reason my memory of that voyage is so vivid is because Marie agreed to give herself to me for the first time.'

He went quiet and wiped his glasses, then replaced them on his nose. He hadn't touched his drink.

'I was happy. The world was my oyster: New York, Boston, Cincinnati, Baton Rouge, New Orleans, then Mexico, Tampico and Vera Cruz. We ended up in Panama, Colombia, just in time to witness the first pickaxe blow that launched the inter-oceanic canal works. Mademoiselle Ferdinande de Lesseps, the canal builder's daughter, invited us to the celebrations. Tell me, where is Marie?'

'I don't know. I was hoping you might be able to tell me.'

'I have to get back. Will you walk with me?'

They crossed the foyer, where the young man in shirtsleeves was setting out the chairs.

'If you're fond of magic, sir, you mustn't miss Cagliostro's mirror in the interval. You'll see your face transformed. And then, it's a secret . . . a real surprise! Monsieur Méliès is a true genius,' the young man said to Victor.

'All right, Michou, save your breath; he's with me. Come in, Monsieur Legris, I must get dressed.'

Baptiste Delcourt slipped into a black suit and began applying powder to his face.

'Where was I? Oh yes, Panama, a terrible climate, unbearably humid, and full of insects. The ants . . . As for the town, it was nothing special. The whole place had burnt to the ground two years before. There were dozens of ruined churches and monasteries that had been turned into shops and barracks, army depots, and a cathedral even uglier than the one in Mexico City. There were shacks and huts where the blacks, mulattos, mestizos, Indians, people from China and India lived — whole legions of cheap labour. And prefabricated houses imported from the United States popped up like toadstools along the route of the future canal. We had shows lined up in Colon, Cali, Medellin and Bogota and then I fell ill and had to cancel. We holed up in Tumaco, a small island to the south of the country, away from the swamps. I became delirious, I lost weight. I nearly died. Indeed, I don't know how I survived. Three months later, when I was fully recovered, Marie was calling herself Señora Palmyra Caicedo and . . .'

'Palmyra?'

Baptiste stopped fastening his floppy bow tie round his neck and laughed.

'What a name! She fancied herself an Empress and you should have seen her holding court.'

'Zénobie, queen of Palmyre,' Victor said under his breath.

'I beg your pardon?'

'Nothing. I was thinking aloud. Please go on.'

'She'd become a kept woman. I should have known. I mean, after that Italian . . . But I loved her, and it's true that love is blind. She seemed pleased to see me well again. She introduced me to her protector, Don Belisario Cortes, a wealthy tobacco planter who owned a hacienda near Cartagena, and told me she was leaving with him. What she most longed for was respectability. "I want people to call me Madame." I made a last desperate bid and offered to marry her. She laughed in my face. I was too old, too sentimental, too nice for her. I came back to France at the end of '82. After a few setbacks I managed to pick up my old act again here in this theatre. I changed my first name to give the illusion of a fresh start.'

'Did you ever hear from Marie?'

'She wrote to me once, about five or six years ago. She'd just bought a hotel in Cali, Hotel Rosalie — I believe that was her grandmother's name. It was a French establishment, offering French cuisine and French wines. She asked me to send her some prints to decorate the rooms — those dreadful daubs they hang above the beds. She knew exactly what she wanted. Like the one her grandmother had on Rue Ramponeau, a picture of the . . .'

'Virgin Mary,' Victor finished the sentence.

'So you are from the police! What has she got mixed up in now? No, I'd rather not know.'

'Could you describe the pictures to me?'

'They were identical. She sent me a colour sketch of a blue Madonna standing in front of a grotto, her hands clasped together. She wanted a dozen of them. I knew a little artisan who turned out pictures of General Boulanger and Opéra

Garnier and I placed an order with him and then sent them on to Marie. That's the last I heard of her. The show is about to start. I won't see you out.'

'Psst, sir,' the young man in shirtsleeves caught Victor's attention as he passed. 'If you put my name in your book, I'll tell you how Monsieur Méliès makes the audience believe Alcofrisbas the magician is running after a skeleton that's stolen his head. I'm sure he wouldn't mind if . . .'

But Victor had already disappeared through the doorway.

As he drifted through the tide of passers-by, Victor felt a vague yet powerful sense of danger. He turned round several times without knowing quite what it was he expected to find, and took a few deep breaths in the hope this might dispel the uneasiness that was dogging him. The two stories he had just heard melded in his mind. The charming Marie Turnerad had changed into the cynical Palmyra Caicedo: angel or devil? He was haunted by the feeling that if he didn't solve this mystery soon there would certainly be another victim. Who can help me? Whom can I turn to? Why not a medium? Why not Numa? You have doubts about spiritualism but in your heart you would like to believe.

He rang the bell five times, but no one came to the door. Angrily, he seized the knocker and rapped loudly until the door to the apartment opened a fraction, and he glimpsed the head of a young girl in a white bonnet above the safety chain.

'It's no use insisting, sir. Madame says Monsieur Winner left for England yesterday.'

'Do you know when he'll be back?'

'Not before the summer.'

'How may I contact him?'

'You'll need to speak to the concierge – he probably forwards his post.'

Victor hesitated for a moment then began, dolefully, to walk down the four flights of stairs. He was just reaching the first-floor landing when his foot caught on something and he plunged headlong, grabbing the banister rail to stop his fall. He managed to stay upright for a split second but the momentum carried him forward and he fell flat on his face, stunned and breathless. A succession of faces flashed before his eyes: Numa, Marie, Palmyra and *The Madonna in Blue*, leering masks, fugitives from the Fêtes des Fous.

After what seemed like an eternity, he managed to stand up, using the wall to steady himself. His knees felt weak and he walked back up the steps to make sure he hadn't twisted his ankle. He swivelled round on the first-floor landing. At eye level, written in large, red letters were the words:

DESIST! A.D.V.

His legs turned to jelly and he stood for a moment at the top of the stairs looking down at the piece of wire he had ripped out of the wall with his foot. He stooped and picked up a nail that had traces of plaster on it, and twiddled it in his fingers. He could hear a distant conversation echoing in the stairwell, the sound of stampeding feet and children's' laughter. A woman's voice rang out:

'Paul, Henri, stop racing about! Just wait till I catch you!'

Brought back to reality by the voices, it occurred to him that his assailant could not be far away. He grabbed the piece of wire, raced back down the stairs and out into the Rue d'Assas. A carriage was picking up a fare close by, the door closed and it moved away, turning into Rue Madame. Victor walked a few paces and then stopped, out of breath, his view of the street ahead blocked by an upholsterer who had appeared from his right carrying a load of furniture.

He collapsed on to a bench opposite a bakery, exhausted. This wasn't an attempt on his life: it was a warning, meant to scare him off. The murderer hasn't found *The Madonna in Blue*, or he'd have scarpered long ago. He stared at the piece of wire in his hand and racked his brains, trying to think where Denise might have hidden the print. Among Tasha's canvases? He would have found it by now, he'd examined them one by one during the move. At a loss, he found himself staring at the bakery windows and then at the piece of wire he was unthinkingly twisting in his fingers. An idea emerged, like the image on a plate in the developing bath, vague at first then gradually becoming clearer. He leapt to his feet. The mirror! I forgot to look at Tasha's mirror!

Monsieur and Madame Ladoucette were in the middle of dinner when Victor appeared in the doorway to their lodge.

'Forgive me for bothering you. I seem to have mislaid the

key to the new lock. Would you lend me your master key?'

Madame Ladoucette leant over and shouted in her husband's ear: 'Aristide, the master key.'

Monsieur Ladoucette wiped his mouth, put down his napkin and pushed his chair back.

'It's not that I like climbing all those stairs, Monsieur Legris, it's a question of discipline. I mount the guard at the outpost, like I did in Sedan, and I won't hand that key over to a soul. The master key is to the concierge what the rifle is to the artilleryman!'

'Don't behave like a fool, Aristide. What about your rheumatism? It's Monsieur Legris, you can trust him.'

'I don't want to get an earful from that German landlady. They won the war – that's a fact – we can't change it. There's always a loser in a war. But there's one thing they can't take away from us and that's our sense of duty!'

'Come now, Aristide,' Madame Ladoucette protested. 'Mademoiselle Becker is a lovely landlady, and anyway she's lived in France for years.'

'All the same. Shall we mount the attack, Monsieur Legris? Choupette will go with us so I can come back and finish my boiled beef and you can take your time. When you're ready to leave, all you have to say is, "Private Choupette, report for duty!" She'll understand, and she'll come and fetch me like a good little soldier so I can lock the room. You know, we call them dumb animals, but they're not as dumb as all that. Madame Ladoucette and I went to Fernando's Circus yesterday, and you should see what they can make those horses do!'

They arrived on the sixth floor and Monsieur Ladoucette opened the door for Victor.

'You know what to say then, Monsieur Legris: "Private Choupette, report for duty!" and I'll come and lock up.'

Victor waited for the concierge to leave before going straight over to the cracked mirror hanging next to the recess containing the bookshelves. He lifted it off the wall. Nothing. How stupid he had been to trust his intuition! And yet, since he was there, why not have one more look around, just to be sure? He gave a bitter laugh. Where to begin? The famous piece of evidence wasn't simply going to appear out of a hat. If you want to compete with Monsieur Lecoq, be meticulous. He started by looking through Tasha's trunks, though without much conviction, and while doing so plunged his hands into her petticoats and corsets, and delighted in the softness of a silk stocking. Then he pulled out the dresser, maybe *The Madonna in Blue* was concealed behind it. All he found was dust. He groped under the sink, felt the mattress, tapped on the walls to see if they sounded hollow, indicating a hiding place. Intrigued, Choupette watched, wagging her tail.

'Come on, dog, sniff it out and I'll give you a bone!'

But Choupette contented herself with frantically scratching her ear.

'There's nothing here. That's it, I've had enough.'

He was perspiring.

'Choupette, go and fetch Papa! No, that's not it. Private Choupette report for duty! Is that it? I've forgotten. Never mind, we'll have to go down. Come on, out!'

As Victor shooed the dog in the direction of the door he stepped on a frame and trapped the end of his shoe between the crosspiece and the canvas. The dog gave a bark that sounded like a hoot of laughter.

'Shut up, pooch!'

Choupette scuttled out into the corridor, head bowed and tail between her legs.

Puzzled, Victor contemplated his trapped shoe. The frame was heavy, it was solid. Bending over to free himself, he remained in a stooped position, pondering.

What if . . . ? No! That would be too easy.

He hopped over, grabbed a book and tried to slip it under the crosspiece, then thought for a moment and put the book aside.

Yes! It has to be hidden in here!

He lifted his leg and brought it crashing down with all his might. The frame exploded and the canvas crumpled.

He rummaged excitedly through the debris.

As he got up, he thought he saw a shadow in the doorway. Instinctively, he rushed over, arms outstretched, just in time to crash into the door as it slammed shut from the other side. He turned the handle, gently at first then more forcefully. It wouldn't open. He stood there, feeling foolish. He was locked in. He put his face up to the door and called out.

'Choupette . . . Choupette . . . Hey! Is anyone there?'

He rattled the handle frantically.

Not knowing how to occupy her mind, Tasha examined the sepia drawing hanging above the bed. Daphne Legris had certainly been very beautiful, and yet how melancholy she looked. Victor was very like her – except for his nose, which he must have inherited from his father. Curiously, he never mentioned his father. She thought of her own parents. She'd lost the only photograph she had of them together. When would she see her mother Djina and her sister Ruhlea again? The Ukraine was so far away! And her father, Pinkus – where was he now? She glanced at the drawing again. No. It was no use trying to be interested in the portrait, she was too anxious. 'He was supposed to pick me up at Bibulus, I know something's wrong!' She went down to the street through the main building and walked briskly over to Rue Visconti. It took Madame Pignot ages to open the door.

'Oh, it's you! One is more careful at this time in the evening, especially a poor defenceless woman like me with a sick person to—'

'Might Joseph know where Monsieur Legris is?'

'Pet, have you seen your boss?'

Joseph hoisted himself up from under the eiderdowns that were almost suffocating him.

'He came round yesterday afternoon to bring your cart back. Is that you, Mademoiselle Tasha? Don't fret. He must have been detained looking at a collection. I'm sure he won't be long.'

'What a good boy,' said Madame Pignot, accompanying Tasha to the door. 'Sick as he is, he still tries to put your mind at rest, just like his father – the blind leading the one-eyed. I'll walk with you part of the way.'

Joseph took advantage of his mother's departure and pounced on his clothes, which lay neatly folded at the end of the bed. He slipped them on hurriedly, rolled his nightshirt in a ball and stuffed it under the pillow with the poultices.

He knew Victor well and sensed his absence must have something to do with the case. 'I should let him stew – that'd teach him to leave me out of his investigations.' He got back into bed and pulled the eiderdowns up under his chin.

Kenji stepped out of the carriage, almost ruefully. It was so mild out he would happily have continued his evening ride. He strolled along the pavement outside the bookshop slumbering behind its wooden shutters. He was pleased with his day and savoured every moment of it: dawn at the Gare du Nord; Iris's pale yellow dress and white parasol standing out against the smoky platform and beside her the porter bearing her heavy trunk. The journey to Saint-Mandé and their arrival at Mademoiselle Bontemp's boarding house, the wild garden where the early hyacinths were sprouting fierce blue buds, the bright room, simply and tastefully furnished. He felt a rush of pleasure as he recalled Iris opening one by one the gifts scattered over the bed, and her cry of delight when she saw the dress the colour of Bengal rose with the little azure lace hat garlanded with primroses. 'It's sheer madness!' She had changed into the frock at once, and put on the *Jasmin de Provence* perfume purchased at La Reine des Abeilles. They had taken lunch at a restaurant near the lake. Throughout the meal, alternately jealous and proud, he had shot sidelong glances at a young man who was clearly bewitched by his companion. They had spent the afternoon strolling in the grass in the Bois de Vincennes, building their plans for the future.

As he walked along the passageway to his apartment he

heard a faint noise coming from Victor's rooms. Ought he to make his presence known? What if Tasha opened the door? He hesitated, deciding to change into his dressing gown first.

The scent of *Cuir de Russie* pervaded his rooms and he opened the windows to air them. He could still picture Ninon lying on the bed, naked but for her mid-length gloves. Undoubtedly the contentment he had been feeling all day was as much due to her as to Iris. He was at one with life, ready to share this blissful feeling, and when he heard another sound from Victor's rooms, he made up his mind to knock on the door. There was no answer. He waited a moment then desisted, not wishing to intrude. And yet someone was moving about in the apartment. He was seized by an irrational fear. Might it be a burglar?

He cautiously opened the door. The gas lamps were lit. He moved towards the dining room and saw a figure crowned with red hair lying motionless on the floor. Tasha! He rushed to her side, but before he could even reach out his hand he was suffocated by a piece of cloth pressed to his face. He felt himself sinking into a quicksand reeking of chloroform.

Feeling queasy in the stuffy carriage, Victor leant out of the window. Under the stark light of the street-lamps the passers-by came into focus for a moment before turning into shadows again, like whoever had locked him in Tasha's room. He would still be there if it hadn't been for old Ladoucette, who was worried when Choupette didn't appear and had gone up and found her locked in the water closet. Alerted by Victor's cries, he freed him next, swearing he'd lock the little joker who was responsible for this in a Mazas cell.[3]

Victor rapped on the glass and ordered the driver to take him to Rue Visconti. There was something he needed to clarify.

Joseph was asleep, snoring with his mouth open. Madame Pignot gave Victor permission to look through the newspapers in the study.

'Just make sure you leave them as you found them. My pet is even fussier than his father, and that's saying something! And then you'd do well to hurry home; Mademoiselle Tasha's having kittens about you.'

He nodded, and picked up the lamp from the night table. Joseph opened one eye, thought of offering to help him, but changed his mind. Never in his life had he been so hot.

Victor had no trouble finding the newspaper, which was sitting on top of the pile. As he moved under the skylight to read it, he felt something soft underfoot and, looking down, thought he saw a scrunched up animal with claw-like legs. He shuddered and recoiled in fright. He'd been terrified of spiders since he was a child and this looked like a huge one. 'No, it can't be. It's the size of a crab!' He overcame his revulsion and bent down, chuckling with relief when he realised it was only a glove.

The dining room! He must go through the canvases again, one by one. Goodness, there were as many as in the galleries of the French school at the Louvre! He gave up, disheartened. He'd examined them all and found nothing – it was maddening. A noise behind him caused him to turn round just as a raised cane, wielded by a schoolboy wearing a cap and uniform, was about to come down on his head. Instinctively, he lifted his arm to protect himself. Just then someone grabbed his assailant firmly from behind. The cane fell to the floor and Victor pounced on it, sending it skittering under the table. He leapt up and ran to help Joseph who was trying with difficulty to immobilise the struggling young man. Dodging a kick, Victor aimed a slap at the boy, whose cap went flying, revealing a thick braid. The scene froze like an image in one of Baptiste Delcourt's projections.

'Delighted to make your acquaintance, Marie Turnerad, alias Ninon Delarme,' said Victor, out of breath. 'I've heard so much about you. Joseph, take the curtain cord and fasten her hands.'

'Marie Turnerad? How did you know, boss?' Joseph quizzed Victor, as he did what he'd been asked.

'He knows nothing,' said Ninon.

'Don't be so sure. Sit down – you must be tired after all your activity. Help me, will you, Joseph.'

They tied her to the back of the chair. She had stopped trying to resist and was looking at them mockingly. Victor walked straight over to the sideboard and, crouching down, slid out his nude portrait. He turned it over and removed a rectangular wooden object wedged behind the canvas. Joseph gasped as Victor waved *The Madonna in Blue* in Ninon's face.

'This is what you were looking for, isn't it?'

She shrugged, smiling.

'What a pity for you that in her distress poor Denise hid it behind the one canvas I didn't want exhibited. Otherwise you'd have found it by now and you'd be . . . Where would you be, Palmyra Caicedo? Or should I call you Zénobie Turner?'

'I can't keep up with you, boss!' cried Joseph.

Ninon's smile broadened.

'You're very good, Monsieur Legris. I like that. I'm glad I didn't disfigure you. I see you are all in one piece. You looked the worse for wear when you came out of that building on Rue d'Assas. You chased after my carriage, no doubt thinking I was getting away. But you were mistaken. I was spying on you. After turning down Rue Madame, I ordered the cabman to go back up Rue de Fleurus and park near the bench you were sitting on. I didn't want to lose you; you're so unpredictable. When you hailed a carriage, I followed you to Rue Notre-Dame-de-Lorette. I had a double of Tasha's key and I improvised to gain time. I locked you in so that I could search your apartment. Unfortunately, it's like a railway station in here – there's no chance of any peace.'

Victor, suddenly anxious, became aware again of the strange smell he'd noticed when he arrived.

'Kenji?' he called out.

'Don't worry about him – he's sleeping. So is Tasha.'

'What have you done to them!' he roared.

'Just a spot of chloroform. I dragged them into your room. They look so sweet lying there side by side on the carpet.'

'Go and see, Joseph!' ordered Victor.

'I'll make the most of this interlude to put you right, Monsieur Legris. I've known the whereabouts of the *Madonna* since the day I helped Tasha fetch her paintings from the framer. So you see I could easily have killed her and taken back what was mine, but I dislike violence. And then the gallant Monsieur Legris offered to store his beloved's paintings here! All I needed to do to gain entry was to seduce Monsieur Mori, which I did, thoroughly – men really are the same the world over. I thought I'd be able to come in here that night, but I was unpleasantly surprised to find the door locked.'

Victor cast a critical eye over the *Madonna*.

'You don't expect me to believe it was the picture's artistic worth that compelled you to carry out this slaughter, do you?'

'What slaughter? Explain yourself, Monsieur Legris.'

'Come now, Ninon, don't take me for a fool. You saved your neck ten years ago but you won't escape justice this time. You played and lost. That's life.'

Joseph came back looking pale.

'She was telling the truth, boss. They're out cold. I'll go and sprinkle some water on their faces.'

'I didn't murder Dante!' Ninon exclaimed. 'I'm innocent – they released me. What do you know about life? You were born with a silver spoon in your mouth. I come from the back streets, miles from the fancy neighbourhoods. Life was a struggle, and just when I had my head above water they threw me in prison, dragged me through the courts. I lost everything in a few months!'

'I know. They charged you because you had a cut on your hand. But this time it's different. You're guilty and you've left a clue,' Victor said, pulling a glove out of his pocket.

'That's one of the gloves I picked up at the Cour des

Comptes!' cried Joseph, walking in holding a damp cloth. 'I wondered what you were doing in the study, boss. Where's the other one?'

'It's not important. This is the one we're interested in because the left thumb is worn through. You wear a prosthesis on your left thumb, don't you, Ninon?'

'Why ask if you already know the answer. How did you work it out?'

'By putting two and two together. Francine Blavette's story revealed to me why you felt nothing yesterday when you caught your thumb in the door. Anyone else would have screamed out in pain and yet you remained perfectly calm. It didn't strike me at the time, but when I found the glove I understood.'

'There's no denying it, boss, you've got a real nose for this. But you must admit I have too, because if it hadn't occurred to me to follow you – whack!'

'Don't congratulate yourselves too soon, dear sirs. This glove may belong to me, but it doesn't prove I was at the scene of any . . . slaughter. You could have picked it up anywhere.'

'But, boss . . .'

'She's right. Go and fetch me a knife, Joseph. We're going to discover the *Madonna*'s inner secret.'

Joseph rummaged in the kitchen, muttering to himself indignantly.

' "Tie up her wrists, Joseph!" "Do this, do that, Joseph." "Go and fetch a knife, Joseph!" Never "Thank you for saving my life, Joseph." It's nice to feel appreciated!'

He came back with a large meat knife, which he held out purposefully, blade first. Victor sliced open the picture and slipped the knife easily between the *Madonna* and the backing board. He extracted an official document drafted in Spanish and covered with various stamps. On it was the name Armand de Valois.

'What is this?'

'The deed of sale to a piece of land in Colombia,' Ninon replied.

'Does it belong to you? I see no mention of the name Palmyra Caicedo.'

'Let's just say it reverts to me by right.'

'And in order to recover it you didn't hesitate to kill three people. No, four, including Armand de Valois.'

'May God receive him in heaven! Dear Armand was a scoundrel, but I was fond of him. We were similar in many ways. Come, admit it, the most you can have me charged with is attempted theft without breaking and entering, since Monsieur Mori invited me on to the premises.'

'How did you get hold of the double key to the garret?'

'Tasha lent it to me. She left some materials behind yesterday and asked me to go and fetch them for her.'

'What happened to Monsieur Turner?'

Ninon burst out laughing.

'Give me some trousers, a frock coat and a bowler and I'll give you Monsieur Turner. I enjoyed playing that dual role, the husband then the wife – they weren't a very close couple, those Turners; you never saw them together. That concierge fell for it. I had a good teacher. I was trailing you when you went into the Théâtre Robert Houdin. Doubtless that fool Médéric told you some sob story. Poor wretch! He was far too sentimental for my liking.'

Irritated, Victor glanced at Joseph, who was jotting everything down in his notebook. This interrogation was leading
nowhere. He needed to change tack.

'You killed Odette, Denise and Père Moscou,' he pronounced.

'Pure supposition on your part.'

'You threatened Madame de Brix. The letter signed by her
dead son nearly killed her, and who knows? She may still die as
a result of her stroke.'

'Although I've never met her personally I am terribly sorry
to hear it. I wasn't aware that her health was so fragile.'

'You posed as a clairvoyant in order to exploit Madame de
Valois's suffering and her gullibility.'

'Suffering! Isn't that a slight exaggeration, dear man? She
was so in love with her husband that she deceived him with you!
At worst I caused her to shed a few crocodile tears. If that's my
only crime, then I plead guilty.'

Joseph stopped writing and, beaming, stuck up the hand in
which he held the pencil.

'Can I have a word, boss?'

He pulled Victor to one side and whispered in his ear:
'I've got proof of her guilt. I'll run home and fetch it,
sharpish.'

Victor nodded and Joseph ran out immediately.

Ninon gave Victor a look of complicity.

'Now we're alone you can let me go and no one will know.
You can say I escaped.'

'What have I to gain from it?'

'Why, everything: riches, love. We'd make a formidable
pair . . .'

'It's very tempting, but I already have all that. And you're wrong, we're not alone.'

He motioned with his chin as he walked over to the bedroom. Reconciled in sleep, the two people he loved most in the world lay like a couple of children, dead to the world. He couldn't help feeling grateful towards Ninon. She could have killed them too.

A tornado appeared to have hit Madame Pignot's usually tidy abode. Joseph's wardrobe doors were flung open and a heap of clothes lay scattered on the floor. At last he found the jacket he'd been wearing on the night of the attack on Père Moscou. He turned out the empty pockets. 'Oh, Maman! What have you done with it? I know you haven't chucked it away; you save everything in case there's another war.'

He tore over to the cupboard where she kept her bits of string and brown paper, and biscuit tins containing pins, pennies and buttons. He spread the contents of the tins over the table and combed through them feverishly. Joseph's fingers closed around his catch, and he made his way back to Rue des Saints-Pères.

'Boss, boss, I've got it – the proof!'

Lying on his outstretched hand was a gold button from a student's uniform. Victor compared it to the matching ones on Ninon's dark frock coat.

'What fools you are! The Lakanal School is swarming with

students dressed in identical rags! All right, so I lost a button, you little cretin, but how will you convince the gentlemen from the police that I lost it at Cour des Comptes?'

'She said it, boss! Boss, she confessed, she said, "Cour des Comptes"! She did it!' shrieked Joseph, still smarting at being called a 'cretin'.

'Of course she did. The question is how do we prove it?'

'Crikey, you're hard to please. I've given you a glove, a button, newspaper articles and . . .'

'And you've just given me an idea that might help expose our dear friend here. I am eternally grateful.'

Joseph went red as a beetroot – he would have hugged Victor only he didn't dare.

And thank you, Numa, thought Victor. 'Follow your instinct.' Isn't that the message he passed on to me from Daphne and Uncle Émile?

'Joseph, go round to the police station, will you? Please,' he added, with a grin.

CHAPTER 11

FOR the third time since the interview began, Inspector Lecacheur stopped in front of the mottled mirror, adopted a flattering pose and smoothed down his thick, black moustache before continuing to circle the desk near which Victor was seated.

'You must admit I've been extremely patient with you. What do you have to say in your defence?'

'A friend of mine disappeared and I thought I was doing the right thing by . . .'

'Obstructing justice?'

'I didn't obstruct anything. I brought you the culprit's head on a platter!'

'And almost got yourself killed again in the process! What attracted you to this case? Did you want to show everyone your brilliant mind in action?'

'Possibly,' Victor replied casually, 'but perhaps also because I see in this woman a murderer who didn't hesitate to take four lives, and I happen to believe she deserves to pay for it.'

'Why don't you stop playing the sleuth and restrict yourself to the company of book lovers, of which I am one? Incidentally, you don't happen to have a first edition of *Manon Lescaut* by the Abbé Provost do you? Excuse me just a moment.'

He tiptoed to the door and pulled it open sharply. Joseph, who was bent over at the keyhole, stood up with a start, and hurried to sit on the nearest bench. Inspector Lecacheur eyed him sternly before closing the door.

'You see? You're encouraging emulators amongst your staff. It's preposterous!'

He stuffed a handful of cachou[1] pastilles in his mouth, which caused him to have a fit of sneezing. When the tornado had blown over, he explained: 'I'm trying to stop smoking. Well, that's all for now. Naturally we'll need you to give evidence during the trial – you're a main witness; it's becoming a habit.'

Victor stood up. He barely reached the shoulder of the inspector, who stooped a little to make himself smaller.

'It's been a pleasure, my dear sir. Oh, before I forget, it's only fair that I should thank you. After hours of unsuccessful questioning I took your advice and asked the accused to fill in a form which I immediately sent to a handwriting expert. It's definitely her writing on all three letters you gave us. She broke down. She made a full conf—'

'So we have our proof!' Victor exclaimed.

'You don't. All you have is the door handle, which you'll be using unless you can listen to the long story I'm about to tell you without interrupting. For you know how Marie killed, but you still don't know why.'

Victor tensed up, assuming an almost military bearing. He listened carefully to the inspector's account, keeping his comments to himself, and when it was over shook the man's hand, and took his leave with a look of triumph on his face. Joseph rushed over, keen to know what had happened, but Victor led him away in silence.

Inspector Lecacheur, sucking on a pastille, watched them go.

'Confound the man!' he muttered. 'Claims to be a bookseller but prefers the smell of blood to the smell of ink.'

Joseph had gone over to the parapet to watch the ship *Charenton-Point-du-jour* draw alongside the quay. Victor was lighting a cigarette when someone tapped his shoulder. He turned to find Isidore Gouvier winking at him.

'Well done, Monsieur Legris. You certainly fooled me with that story about writing a novel. Don't you think it's about time we began exchanging information?'

'You're a dangerous man. I'm afraid you'd misuse anything I passed on to you.'

'*Le Passe-partout* lives off information, but it doesn't mean we divulge everything. And, anyway, you owe me for having put you on the trail of Marie Turnerad.'

'That's true. Let's say eleven o'clock tomorrow at the Jean Nicot then.'

'Boss! Mademoiselle Tasha and Monsieur Mori are here.'

Victor could hardly believe his eyes. Arm in arm, Tasha and Kenji were walking towards them, beaming. He hurriedly took leave of Isidore Gouvier.

The four of them sat on a bench in Place Dauphine. Plied with questions by Joseph and Tasha, Victor tried to avoid looking at Kenji, whom he assumed was feeling uncomfortable. It was Kenji, however, who turned to him and asked in a natural voice, as if sensing Victor's uneasiness: 'I understand Mademoiselle

Ninon Delarme has confessed. So what is it that's bothering you?'

'Me? Why, nothing. Ninon finally came clean and Inspector Lecacheur enlightened me as to the motive for her crimes. It all began in Panama in the spring of last year. You probably know as well as I do that seven years after the Inter-Oceanic Canal Company began construction it was drowning in debt.'

'Yes, I remember reading about it in the papers at the time,' Kenji said. 'At the end of 1888 the Canal Company asked the government for a further three months in which to repay its debts. They refused and in February 1889 disaster struck. Over eight hundred thousand small investors lost their savings, if I'm not mistaken.'

'Exactly right,' said Victor. 'The suicide rate shot up and the cessation of the canal works plunged the Panama region into chaos. There were riots in the villages and workers scoured the country looking for non-existent jobs. Crime and theft rates went up and the British government sent special emergency vessels to evacuate ten thousand of their citizens to Jamaica. The United States did the same. Chile, which needed immigrants, welcomed any volunteers, offering them a free passage to Valparaíso.'

'Would you mind if I take notes, boss?'

'Please do, Joseph, please do. Armand de Valois, convinced that Ferdinand de Lesseps's project would be a success, imprudently invested all his money in the canal. After the débâcle he was left with no money and no job. He put off his return to France to give himself a chance to recoup his losses. He was sure that sooner or later the United States would take over the digging of the canal through the isthmus. He heard talk of a little port town called Tumaco, on the frontier between Colombia and Ecuador, and went there with the intention of setting up a trading post. And that is where, during a reception at the French Consulate, he made the acquaintance of Palmyra Caicedo.'

'Marie Turnerad,' Joseph volunteered, with a knowing air.

Victor leant back against the bench.

'Palmyra and Armand became lovers. He told her about his plans to buy land in Tumaco. She was interested, and offered to put him up at the hotel she ran in Cali, where they could begin raising the money they needed. Armand offered his services as a geologist to prospectors who were combing the region and purchased small quantities of gemstones, and Palmyra managed the profits. And this is when Lewis Ives arrived on the scene.'

'Who?' asked Kenji.

'An American. He'd lost his job as foreman at the canal works.'

'Was he the St Nazaire corpse?'

'No, that was Armand de Valois. Patience, please! Lewis Ives was penniless. He decided to try his luck prospecting for gold. After months of travelling, he arrived in the south. There he heard about a legend. It was said that at the beginning of the century, native people reported finding pieces of gold weighing several pounds in remote parts of the south. It was the promise of an Eldorado! Lewis Ives ended up in Cali, where he rented a room at the Hotel Rosalie. He set about exploring the region around the River Sipi, reputed to be rich in minerals. One day he met an old Indian who had dug up some green crystals believing them to be *gold that is unripe*. In exchange for a machete and a few pickaxes, Ives persuaded the old man to show him the place in the mountains where he'd been prospecting.'

'What a great beginning for an adventure story!' said Joseph.

'If you keep interrupting, I'll lose the thread.'

'I'll shut up, boss. Not another word, I promise.'

'Lewis Ives was a novice where mineralogy was concerned and needed some expert advice. He went to Armand, whom he'd met at the hotel. Armand examined the pieces of stone. He instantly recognised them as emeralds, but was careful to tell Ives they were worthless quartz crystals. Nevertheless, he also told Ives he'd like to analyse the rock where they came from for other possible mineral deposits. The unsuspecting Ives showed him on a map the exact location of the seam, a remote region of the central cordillera only accessible on foot. Armand offered to finance an expedition. He told Palmyra about the emeralds, but craftily omitted to say he knew the exact whereabouts of the seam.'

'The villain!' exclaimed Joseph.

'Palmyra hatched a plan. Armand would go with Ives to find the place and on the way back he would get rid of his unwanted companion. Then the two of them would become partners and mine the emeralds. Only Armand was a crafty devil, and had no intention of going into partnership. Just before setting out, he secretly purchased the piece of land and with it the mining concession. He sent the deeds to his wife Odette, hidden inside a chromolithograph hanging above his bed.'

'*The Madonna in Blue*,' Joseph gasped, forgetting to note it down.

'He asked Odette to send him a telegram telling him it had arrived safely, which she did and, convinced he'd got away with it, booked his passage to France on the *La-Fayette* in the name of Lewis Ives.'

'I can guess what's coming next,' murmured Kenji. 'He killed Ives and assumed his identity. One thing remains unclear, though. How could he mine the emeralds as Lewis Ives if the deeds were in his name?'

'He probably intended to disappear for a while and resurface miraculously after three or four months – there exist vast, unexplored areas of Colombia.'

'Every bit as good as a Gustave Aimard story!' cried Joseph. ' "Captured by Indians he manages to escape . . ." So far Ninon's innocent then.'

'In principle. She still had no blood on her hands, but she was just as cunning as Armand, and after he left she searched his room and found at the bottom of the wastepaper basket some torn up bits of paper that she painstakingly pieced together. A telegram. "Received *Madonna in Blue*. Will take good care of her. See you at Christmas. Odette."

She ascertained that *The Madonna in Blue* was missing from his room and went to the concession office, where she discovered she'd been tricked. At the shipping office she found a Lewis Ives on the list of passengers sailing for France. She resolved to buy a passage herself on the same boat, kill Armand and retrieve *The Madonna in Blue* from Odette's apartment.'

'It's as clear as crystal, boss. She bumped off her lover in St Nazaire!'

Sensing Kenji's uneasiness, Tasha quickly asked: 'Did Odette have any idea that *The Madonna in Blue* contained the deeds of sale?'

'No. And Ninon knew she didn't.'

'How foolish I've been!' muttered Kenji, smiling feebly. 'I should have . . .'

'You couldn't possibly have known,' said Tasha. 'I liked her too.'

Victor stood up and straightened his hat.

'Let's go home. I'm exhausted.'

'They walked back to the bookshop. Not one of them would have admitted it, but they were all thinking of Ninon. Tasha recalled the intrepid young woman posing nude in the studio at the back of the *Bibulus*, and found it impossible to imagine her as a criminal. Kenji wondered, shamefully, whether his name would come up during the trial. Joseph was relieved that the shadow he'd mistaken for the ghost of Père Moscou had only been a woman. As for Victor, he was reflecting on the unwitting part little Denise had played in all this. Had she not fallen in love with that chromolithograph she, Odette and Père Moscou would all still be alive. He came to the conclusion that in matters of art, good taste can sometimes be crucial.

With a look of disgust on his face, Isidore Gouvier tossed some drawings by *Le Passe-partout*'s new caricaturist on to a table covered in glasses.

'Honestly, Monsieur Legris, he's no match for Tasha. Look what he's come up with, the joker! He wanted to poke fun at the spiritualists and he thought it would be clever to show a ghost brandishing a cane. Only the ghost looks like an epileptic sheik and you couldn't hit your way out of a paper bag with that cane! By the way, Monsieur Legris, you had a lucky escape. Did you know that the handle of the murder weapon contained a piece of lead?'

'Naturally, since I read your detailed articles about the state of the corpses they dug up at the Cour des Comptes,' murmured Victor. 'Poor Odette, she was so trusting! Why did Ninon – or should I say Marie – have to kill her?'

'My contact at police headquarters gave me a few tips and I can tell you one thing. Marie didn't mean to kill Odette de Valois. In fact it was an accident. When she went to the cemetery to get the picture back, as arranged, Madame de Valois thought she was seeing Armand's ghost and started screaming hysterically. To shut her up Marie hit her, but a little too hard, and the rest you know . . . And now it's your turn to shed a bit of light, Monsieur Legris, fair's fair.'

Victor swallowed his vermouth cassis.

'On condition you don't mention my intimate association with Odette de Valois.'

'I'd willingly oblige, old chap, but I can't vouch for my fellow journalists. The concierge at Boulevard Haussmann, a certain Hyacinthe, has already been raging about you quite a bit. I suppose I could edit his declarations. The written word outlasts the spoken word. Will that do?'

'It'll do. When Denise came to see me at Rue des Saints-

Pères, to tell me about Madame de Valois's disappearance I took her to a local café. I suppose Ninon must have been sitting in an adjoining booth, in which case she would have overheard our entire conversation.'

'What did you talk about?'

'About what had happened the previous evening at the cemetery and then in the apartment at Boulevard Haussmann, and about Madame de Valois's strange behaviour – I wasn't paying attention to everything she said. Afterwards I went to see Mademoiselle Kherson to ask if she'd agree to let the girl stay in her room. When I came back to Rue des Saints-Pères I noticed a student browsing in the shop – it was Ninon, but naturally I couldn't have known that then. She presumably followed Denise and my assistant to Rue Notre-Dame-de Lorette and . . .'

'Monsieur Legris, let's stop all this beating about the bush. What interests me is the methodology of your investigation, the rest I can get from my sources.'

'It might take a while.'

'I've plenty of time; it's not yet midday.'

'I'd like another drink, how about you?'

'I wouldn't say no. Alphonse! Two vermouths! I'm all ears, Monsieur Legris.'

Victor tousled his hair and waited for the waiter to leave again before he began telling his story.

By the time he'd finished, the minute hand and the hour hand were both pointing at two.

'It only came to me at the very last moment,' he concluded. 'Whoever would have suspected such a pretty woman?'

'Yes, she's a handsome creature,' declared Gouvier. 'I saw her in Lecacheur's office. She possesses the sort of poise a lot of our Comédie-Française actors wouldn't mind having.'

'Don't fall into the trap of glamorising the most despicable criminals. Journalists are so good at it that they end up turning murderers into heroes.'

'Novelists too, Monsieur Legris.'

Victor greeted Madame Ballu, who ignored him. She was busy reading aloud from the front page of a daily newspaper. Her audience consisted of Madame Pignot and son, who were all ears.

'Don't forget to come to work, Joseph!' Victor called out.

'The bitch!' cried Madame Pignot, snatching the newspaper from Madame Ballu who looked daggers at her. 'Listen to this! "I went to spy on the little redhead at Rue des Saints-Pères."'

'She's referring to Madame Tasha,' Joseph explained.

'"She took an omnibus to Montmartre, where she entered a cheap eatery called the Bibulus. When I discovered the studio I realised my task would be a lot easier than I'd thought. Befriending the artists was child's play."'

'She's got a nerve, that one!' Madame Ballu opined loudly, snatching back her paper. "I was sitting in the Temps Perdu when to my astonishment I saw the old man from the Cour des Comptes go past on his way to spy on the bookshop. I discovered he'd taken up residence in one of the court-yards . . ." Number 23!' cried Madame Ballu. I knew he was up to no good the moment I saw him prowling around . . .'

'My turn! My turn!' screeched Madame Pignot and grabbed the newspaper, tearing it in the process. ' "I decided to return early the next morning. I was nervous. I saw the old man being chased down the street by a concierge." She means you, doesn't she?'

'I was chasing him all right. He was rude to me! Here, let me see that! ". . . I had spent the night with Laumier who was in a hurry to start the life-drawing sessions . . ." '

'The shameless hussy!' Madame Pignot cried.

'And to think she was slipping in and out of here. You can say what you like, but even so, Monsieur Legris and Monsieur Mori are hardly . . . Well, I know what I mean.' Madame Ballu went quiet, shooting a sidelong glance at Joseph, who had managed to get hold of the paper.

' ". . . I had to act quickly to get rid of the old man from the Cour des Comptes. It would have all been all right if the little upstart hadn't caught me in the act . . ." Hey, Maman, did you hear that? The upstart, that's me! Look! There's my name, spelled out, Joseph Pignot!'

'Jesus, Mary and Joseph! Where? I can't see a thing!' bellowed Madame Pignot.

'Give me back that paper. It's mine!' brayed Madame Ballu.

Each of the women pulled at the paper in an effort to snatch from the other, with the result that the ground was soon strewn with bits of paper and the two women, red in the face, their hair ruffled, began hurling insults and aiming kicks at one another. Joseph placed himself between them, arms akimbo. Regardless of the blows he received during this valiant intervention, there was but one thought running through his mind: 'My name's in the paper! My name's in the paper! Valentine will be proud of me!'

CHAPTER 12

A STREAM of light poured in through the window on to a little table covered in palettes and tubes of gouache. Nonchalantly seated in an armchair, legs crossed, holding a book and with a faint smile on his face, Kenji Mori looked for all the world as if he were about to utter one of his favourite proverbs. With an air of satisfaction, Tasha took a step back to admire her canvas, then added a white fleck to the corner of Kenji's eyes to bring them alive.

'What do you think?' she asked Victor who was struggling, hammer in his hand, with a recalcitrant nail.

'I'm not sure. I think I'm about to have a fit of jealousy. I find this sudden friendship very suspicious.'

'I'll never be able to fathom men. You've been waiting for a truce between us for months, and when it finally comes . . .'

'I am comforted by the fact that he poses for you with his clothes on.'

'Don't be too sure; this is only a beginning.'

'No, you're not his type, he prefers brunettes. Ninon was . . .'

'She still is.'

'. . . And perhaps Iris is too. Little redheads don't interest Kenji; he leaves them for me.'

He put down his hammer and she her paintbrush and they kissed.

'So, do you like it?' he whispered in her ear.

'You mean the way you kiss?'

'No, idiot, the studio.'

'If you insult me, I'll go back to Helga Becker! Of course I like it. I'd be hard to please if I didn't. Do you know what I like most about it, though?'

'The bed?' he said, pointing to the alcove, which was now home to a double bed draped in liberty satin.

She shook her head.

'The water closet?'

'No.'

'The furniture?'

She looked at the various pieces of furniture Victor had bought at the auction house on Rue Drouot: the two Henry IV armchairs, the Regency sofa and the Tudor tables and chairs.

'They're truly lovely, but no. The thing I like most is the running water.'

'Women are beyond me,' sighed Victor.

There was a knock on the door. Tasha let in Madame Pignot and Joseph, who presented her respectively with an enormous fruit basket and a potted palm purchased at L'Île de la Cité flower market. When they'd set their gifts down in front of the ceramic stove she gave them each a kiss.

'I won't wash my cheeks for a whole year!' declared Joseph.

'Is Monsieur Mori here yet?' whispered Madame Pignot.

'We're expecting him soon. In any case Germaine has prepared a cold buffet supper,' Victor replied, pointing to the sideboard creaking under the weight of terrines of braised beef and chicken, platters of *foie gras*, salad bowls filled with cress and red lettuce, strawberries and cream, cakes and bottles of champagne.

'Rustic but plentiful,' he added. 'Have you made your peace with Madame Ballu?'

'Yes, but it cost me two pounds of oranges and five of pears,' muttered Madame Pignot.

'Don't forget to tell them she gave you a brand new broom,' Joseph remarked, eyeing the braised beef.

There was another knock, and the door opened to a young delivery boy hidden behind a bouquet of lilies.

'Is this the house warming at Madame . . . Sacha Kherson's?'

'Tasha,' Victor corrected him as he took the flowers from the boy. 'Would you care for a glass of champagne?'

'Oh! There's a card! It's from Kenji!' cried Tasha.

'No thanks, sir, not while I'm working. But I'd love a bit of pâté.'

Clutching his slice of bread and pâté, the delivery boy made way for Kenji who had just walked in carrying a large package.

'This is for you,' he said to Tasha.

'More! You're spoiling me – your flowers are gorgeous.'

She tore through the wrapping paper and carefully lifted out a yellow tea set with flecks of green resting on a lacquered tray.

'It's so beautiful,' she murmured.

'It's seventeenth century. Nothing is too beautiful for a pretty woman.'

'Careful, Kenji!' Victor groaned.

'Why don't we eat?' Joseph suggested, to defuse the atmosphere.

He went and stood in front of the potted palm clasping his plate, and said with his mouth full: 'They need plenty of light and heat these things. By the way, do you know what I read in

Le Passe-partout yesterday? It wasn't on account of a palm tree that Marie Turnerad chose that funny name Palmyre, it was because when she was a girl her grandmother had a Siamese cat called Palmyre. And the other name she used, Delarme, wasn't just any old name either. You'll never guess what it stands for, not in a million years: emerald. An anagram! What a plucky woman she was.'

He had just realised why Tasha kept looking at him frantically and signalling to Kenji, when the latter observed: 'Why do you speak of her in the past tense? She's rapidly becoming famous. Her cell, it seems, is filled with flowers sent from all over France by her many admirers. The Prince of Wales visits her twice a week, and they say the Duc de Frioul has offered to marry her. She's even begun writing her memoirs. I hope to goodness she doesn't mention my name.'

He looked at them defiantly and they admired his courage. Victor wondered whether Iris knew anything about her Kenji's peccadilloes. He remembered the words Numa Winner had attributed to Daphne: 'You can be reborn if you break the chain.' Whether this advice came from her or from the clairvoyant, its meaning was becoming clear. Victor realised that the bond between him and Kenji had changed. They were no longer father and son, but two men on an equal footing.

'This fascination for criminals amazes and disgusts me. One mustn't forget their victims.'

'Rest assured, I am not in the slightest bit fascinated,' Kenji replied, walking over to Tasha. 'I appreciate your concern,' he added in a low voice, 'but it is useless to try to spare me. My pride has suffered, but, as we all know, such wounds are superficial. Your friend Maurice Laumier appears far more upset by his lover's duplicity than I am. He's still fuming.'

'How do you know?'

'I've been to the Soleil d'Or.'

'Really? I'm touched.'

'I very much liked your work.'

'The portraits most of all, I'll wager,' mumbled Victor, who was hovering around them, eavesdropping.

'I confess I think I've turned out rather well,' retorted Kenji, standing in front of his portrait resting on the easel. 'Have you sold any paintings?'

'Only one. My favourite, the Paris rooftops at dawn.'

Kenji poured himself some more champagne and wondered how long he'd have to keep his acquisition hidden at the bottom of a chest.

'But the most wonderful reward of all was that Anatole France went out of his way to come to the exhibition and encouraged me to remain faithful to my ideal.'

'Only he who remains faithful to his ideal can feed at the table of Art,' Kenji announced, cutting himself a large slice of apple tart.

'You just made that up!' exclaimed Victor.

'By the way, the battleaxe came to the shop two days ago. You wouldn't happen to have *Betrayal* by Maxime Paz in the Ernest Kolb edition, would you?'

'Joseph, I've told you not to use that expression. You must say, La Comtesse de Salignac,' declared Kenji, frowning.

'But it's not an insult, boss. Mademoiselle Tasha calls me the moujik and I don't make a fuss about it. If you prefer, I'll call her the *Mousmé*, it's more flattering if less suitable. It means "young girl" in Japanese . . . doesn't it? Since it's like that, I shan't tell you the end of the story about the horses' manes.'

'Oh please do, Joseph, even though I haven't the faintest idea what you're talking about!' implored Tasha.

'Well, it's like this. A while ago, some individuals broke into the stables owned by the omnibus company on Rue Ordener, and chopped the manes off twenty-five horses. The mystery's just been solved. They sold the hair to the wig makers who supply the Opera.'

'Bravo, my pet! You're following in the footsteps of Inspector Lecacheur!' exclaimed Euphrosine Pignot.

'But, Maman, I didn't solve the case. I'm just telling you the . . .'

'Nonsense! Don't be so modest; I know it was you. Let's drink a toast to my pet!'

They clinked their champagne flutes and a ray of sunlight refracted through the cut glass shone on to the eyes of Kenji's portrait, making them twinkle. Tasha whispered in Joseph's ear: 'Thank you, my little moujik, or should I say my guardian angel. You saved Victor's life and for that you deserve a kiss and my eternal gratitude.'

APPENDIX

A FEW HISTORICAL NOTES ON FRANCE IN 1890

In 1890 there was a new air of liberty in Paris. At the Moulin Rouge the cancan was all the rage and the dancers' skirts were daringly short. The style of dress of both men and women became less formal and the term *fin de siècle* began to be heard.

The start of 1890 was nonetheless grim. Paris was in the grip of an influenza epidemic that had claimed 370 deaths by fourth January. In Panama the deaths were counted by the thousand. Of the 21,000 Frenchmen who had gone to Panama since the start of the digging of the canal nine years previously, 10,000 had died of yellow fever.

The fever was not the only hazard of the canal. The project started in 1878 when Prince Louis Napoleon Bonaparte was granted a concession to build a canal in Panama by the Colombian government. Ferdinand de Lesseps headed up the construction company, and the project was financed by hundreds of thousands of French investors, many of them of modest means, who put their faith in 'the great Frenchman' as de Lesseps was known because of his success in building the Suez Canal. Work began on February 1st 1881. The canal was intended to link the Atlantic and Pacific Oceans. Seventy-five kilometres in length, it was to be dug across the narrowest place on the continent, in the Colombian state of Panama. De Lesseps insisted on using the same construction methods as in Suez making no allowances for the different climatic and geographical conditions. For example, the geology of the Culebran hills created enormous technical difficulties. Under the tropical rain, machinery sank into mud and trenches collapsed. In the dry season, work was possible, but there were monsoon conditions for seven months out of the year, along with constant humidity. Along the coast the many lakes were breeding grounds for mosquitoes. In the 1880s, no-one knew that mosquitoes carried yellow fever. In fact, to counteract the invasion of ants in their homes, people would put the feet of their beds in water, where mosquitoes multiplied. The result was the spread of yellow fever.

After seven years of work, it was discovered that the company was in serious debt. In December 1888 it applied to the French government for a deferment of its liabilities which was refused. In February 1889, the company was dissolved and liquidated. More than 870,000 investors did not receive their payment and were subsequently ruined. Suicides rates soared.

Back in Paris, predicting the future was all the rage. Everyone was turning to occultists, cabbalists and necromancers, pseudospiritists who claimed to be able to reveal the future and communicate with those beyond it. These characters abounded in the city with small announcements appearing in the newspapers such as 'Madame Duchatellier, 45 rue Sainte-Anne, answers all questions about the future', or even 'Madame Berthe, the famous somnambulist, 23 rue Saint-Merri, receives every day between one and six, by appointment only.' 'How is one to distinguish between the real mediums and those who only claim to possess the gift of divination?' asked the French painter James Tissot who became very interested in spiritualism when his mistress died. From 1869, the London Dialectical Society selected a committee of 33 members to study supernatural phenomena. Victor Hugo, Théophile Gautier, Victorien Sardou and Conan Doyle stuck to the spiritualism that Allan Kardec (Hippolyte-Léon Rivail to use his real name) shed light on, defining the following principles: man is not solely composed of solid matter, there exists within him a thinking soul linked to the physical body by the perispirit. This thinking body controls the physical body, which it then leaves, as one would remove a worn-out piece of clothing, when its present incarnation has completed its course. Once dis-incarnated, the dead can communicate with the living, either directly, or through mediums, visibly or invisibly. Opinions varied but many were convinced that spiritualism was scientific proof of life after death.

The interest in spritualism sat alongside significant scientific progress, but not everyone embraced the changes that this brought. Some people in 1890 looked back nostalgically to the past and vigorously denounced the lack of manners, the de-population of the countryside, the pessimistic and pornographic literature, socialism, soaring crime rates, and the influx of immigrants from Belgium, Italy, Switzerland, Spain, Russia and Poland. As the end of the century approached, France was having to open itself to the rest of the world.

NOTES

CHAPTER ONE

1. Grouchy (Emmanuel de, 1766–1847): Marshal of France. Charged with giving chase to the Prussians routed at Ligny, he lacked initiative and failed to come to Napoleon's aid at Waterloo.

2. The ruins of the Palais d'Orsay which housed the Conseil d'État (Council of State) and the Cour des Comptes (Court of Accounts) stood on the Quai d'Orsay until 1898, when the Compagnie des chemins de fér d'Orleans built the Gare d'Orsay. Today the building houses the Musée d'Orsay.

3. A *grognard* is an historical term for the soldiers of the old guard of Napoleon I.

CHAPTER TWO

1. Japanese artist, famous for his paintings, illustrations and etchings (1752–1815); celebrated for his works depicting the theatrical world and for his portraits of women.

2. Japanese painter and printmaker (1797–1858); celebrated especially for his landscape prints, which transmuted everyday settings into intimate, lyrical scenes.

3. Joseph Fouché (1759–1820) served as Minister of Police under Napoleon and was instrumental in the return of Louis XVIII to the throne in 1815.

4. This is a play on words, Père Moscou is spelling out the sound of the name Josephine de Beauharnais, later Josephine Bonaparte, as if speaking in code.

CHAPTER THREE

1. A Parisian popular daily newspaper founded in 1879, which lasted until the outbreak of World War I.

2. This affair began with the disappearance of a porter named Gouffé on 26 July 1885 and concluded with the arrest of two men, Michel Eyraud and Gabrielle Bompart.

3. In the fifth arrondisement, now known as the Marché Maubert.

CHAPTER FOUR

1. *Gargantua and Pantagruel* by François Rabelais.
2. Popular novelist (1823–1902) and author of a considerable body of work. His most famous work is *La Porteuse de Pain* (The Bread Delivery Girl).
3. Crébillon fils, Claude Prosper Jolyot de Crébillon (1707–1777), Parisian novelist, son of the famous tragedian Prosper Jolyot de Crébillon.
4. *Tripes à la mode de Caen*: A traditional recipe of tripe baked in a casserole dish for twelve hours, with layers of onions, beef suet and a calf's foot, topped with a pie crust.

CHAPTER FIVE

1. Pierre François Joseph Lefebvre (1755–1820), duke of Danzig, Marshal of France.
2. A policeman and hero of many of Émile Gaboriau's detective novels.

CHAPTER SIX

1. A popular figure of the Latin Quarter during the 1890s. He was a bohemian and autodidact, who supported himself doing odd jobs, and became the right-hand man of the poet Verlaine, selling off his mementoes of the poet after Verlaine's death in 1896.
2. (1755–1842) French painter, most famous for her portraits of European aristocrats.

CHAPTER SEVEN

1. Catholic journalist (1844–1917). In 1890, Maurice Barrès said of him: 'Antisemitism had not been a well-established tradition in France until, in the spring of 1886, Drumont reawakened these sentiments in a way that caused an uproar.' It was in this year that he published *Jewish France*, one of the great bestsellers of the second half of the nineteenth century.
2. Mentioned by Jules Verne in *Journey to the Centre of the Earth* (1864), this

portable apparatus with an electrical charge gave off a light strong enough for use in intense darkness.

CHAPTER EIGHT

1 Adolphe-Léon Willette (1857–1926). A painter who did illustrations, lithographs, pastels and posters and first became known at the *Chat-Noir* cabaret. Creator of popular impish versions of the figures Pierrot and Colombine. He was a virulent anti-semite.

2. French painter, engraver and sculptress (1858–1927).

3. The panorama, from the Greek pan (all) and orama (view) was invented by an Irishman called Robert Barker. It consisted of a series of gigantic landscapes painted in *trompe-l'oeil* on canvases and placed inside rotunda.

CHAPTER TEN

1. His real name was Étienne Marin (1807–1874). He began his acting career at the Théâtre de Belleville. Such was his success that in 1831 he played in Paris where Alexandre Dumas introduced him into the Théâtre de la Porte Saint-Martin.

2. Jean Eugéne Robert-Houdin (1805–1871), a conjurer who first had the idea of performing his magic acts wearing a black suit to banish from the audiences' minds any sense of watching an illusion. This brilliant inventor of electric automatons first opened his spectacle, *Magical Evenings*, in 1845 at the Palais Royal, and then in 1854 on Boulevard des Italiens.

3. The Prison de Mazas was opened in Paris in 1841 and located near Gare de Lyon.

CHAPTER ELEVEN

1. Powerful licorice pastilles, developed in 1880 by a French pharmacist as a breath freshener.

Turn the page for a sneak peek at
Claude Izner's New Book

THE MONTMARTRE
INVESTIGATION

Coming in September 2010

CHAPTER 2

Paris, Thursday 12 November 1891

Paris slumbered under a waxing moon. As the Seine flowed calmly round Île Saint-Louis, patterned with diffuse light, a carriage appeared on Quai Bernard, drove up Rue Cuivier and parked on Rue Lacépède. The driver jumped down and, making sure no one was watching, removed his oilskin top hat and cape and tossed them into the back of his cab.

Just before midnight, Gaston Molina opened the ground-floor window of 4 Rue Linné and emptied a carafe on to the pavement. He closed the shutters and went over to the dressing table where a candle burned, smoothed his hair and reshaped his bowler hat. He cast a quick glance at the young blonde girl who lay asleep, fully dressed, in the hollow of the bed. She had sunk into a deep slumber as soon as she swallowed the magic potion. Mission accomplished. What happened to her next was of no concern to him. He stole out of the apartment, careful not to attract the attention of the concierge. One of the tenants was leaning out of an upstairs window. Gaston Molina hugged the wall, lighting a cigarette, and passed the Cuvier fountain before diving down the street of the same name.

A man in a grey overcoat lying in wait on Rue Geoffroy-Saint-Hilaire gave Gaston a head start before setting off behind him.

Gaston Molina walked alongside the Botanical Gardens. He froze, his senses alert, when something growled to his right. Then he smiled and shrugged. Calm down, my friend, he thought, no need to panic; it's coming from the menagerie.

He set off again. The silence was broken by the coming and going of the heavy sewer trucks, with their overpowering, nauseating smell. Going unobtrusively about their business through the sleeping city, the trucks rattled as far as the quayside at Saint-Bernard port and emptied their waste into the tankers.

Gaston Molina was almost at the quay when he thought he heard the crunch of a shoe. He swung round: no one there.

'I must be cracking up; I need a night's sleep.'

He arrived at the wine market.[2] Sometimes tramps in search of shelter broke in and took refuge in the market. Beyond the railings, the barrels, casks and vats perfumed the air with an overpowering odour of alcohol.

I'm thirsty, thought Gaston. Ah, what I wouldn't do for a drink!

Something skimmed past his neck, and a silhouette appeared beside him. Instinctively he tried to parry the blow he sensed coming. An atrocious pain ripped through his stomach and his fingers closed round the handle of a knife. The moon turned black; he collapsed.

As always, Victor Legris reflected on the soothing effect of half-light.

He had woken in an ill temper in anticipation of the stories his business associate would invent to avoid taking Dr Reynaud's prescriptions.

'Kenji! I know you're awake,' he had shouted. 'Don't forget the doctor is coming later this morning!'

Receiving nothing in reply but the slamming of a door, Victor had gone resignedly down to the bookshop, where Joseph the bookshop assistant was perched precariously at the top of a ladder, dusting the bookshelves with a feather duster and belting out a song by a popular young singer.

> *I'm the green sorrel*
> *With egg I've no quarrel*
> *In soup I'm a marvel*
> *My success is unrivalled*
> *I am the green sor-rel!*

His nerves on edge, Victor had failed to perform the ritual with which he began each day: tapping the head of Molière's bust as he passed. Instead he had gone swiftly through the bookshop and hurried down the basement stairs to closet himself in his darkroom.

He had been here for an hour, savouring the silence and dim light. No one disturbed him in this sanctuary where he could forget his worries and give himself over to his passion: photography. His collection of pictures of the old districts of Paris, started the previous April, was growing. He had initially devoted himself to the 20th arrondissement and particularly to Belleville, but recently he had started on Faubourg Saint-Antoine, cataloguing the streets, monuments, buildings and studios. Although he had already accumulated a hundred negatives, the result left him profoundly frustrated. It was not for lack of all the best equipment; it was more because there was nothing of his own personal vision in his work.

All I have here is the objective view of a reporter, he thought.

Was he relying on technique at the expense of creativity? Did he lack inspiration? That often happened to painters and writers.

The meaning of the pictures should transcend the appearance of the places I photograph.

He knew that a solution lurked somewhere in his mind. He turned up the gas lamp and examined the picture he had just developed: two skinny urchins bent double, struggling with a sawing machine that was cutting out marble tablets. The image of a frightened little boy stammering out one of Chaucer's *Canterbury Tales* under the watchful eye of an imposing man in a dark frock coat sprang to mind. Those poor brats reminded him of the terrorised child he had been faced with his domineering father's displeasure. And suddenly he had an inspiration:

'Children! Children at work!'

Finally he had his theme!

He put his negatives away in a cardboard box with renewed energy, smiling as he glimpsed a large picture of two interlaced bronze hands above an epitaph:

My wife, I await you
5 February 1843

A photograph slipped out of the packet and drifted slowly down to land on the floor. He picked it up: Tasha. He frowned. Why was this portrait of her hidden among views of the Père-Lachaise cemetery? He'd taken it at the Universal Exhibition two years earlier. The young woman, unaware she was being photographed, wore a charming and provocative expression. The beginning of their affair, recorded in that image, re-awakened his sense of their growing love. It was wonderful to know a woman who interested him more with each encounter and with whom he felt an unceasing need to talk and laugh, to make love, to hatch plans . . . He was again overcome by the bitter-sweet feeling that Tasha's attitude provoked in him. Since he had succeeded in wooing her away from her bohemian life and installing her in a vast studio, she had devoted herself body and soul to her painting. Her creative passion made him uneasy, although he was happy that he had been able to help her. He had hoped that after the show at which she had exhibited three still lifes, she would slow down. But the sale of one of her paintings to the Boussod & Valadon gallery had so spurred her on that some nights she would tear herself from his arms to finish a canvas by gaslight. Victor sought to prolong every moment spent with her, and was saddened that she did not have the same desire. He was becoming jealous of her painting, even more than of the artists with whom she consorted.

He paced about the room. Why was he unable to resolve this contradiction? He was attracted to Tasha precisely because she was independent and opinionated, yet he would secretly have liked to keep her in a cage.

Miserable imbecile! That would be the quickest way to lose her! Stop tormenting yourself. Would you rather be with someone dull, preoccupied with her appearance, her house and her make-up?

Where did his unreasonable jealousy and desire for certainty and stability come from? With the death of his overbearing father, Victor had felt a great weight lift, but that feeling had quickly been succeeded by the fear that his mother loved another man. This threat had haunted him throughout his adolescence. When his mother Daphné had died in a carriage accident, he had decided to stand on his own two feet, but Kenji had joined him in Paris and, without knowing it, had limited Victor's choices. Through affection for him, Victor had submitted to an ordered existence, his time shared between the bookshop, the adjoining apartment, the sale rooms and passing affairs. As the years had drifted down he had grown used to this routine.

He looked at the photo of Tasha. She had a hold over him that no other woman had ever exercised. No, I don't want to lose her, he thought. The memory of their first encounter plunged him into a state of feverish anticipation. He would see her soon. He extinguished the lamp and went back upstairs.

An elderly scholar, taking a break from the Collège de France, was reading aloud softly to himself from Humboldt's *Cosmos*, while a balding, bearded man struggled to translate Virgil.

Indifferent to these potential customers, Joseph was massacring a melody from *Lohengrin* while working at his favourite hobby: sorting and classifying the articles he clipped from newspapers. He had been behaving unpredictably of late, lurching from forced gaiety to long bouts of moroseness punctuated by sighs and incoherent ramblings. Victor put these changes of mood down to Kenji's illness, but since he too was rather troubled, he found it hard to bear his assistant's capricious behaviour.

'Can't you put those damned scissors down and keep an eye on what's going on?'

'Nothing's going on,' muttered Joseph, continuing his cutting.

'Well, I suppose you're right, it is pretty quiet. Has the doctor been?'

'He's just left. He recommended a tonic; he called it robot . . .'

'Roborant.'

'That's it, with camomile, birch and blackcurrant, sweetened with lactose. Germaine has gone to the herbalist.'

'All right then, I'm going out.'

'What about lunch? Germaine will be upset and then who will have to eat it? I will! She's made you pork brains in noisette butter with onions. Delicious, she says.'

Victor looked disgusted. 'Well, I make you a present of it – treat yourself.'

'Ugh! I'll have to force it down.'

As soon as Victor had climbed the stairs to the apartment, Joseph went back to his cutting out, still whistling Wagner.

'For pity's sake, Joseph! Spare us the German lesson,' shouted Victor from the top of the stairs.

'*Jawohl*, Boss!' growled Joseph, rolling his eyes. 'There's no pleasing him . . . he's never happy . . . if I sing "Little Jack Horner sat in a corner", he complains. If I serve up some opera, he complains! I'm not going to put up with it much longer, it's starting to wear me down, and I'm fed up! One Boss moping in quarantine, the other gadding about!' he said, addressing the scholar clutching the Humboldt.

Victor went softly through his apartment to his bedroom. He put on a jacket and a soft fedora, his preferred headgear, and crammed his gloves into his pocket. I'll go round by Rue des Mathurins before I go to Tasha's, he thought to himself. He was about to leave when he heard a faint tinkling sound.

The noise came from the kitchen. Victor appeared in the doorway, surprising Kenji in the act of loading a tray with bread, sausage and cheese.

'Kenji! Are you delirious? Dr Reynaud forbade you . . .'

'Dr Reynaud is an ass! He's been dosing me with sulphate of quinine and broth with no salt for weeks. He's inflicted enough cold baths on me to give me an attack of pleurisy! I stink of camphor and I'm going round and round in circles like a goldfish in a bowl! If a man is dying of hunger, what does he do? He eats!'

In his slippers and flannel nightshirt Kenji looked like a little boy caught stealing the jam. Victor made an effort to keep a straight face.

'Blame it on the scarlet fever, not the devoted doctor who's working hard to get you back on your feet. Have a glass of sake or cognac, that's allowed, but hang it all, spare a thought for us! You can't leave your room until your quarantine is over.'

'All right, since all the world is intent on bullying me, I'll return to my cell. At least ensure that I have a grand funeral when I die of starvation,' retorted Kenji furiously, abandoning his tray.

Suppressing a chuckle, Victor left, one of Kenji's Japanese proverbs on the tip of his tongue: 'Of the thirty-six options, flight is the best.'

'Berlaud! Where have you scarpered to, you miserable mongrel?'

A tall rangy man with a cloak of coarse cloth draped across his shoulders was driving six goats in front of him. At the entrance to the Botanical Gardens, he struggled to keep them together. Cursing his dog for having run off, he used the thongs attached to their collars to draw them in.

The little flock went off up Quai Saint-Bernard, crossed Rue Buffon without incident and went down Boulevard de l'Hôpital as far as Gare d'Orléans,[3] where the man stopped to light a short clay pipe. The silvery hair escaping from under his dented hat and his trusting, artless face gave him the look of child aged suddenly by a magic spell. Even his voice was childlike, with an uncertain catch to it.

'Saints alive! I'm toiling in vain while that wretched mutt is off chasing something to mount.'

He put two fingers in his mouth and gave a long whistle. A large dog with matted fur, half briard, half griffon, bounded out from behind an omnibus.

'So there you are, you miscreant. You're off pilfering, leaving me yelling for you and working myself to death with the goats. What you lookin' like that for? What you got in your mouth? Oh, I see, you went off to steal a bone from the lions while I was chatting to Père Popèche. That's why we heard roaring. But you know dogs aren't allowed in the Botanical Gardens, even muzzled and on the leash. Do you want to get us into trouble?'

Berlaud, his tail between his legs and teeth clamped round his prize, ran back to his post at the back of the herd, which trotted past the Hospice de la Salpêtrière, before turning towards Boulevard Saint-Marcel and into the horse market.

Each Thursday and Saturday the neighbourhood of the Botanical Gardens witnessed a procession of miserable worn out horses, lame and exhausted but decked out with yellow or red ribbons to trick the buyers. They were kicking their heels in resigned fashion, attached to girders under tents held up with cast iron poles where the horse dealers rented stalls. Ignoring the auctioneers proffering broken-down old carriages just outside the gates, the goatherd pushed his flock in among the groups of rag and bone men and furniture removers in search of hacks still capable of performing simple tasks. Each time he visited, the goatherd found it heart-rending to see the dealers with their emaciated nags, whose every rib could be seen, making them trot about to display their rump, their face and their flanks to possible buyers.

'Savages! Tormenting to death these poor beasts worn out by pulling the bourgeois along the streets of Paris! My brave horses, you certainly know what it is to work hard. And the day you're of no use you'll be sent to the knackers' yard or to the abattoir at Villejuif! Dirty swindling dealers!'

'So, here comes our friend Grégoire Mercier, the purveyor of milk direct to your home, the saviour of consumptives, the ailing and the chlorotic! Well, Grégoire, still heaping invective on the world? I'm the one who should grumble – you're late, my fine fellow!'

'I couldn't help it, Monsieur Noël. I had so much to do,' replied the goatherd to a horse dealer who was impatiently waving a household bottle at him. 'First, at dawn I had to take the she-kids to graze on the grass on some wasteland at the Maison-Blanche. Then I had to visit a customer on Quai de la Tournelle with a liver complaint; she has to have milk from Nini Moricaude – I feed her carrots. After that it was straight off to do some business at the menagerie at the Botanical Gardens.'

'You're curing the chimpanzees with goat's milk?'

'Don't be silly, Monsieur Noël! No, I had to speak to someone and . . .'

'All right, all right, I don't need your whole life story.'

Grégoire Mercier knelt down beside a white goat and milked it, then held out a bowl of creamy milk to the horse dealer, who sniffed it suspiciously.

'It smells sour. Are you sure it's fresh?'

'Of course! As soon as she wakes up Mélie Pecfin gets a double ration of hay fortified with iodine; it's the best thing for strengthening depleted blood.'

'Depleted, depleted, my wife is not depleted! I'd like to see how you'd be if you'd just given birth to twins! I'll take it to her while it's still warm.'

The man dropped a coin into the goatherd's hand and snatched up the bowl.

'Tomorrow, do you want me to deliver to your house on Rue Poliveau?'

The horse dealer turned his back without even bothering to say thank you.

'That's right, run off to your missus. You may treat her better than you do your horses, but you don't cherish her the way I cherish my goats when they have kids! Isn't that right, my beauties? Papa Grégoire gives you sugar every morning and he nourishes your babies with hot wine. Come on, Berlaud, let's go!'

As he reached Rue Croulebarbe, Grégoire Mercier regained his good humour. Now he was back on home turf, the borders of which were the River Bièvre[4] to one side and to the other the orchards where the drying racks of the leather-dressers were lined up.

Freed from the strap holding them prisoner, the goats gambolled between the poplar trees bordering the narrow river, its brown water specked with foam. The Bièvre snaked its way along by tumbledown houses and dye-works whose chimneys belched out thick smoke. Although he was used to the sweetish steam of the cleaning tubs and the fumes from the scalding vats where the colours were mixed, Grégoire Mercier wrinkled his nose. Piled up under the hangars, hundreds of skins stained with blood lay hardening, waiting to be plunged in buckets of softening agent. After a long soaking, they would be hung out and beaten by apprentices, releasing clouds of dust that covered the countryside like snow.

Determined not to drop his find, Berlaud guided the goats on to the riverbank where tomatoes, petits pois and green beans grew. He hurried past the wickerwork trays of the peat sellers and the coaching-shed of Madame Guédon who leased hand-carts for use on Ruelle des Reculettes, which opened out just beyond the crumbling wall behind the lilac hedge.

Old buildings with exposed beams housed the families of the curriers. Blackened twisted vines ran over their packed earth façades. The sound of pistons, and the occasional shriek of a strident whistle, served as a reminder that this was the town and not the countryside.

Letting his dog and beasts trot ahead, Grégoire Mercier stopped to greet Monsieur Vrétot, who combined work as a concierge with his trade as a shoemaker and cobbler to make ends meet. Then the goatherd started up the stairs, whistling on every landing. Thirty years earlier he had left his native Beauce for Paris, and settled at the heart of this unhealthy neigh-bourhood, ruled by the misery and stench of the tanneries. A delivery boy for the cotton factory by Pont d'Austerlitz, he had fallen in love with a laundress, and they had married and had two little boys. Three happy years were brutally cut short by the death from tuberculosis of Jeanette Mercier. Moved by the plight of the little motherless boys, public assistance had given them a goat to provide nourishment, until consumption carried the little boys off in their turn. When he had overcome his grief, Grégoire decided to keep the goat and take in others as well. He had never remarried.

He reached the fifth floor, where his flock were massed before a door at the end of a dark corridor. As soon as he closed the door of his garret, the goats went into the boxes set up along the wall. He went into a second room, furnished with a camp bed, a table, two stools and a rickety sideboard, shrugged off his cloak and hurried to prepare the warm water and bran that his goats expected on returning from their travels. He also had to feed Mémère the doyenne a bottle of oats mixed with mint, before opening the cubby hole where Rocambole the billy goat was languishing. Finally he heated up some coffee for himself and took it to drink beside Mélie Pecfin, his favourite. It was then that he noticed Berlaud. He was sitting on his blanket, wagging his tail, his find from the Botanical Gardens still between his paws, but with his eyes fixed on the sugar bowl. Grégoire pretended not to know what his dog was after and Berlaud growled meaningfully.

'Lie down!'

Instead of obeying, the dog adopted an attitude of absolute servility, flattened his ears, raised his rump and crept stealthily forward, begging for his master's attention. Grégoire distracted him by throwing him a sugar cube and grabbed the dog's spoils.

'What's that? That's not a bone, that's . . . that's a . . . How can anyone mislay something like that? Oh, there's something inside . . .'

Grégoire was so puzzled he forgot to drink his coffee.

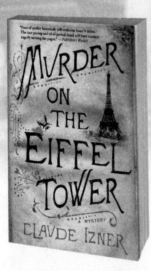
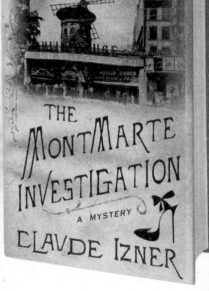